JOANNE PERELLA

Vanishing Act

First Stillwater River Publications Edition

ISBN: 978-1-960505-90-3

Library of Congress Control Number: 2023921752
Names: Perella, Joanne, author.
Title: Vanishing act / Joanne Perella.
Description: First Stillwater River Publications edition. | West Warwick, RI,
    USA : Stillwater River Publications, [2023]
Identifiers: ISBN: 978-1-960505-90-3 (paperback) | LCCN: 2023921752
Subjects: LCSH: Older women—Fiction. | Congregate housing—Fiction. |
    Autonomy (Psychology)—Fiction. | Self-realization in women—Fiction. |
    Escapes—Fiction. | Love—Fiction. | Friendship—Fiction. | Aging—Fiction.
    | LCGFT: Action and adventure fiction.
Classification: LCC: PS3616.E741 V36 2023 | DDC: 813/.6—dc23

1 2 3 4 5 6 7 8 9 10

Written by Joanne Perella.
Cover and interior design by Elisha Gillette.
Published by Stillwater River Publications, West Warwick, RI, USA.

This story is dedicated to my mother, Rose,
who has been my biggest inspiration.

VANISHING ACT

One

I couldn't believe I was still alive.

It seemed incredible that just a year ago, I was shuffling around my kitchen trying to pretend my life was fine. With a cursory look from the outside, my house seemed normal. But I wasn't.

The truth was I hadn't eaten for days except for a package of Little Debbies and a half-pint of coffee ice cream. I had stopped cooking weeks before; it was much easier to open a bag of cookies if I got hungry. There was no one to cook for anyway.

My health was taking a nosedive; I stopped showering every day and my laundry piled up. Sometimes my neighbor would drop off some groceries, but the healthy stuff she bought me just piled up in the refrigerator where it turned into a slimy mess. The TV was on all day long, but I didn't watch it. The change from the vibrant, active woman I used to be into a smelly old lady was my little secret. I basically stopped answering the door and the phone. I reasoned that it seemed to matter to no one, especially me.

It was Tuesday—garbage day. I knew this and decided it was time to throw out the bag of rotting vegetables that had begun to stink up the refrigerator. As I was throwing them out, my slipper, which was half off and half on, slid sloppily off the pedal of the garbage can. Next thing I knew, I was face down on the floor. Something warm and sticky dribbled down my face. That's where my oldest daughter Gina found me the next day.

Gina made it clear she was horrified that I had been lying there for God knows how long (her words). I could picture the gruesome sight that greeted her as she walked in the door. But what I suspected really upset Gina most that afternoon was the fact that she was missing the royal wedding. She *always* loved celebrity gossip; actually, we both did. Gina always took after me. The British weddings were the best. Those hats! I thought they called them fascinators. We were certainly fascinated by them. We could have had fun laughing about them together.

Looking back, I realized my life would have been so much easier if Gina had not known about my little mishap. After all, that was not the first one by any means. There were quite a few and they weren't *that* bad.

Except for my car accident.

Gina didn't really know the whole story behind that mess, and I wasn't about to reveal the sordid details. It was enough that she saw the car after it was towed (the nice state trooper called the tow company for me after the car slithered into a ditch). I told him that a tractor trailer cut me off, but that was a lie. I missed the exit because I was singing along to Frank Sinatra and sort of forgot where I was going. When I tried to get back into the exit lane, it was too late. I felt terrible about lying and confessed it all to Father Keith the next week. He gave me ten Hail Marys and five Our Fathers and told me to stay off the road. It wasn't too hard to do since my car was totaled. Gina said I was lucky to be alive, but I didn't feel so lucky.

That was the end of my driving days. I felt bad about my car. My husband Tony and I had bought the big black beauty from Bishop Gelineau. We called it the Blessed Bomber. Even though it was ten years old, the 1996 shiny Mercury Grand Marquis positively glistened after we drove it through the car wash on Saturday afternoons. After Tony died, I still loved gallivanting around in it with the rosary beads hanging from the rearview mirror. Before the tow truck man took it away, I asked him for my rosary beads back. It was sweet of him to get them for me.

I hoped that Gina would not fly into a full-blown panic after finding me on the floor, but I was wrong. As I feared, she insisted I go to the emergency room for an evaluation. I should have known that this evaluation would really be a closed-door discussion between Gina and a bunch of doctors who were trying to decide what to do with me. Gina said I couldn't go home at the time but had to go to rehab. Rehab turned out to be a crappy nursing home. After a month there, I was transferred to Peaceful Havens. It was an assisted living place, but there wasn't much living going on there. It was more like a place where people went to die.

Gina said she chose Peaceful Havens for me because my friend Emma was there, and it would be fun for me to hang out with her. *Really?* She should have stayed there for a night or two. Those nurses and social workers treated me as if I were deaf and dumb, always talking at me in loud measured voices with all-too-bright expressions on their faces. I guessed that was what they got taught in nursing school or wherever it was where they got their degrees.

Gina was here a lot, probably out of guilt. Mario, my son, came sometimes too, but usually with Maria, my other daughter. Maria bustled in like a drill sergeant, rearranging my stuff and telling me what clothes to wear. I felt like ordering them to bring me *all* my clothes, not just the dull things they decided I should be wearing. Where the hell were my favorite black pants? Or my long pearls I got for my first anniversary? And my shoes! I really didn't want to wear cloddy orthopedic shoes for the rest of my life... however long that might be. Honestly, if I stayed in this place, I would have to shorten my life somehow or begin to drink heavily. Sometimes I really wished I had lost my mind. It would be easier than putting up with the daily horror of realizing where you were.

I also didn't smell like I used to. I knew I smelled like this place and like old people. Some of the people there—they called them "residents"—smelled even worse. There as Dolly who wore adult pampers and forgot to change them. Of course, the nurses were supposed to do that for you, but we all knew which nurses were nice and which ones were mean. Emma frequently complained about her mean nurses, but Emma complained about everything. I always thought of her as a pampered princess. Emma was living in the best apartment there. It was a corner one with a real bedroom and a patio, which of course she never used. Her kids felt so guilty about sticking her in there that they got her the most beautiful apartment they could afford—rather what Emma could afford, since it was her money—moved all her furniture in, and decorated it for her as a "surprise" one day. Some surprise. Emma always used to pretend her kids were just the most special, loving children anyone could have. Her oldest son is Father Keith, who is worshipped and adored by everyone, including me. The other kids go around smiling but resentfully know they can never live up to their angelic brother Keith. Lately, Emma had been shutting herself in her room and not coming down for meals. This was making the staff at Peaceful Havens very unhappy. And nervous. All the residents must socialize at mealtimes so it appeared we were all one big happy family.

Right now, everything was decorated for Easter coming up in two weeks. Large pink bunnies and Styrofoam eggs with plastic grass adorned the lobby. Fake lilies were everywhere. There were never any live things here. At Christmastime, the tree and all the holly were plastic. I would have loved to see one plant that needed watering. When a visitor walked into the lobby, he was greeted by a large arrangement of tired seasonal decorations. They had just put away the dusty green shamrocks from St. Patrick's Day. Last week, some washed-out crooner came and sang "Danny Boy" along with other "Irish favorites" at our sing-along night. Usually, I avoided those nights like the plague. They consisted of a bunch of the most senile residents being wheeled into the front lobby to "enjoy" some music. Most slept through it or stared into space. Occasionally, some resident who could walk would wander in and start gyrating to the music in an attempt to dance. The activities director, elated at the prospect that someone was enjoying the music, would begin to clap furiously to encourage others to participate as well.

This resulted in a rather comical routine where the singer got louder and the clapping got louder, and the music would end in a big loud frenzy. Since the only two people clapping were the singer and the activities director, it would suddenly stop, and everyone would be wheeled back into their rooms. This commotion once woke me up from a nap, and I thought I was having a nightmare.

My room was right next to the nurses' station and across from the laundry room. This was the only room available when Gina and Maria moved me in here. It was a "model" room and was supposed to be only temporary. After I was here a month or so, Gina and Maria took me around to see the other rooms I might want, some with a bedroom or sink in a kitchen area. But after they saw the price and how far they were from the elevator, they decided the best plan for me was to stay in my model room, which was fine with me. It was called an efficiency, which was one big room like a cheap hotel room. Sometimes I felt like I was in a Motel 6.

Most hotel rooms I stayed in, though, were much better than this dump. The service was better too. I was paying for laundry service. That meant every week someone gathered up all my dirty clothes (I put them in a large burlap bag in the corner, no hampers here) and brought them to the washing machine across the hall. God knows how many other people's clothes were swishing around in the dirty water with mine. The thought of that made me cringe. So, I started washing my clothes myself right after a few of my bras went missing. I couldn't believe these CNAs put my bras in the washing machine. I wouldn't have wanted them back anyway. *What if they washed my clothes in with smelly Dolly's down the hall?* Since, whenever I saw the washer was free, I brought my clothes over there and washed them myself. I waited and then put them in the dryer too—except for the towels and sheets, which they wouldn't allow the residents to wash. Most of the towels smelled as bad as the residents there.

One day I snuck a look at the detergent they used. It was a huge container of Arm & Hammer that they probably got at the Dollar

Store. It didn't produce any suds at all, so all the clothes swam around in disgusting-looking gray bile. How was that sanitary? I made Gina get me some Clorox detergent with bleach in the hopes that maybe I wouldn't develop some infection from the nasty germs floating around there. Sometimes when I ran out of my own towels, I had to dry myself with their industrial towels. They were scratchy, stiff, and smelled like the nurses' station. It was the same with the sheets. At first, I didn't even want to get into bed surrounded by sheets that had been washed with Arm & Hammer, but I was getting used to it. That was what worried me. It was like how prisoners must feel after being locked up in jail for a month or two. You stopped realizing how demoralizing it was to live like that. After a while, it became normal. That was what scared me more than anything.

I lived in my head most of the time. Tony used to call me Walter Mitty because I daydreamed my life away. Most of the time, people never knew what I was thinking. I didn't usually share my thoughts because I really didn't want to. Lately I'd discovered that I was beginning to feel back to normal, whatever that was. I knew there would come a time, maybe sooner rather than later, when I needed to take responsibility for my own sordid role in landing there. It was my fault, and I was embarrassed that my poor choices resulted in me sliding into despair. Maybe, in a way, I wanted to bring everything to a head, a cry for attention, but right now, I couldn't believe I was still there.

My children thought I had gotten to like it there. The social workers who evaluated me said that I had "adapted well" and adjusted to life here. Last week I heard one of them tell Gina that I was "calling this place home." Of course, that was a bald-faced lie, and the lie sickened me, but it also reminded me how easy it was to get brainwashed around there. You basically had two choices: stay and live the rest of your life like that or leave. Leaving meant either falling (to waste away in a nursing home) or dying.

But perhaps there was another way to leave. Most of my thoughts in the last few weeks had been about my escape plan. I thought it was a good one.

Two

Ben stared out his windows that were streaked from the previous night's snow. His room, 342, was on "the west wing," whatever that was It was a joke to think that Peaceful Havens could call parts of this prison a wing when it was just another corner of the main building. His room was described as "sun-filled and quiet." Ben couldn't imagine it being sun-filled, even if the sun was out. It would have helped if someone washed the windows. It was quiet, but that was because most of the residents were either sleeping or in a coma.

How did he end up here? Well, the truth was, he was not surprised he was no longer at home. Home had become a scary place because he had filled it up with so much stuff that he could no longer move around. Ben always liked to buy stuff. A consumer junkie, he was fascinated with gadgets and vintage trains. Ben was a retired Amtrak dispatcher and a real railroad historian. More than one room in his 1794 colonial was filled almost to the ceiling with his old train sets, not to mention all the timetables from every train depot in the country. He was never a computer guy, but once he discovered Amazon, he was hooked. A friend gave him his old laptop and taught him how to open an Amazon Prime account. Wow! Suddenly everything was within reach and the possibilities were endless. Soon the postman was groaning under the weight of all Ben's new toys. He discovered he could buy his favorite jams from Vermont, old Three Stooges movies, and, of course, more trains. He even won a few eBay auctions (a twelve-gauge locomotive circa 1950 was a real steal). Boxes of stuff soon filled up most of the rooms on the first floor (he hadn't gone up to the second floor in years, and Lord knows what was on the third floor). Disposing of the Amazon boxes became a problem because they wouldn't all fit in the recycling bin, so he threw them on the pile of stuff in the front living room. Soon it was even hard to get in the kitchen, so he stopped eating at home. Then the toilet backed up. Because he was too embarrassed to call a plumber, he began to use the bathroom at Whole Foods, and in the middle of the night, there were always Depends. That didn't solve the problem of showers though. Soon, he began to smell pretty ripe. Sponge baths really don't work for the whole body. He knew it was a matter of time before his secret would be discovered.

One day, Ben forgot to lock the back door and his sister Teresa barged in. She was tired of Ben not answering his phone. She took one look at his deplorable living conditions and called the rescue. That's when his life began to unravel.

First, they put him in the hospital for three days for dehydration and malnutrition. Then he was transferred to rehab for a month until they figured out what to do with him. No one wanted him to live with them, which was not surprising. The obvious answer was assisted living. Ben had thought of that possibility in the past and Peaceful Havens came to his mind. The reason it did was because it was in Smith Hill near where Gina lived. Ben was very close to Gina, whom he'd met through his old train pal Bill. Bill and Gina had been dating for years, and they all became good friends. Gina would frequently have Ben over to her house for lasagna and tiramisu. Her Christmas cookies were also to die for. Ben knew Gina's mother Angie was in Peaceful Havens so Peaceful Havens was Ben's choice. Teresa wanted him to go to St. Anthony's which was closer to his nephew Russell, but Ben dug in his heels. It was bad enough he had to go into one of these institutions! It was his damn money, so he was going to decide where to go. Now Gina could spend more time with him because she had to come here anyway to visit Angie. It was kind of a win-win. Except he really hated the place. His mind was still as sharp as a tack, and it was demoralizing to be treated as if half his brain was missing; kind of like going back into kindergarten when he really belonged in high school.

The food here left a lot to be desired. Ben never cooked but he enjoyed a good meal. He knew the difference between roasting and blanching. Whoever worked in the kitchen didn't. Ben wondered what culinary school these chefs graduated from. The vegetables looked as if someone had already eaten them. Except for salt and pepper, no seasonings were used, probably because most of the residents had gastric problems or didn't even realize what they were eating. He had been here almost two months and had never tasted any garlic. At first, he was elated at the thought that he could order anything he wanted like he was on a cruise ship. On his first morning, he went to breakfast and ordered waffles with fresh strawberries and real maple syrup. His request was met with a blank stare. It soon became obvious that Ben's expectations were a bit high. It turned out there was no waffle maker. No pancakes were ever served that weren't frozen Eggos either. Real bacon? Sorry, too crispy. Residents liked soft. And bland. If you wanted poached eggs, you were in luck—or poached anything. Apparently, the chefs never went beyond the class on poaching in Culinary 101. It was a hard reality for Ben. It soon became apparent that any tasty food Ben was longing for was not going to be found at Peaceful Havens.

Luckily, the Smith Hill Creamery was right across the street. Ben loved their fish and chips on Friday and their homemade ice cream. He still had his cane and walked slowly from his unproductive month at rehab, but he could get there, and that was what mattered. He also still had his car, his old Buick LeSabre sitting out in the parking lot. He scored a great handicapped parking spot right outside the door (aren't they all handicapped?) because most of the residents didn't drive, let alone walk. At least Ben was able to come and go at will. Of course, his sister Teresa told him not to drive and so did his nephew Russell, but who cared what they thought? If they had to eat that food, they would get in their cars and never come back. The staff made you sit with people *they* felt you were suited to. Why couldn't he go down to the dining room and sit alone, staring out the windows like he wanted to? Instead, he must sit with a married couple, Ester and Ralph. Ralph was even deafer than Ben was, and Ester spoke so softly that when she did talk, it was impossible to hear her. They barely ate. Maybe they had kids who took them out for a meal, but who knew what their situation was. Neither one could hear the other one anyway. It seemed like that was the norm in the dining room, no lively conversations coming from any of the tables.

Ben was sitting at breakfast one morning when he heard a crash. He looked over to the other side of the room and saw a feeble lady on the floor. Her walker was flung aside, probably the reason for the fall. The waitstaff looked confused and nervous until the folks from Gold Star Ambulance showed up to carry her away. This was a regular occurrence, mostly after the evening meal. Ben knew they served wine and beer here and suspected that some residents indulged too frequently, causing them to lose their footing. This excitement sometimes livened up his mealtime. Other than that, Ben would rather eat in his room with his laptop. For now, it made more sense for Ben to just make the best of it. He had his computer set up (yes, there was Wi-Fi!) and his little radio so he could listen to his talk shows. His TV was not set up yet but that was okay. He could watch his Three Stooges through his Netflix on his laptop computer. Ben recalled his life a few months ago which involved daily trips to Whole Foods to relieve his bowels. After spending a few months in his cold house with no heat, running water, or plumbing, Ben had to admit Peaceful Havens was an improvement.

So far, he hadn't been there long enough to feel too claustrophobic. Teresa was in Florida where she lived in the winter. She would be returning in a couple of months, but until then, Ben could pretty much do as he pleased. His Amazon account was running like an express train.

The folks here were only mildly curious about all the packages that were being delivered to room 342. It hadn't gotten out of control... yet. But it made Ben very happy to have daily presents waiting for him. It filled the void. God knows there were plenty of voids to fill.

Ben's nephew Russell came occasionally to visit and brought his daughter Chloe, who was ten. Russell and his wife Miriam both worked full time, though, so really, Gina was Ben's support system until Teresa came back for the summer. Gina brought Cubano sandwiches for Ben and took him to dinner when he started to hint that he needed to get out of there. When Gina took Ben out, she waited outside with her car running. That was because if Angie saw her picking him up, she would get jealous and want Gina to take her out too. Poor Gina. She was dealing with a lot, especially with her mother, who had been more verbal about her dissatisfaction with being "locked up." Angie appeared to be getting better mentally, and that was the reason. The residents who were the happiest were the ones who had absolutely no idea where they were or what it was costing them to live there. Ben gulped. He did know what it was costing him to stay here, and his money was not going to last forever.

Three

It was Sunday morning and I decided to watch *Meet the Press*. Tony always laughed about my obsession with politics and people in the spotlight. Despite his teasing, I loved the theatrics of it all. Buddy Cianci, our mayor/convicted-felon-turned-talk-show-host was quite a character, even though he was probably a mobster. I always loved talking about the latest scandals, but there was no one here to talk to. Aside from the weather, there was no interest in anything going on in the outside world. I didn't know why they cared about the weather. It had absolutely no effect on them. Unless the power went out (although I assumed we had a generator based on all the money we spent on this place), weather had no impact on the lives of any of these residents. Still, if a blizzard or hurricane was forecast, a huge wave of panic swept throughout Peaceful Havens—probably because everyone here had their TVs blasting twenty-four seven. Peaceful Havens was the TV media's perfect target audience. It was almost comical to see how an inflammatory headline, even about a Kardashian, could cause such widespread gossip. I really hoped if I ever got to that stage in my life, someone would put a pillow over my head until I stopped breathing.

I should have been going to church that morning, but I decided to skip it. Here, "church" was just a room down the hall decorated with a fake altar and the usual plastic flowers. A priest came over from St. Pius to say Mass and give communion. I had gone a few times out of guilt, but it didn't seem to count as a real Mass. I doubted if there was even real wine in the chalice—and forget a tabernacle. Of course, the candles didn't light either. Upon close inspection, I realized the wicks were plastic and the altar was nothing more than a folding card table draped with a plastic tablecloth. Jesus would be horrified if he was anywhere around here. For these reasons, I found it too depressing to walk down the hall to church. Sometimes if I whined, Gina would take me over to St. Pius. Or, if it was a good day, Father Keith would visit Emma and take me along to Mass and even dinner at the Pine Tree Grille. I missed my shrimp scampi!

Someone was knocking at my door. It couldn't be my kids; they didn't come unless they called first. It was probably one of the nurses here wanting to know if I had taken a shower yet—which was none of her damn business. I would like to remind them that the only time I needed help was when I pushed the button on this contraption around my neck. They pretended this thing was for my safety, but I knew better. The truth was, it allowed them to know where we were every minute of every day. So far, I had only had to push the button once when I couldn't get the TV to work. It turns out none of the staff members could either.

When I first came here, they put a band around my ankle. They did it during my initial exam, so I wasn't aware of it right away. I assumed it was a way of identifying me, like those bands you were forced to wear in a hospital so they don't operate on the wrong person, but after a while, it was not removed. I asked about it several times. The answers I got were always vague, sidestepping my concerns. Finally, one of the more lucid residents told me those were monitoring devices, fastened to my ankle because they assumed I was a flight risk. I was humiliated when I discovered this. Sure, I did not come here willingly, but who did? I asked Gina nicely a week later if I could have it removed because it was causing my foot to be chafed. I hid my feelings of resentment and anger knowing they would not get me what I wanted. It was removed shortly afterward. I realized that I somehow had developed a reputation of being "a sweet lady" among the staff. I could only assume that it was because, compared to the other residents here, I really was low maintenance—but that was because I didn't belong here!

I grabbed my walker and made my way to the door. It took me a few minutes, but when I opened the door, Ben, Gina's friend, was smiling as if he had all the time in the world. In his free hand, he had a box of my favorite Whitman's chocolates. Gina must have told him that I loved them.

"Ben, you sweet man, come on in." I opened the door wide, and Ben shuffled in slowly with his cane. "I hope you'll share these chocolates with me. You know I can't eat them all."

"Sure, Angie, I would love a couple, but they're mostly for you. I know when it's late at night and you can't sleep, you are always looking for a nice treat, right?"

"Yes, you must have been talking to Gina. Have a seat." I took the Sunday papers off the couch, and we both plopped down happily.

Ben surveyed the room approvingly. "Gee, Angie, your apartment is about the same size as mine, but there are no messy piles of clothes on the floor. How do you get the corners of your bed tucked in so neatly?" He grinned sheepishly. "And I recognize that lovely scent in the air. It's Jean Nate, right? My late wife, Sue, wore it all the time." Ben looked down embarrassed by this sudden disclosure.

I looked at Ben critically. Despite his sad moment, he looked better now than the first day he arrived at Peaceful Havens about a month ago. He had been thin and disheveled. Now he had some meat on his bones and had shaved. His hair had been trimmed and his clothes looked clean, although they did not match. Ben could certainly use a woman in his life.

"So, how are you doing? Do you like it here?" I asked rather brightly.

Ben looked at me as if I had lost my mind, but he was still very polite about taking his time to answer. Ben always took his time when he did anything—especially eating. I could eat a whole plate of spaghetti and meatballs and Ben would still be laboring over his first bite.

"I know this is the best place for me right now," Ben began slowly, searching for the right words. "It's my fault I'm in here, and I know this. I feel extremely guilty about letting my house get to the point where it almost needed to be condemned. I'm afraid my sister and nephew have not forgiven me. I doubt they will ever forget what I did. That was my family home, you see. I was raised in that house. We all were. I had two sisters. My sister Ramona died fifteen years ago." Ben gulped and paused with that remark. Then he regained his composure and went on. "The reason I didn't take care of my house is that, quite frankly, I didn't expect to live this long."

Ben stopped talking and gazed out the window. He had a habit of doing that. Tony always spoke slowly and deliberately too, and it drove me out of my mind. I spoke hastily, sometimes too hastily. My words came out jumbled, just the way they were in my head seconds before I said them. One of my many shortcomings, as I have aged, was my impatience. The doctor referred to it as "impulsivity." Mario scratched his head at that one—so did I—but apparently it was a real bona fide medical term now—like *oppositional defiance disorder*, which just meant that your kid needs a good spanking. But I also knew Ben, like Tony, could not be rushed, so I waited for him to continue.

"My family doesn't have a lot of longevity." Ben paused again and leaned forward a bit on the couch. "My parents died early. So did my sister Ramona. I have had heart problems since my wife died back in the eighties. I've had four stents so far, and my cardiologist told me a while ago that four is the maximum. I assume by that he meant that the next cardiac episode would result in my demise. Quite frankly, I am okay with that. I have lived a good life with a career I loved. Still love my railroads and can't quite get enough of them. I got to travel with my wife to almost all the places I wanted to, although that didn't last as long as I had hoped. Still, I've had a long and full life, got to see some of my grandnieces and grandnephews get married and have kids. About ten years ago, I felt like I was ready to meet my maker, so to speak." Ben paused again.

I noticed that "so to speak" was one of Ben's favorite expressions along with "time marches on." I was sure there were others I would discover soon.

"So, I sort of stopped caring about my health and my surroundings. I knew the house would be passed on to my nephew, so I figured, 'why fix it up?' I wouldn't be around to enjoy a new kitchen or the new plumbing or the wiring it would need. My money was safe in the bank, and that's where I wanted it to stay. I didn't think the damage to the house would be so extensive because I thought my time here on earth was going to be short. But as time went on, I began to realize with some embarrassment that I was wrong. I realized I was living way beyond my expiration date."

"Well, I can certainly relate to that point of view." I interjected. I knew I should let Ben talk, but once again, my impulsivity got the best of me. "How do we deal with the fact that we have outlived our money and usefulness, but we are not allowed to leave?"

I asked Father Keith that question several weeks ago, but he became alarmed and looked very uncomfortable. Apparently, this was not the type of question he was used to answering. It was probably because an honest answer would mean he would have to confront the thorny issue of euthanasia. *Good grief,* as Tony used to say. It was bad enough Catholics had not yet even learned how to deal with contraception or abortion. Catholicism had never been good with managing end of life issues either.

Ben sighed. Again, he became lost in thought. Finally, he looked up at me sadly. "I guess it's all water under the bridge now. I know this is the place I will stay, and I will have to make the best of it. I don't like it here, and the food is awful, but if I can continue to have some measure of freedom, by which I mean I can still drive, I will still have some quality of life, so to speak."

"Well, I don't," I burst out emphatically. "Look at the things I loved to do in my life: cooking, baking, eating, and most importantly, my independence. They're all gone now. I've been placed in here against my wishes, and there is no way I can fight my kids. My house will be sold soon and at that point, I really have nothing left. Most of the people here, as you know, cannot think straight. That's why they're put in a 'memory care' unit, which really means they have dementia. I admit I was not thinking perfectly straight for a while there when I wasn't eating right. I had a car accident and needed to be hospitalized, but I'm fine now." My voice took on a higher pitch, something that happened when I felt desperate.

Ben did not look alarmed as my kids usually did when I started to screech. He just let me finish my rant.

"Why can't a doctor look at the results of my most recent mental evaluation and realize I don't deserve to be locked up in this godforsaken place?"

Ben sighed again. "Angie," he began slowly, "I think we both know the answer to that question. It's very hard to admit this, but the people we love want us to be here. They don't want to have to worry about us anymore, but more importantly, they want peace of mind so they can go on with their lives without the fear that a late-night phone call from the police or hospital will disrupt their lives once again. Is it selfish? Damn sure it is. But how many kids do you know that want their parents to continue living in their big scary house when the responsibility for the house and them ultimately falls on their shoulders? Not many, barely even a few. In my case, Teresa didn't want to deal with any of that either. I even overheard my brother-in-law tell her to 'put me in a place where we don't have to worry about him anymore, sell the damn house and everything in it.' And to tell you the truth, I can't say I blame him. I never wanted to be a burden to anyone, did you?"

"No." Now it was my turn to sigh and shift in my seat. I gazed out the windows for a minute or two to put my thoughts together. "But I do want to talk about something that has been on my mind, Ben, and I hope you can listen and give me some advice. I also hope you will realize everything I am about to say is spoken in complete confidence. Up until now, I have not shared my thoughts about this with anyone else."

Ben seemed surprised but smiled in his relaxed way. "Of course,

Angie. I am very good at keeping secrets, and I am happy to help you in any way I can."

"Thanks, Ben. It's a huge relief to be able to finally talk to someone about all the stuff that has been bouncing around in my mind. I have no one to talk to really. Probably that is the most frustrating thing about my life right now. While I have always been a Walter Mitty, most of my life was not lived in my head. But now, everything that I think about is part of this big secret plan that I haven't been able to share. So, I want you to know how much it means to me to finally unburden these ideas, in the hope I can finally make sense out of them."

I took a deep breath and continued. "You are so right when you say that we don't have any say in our lives here. You are very honest in your assessment of the reasons we're here and the reasons no one will let us leave. It hurts me, though, to know that my family really wants me here for their own selfish reasons. In their own minds, they have convinced themselves this move is to 'keep me safe,' and I am sick to death of hearing this, but I know it is a way for them to justify their own actions. They would feel extremely guilty if they just once admitted the real reason I am here. That being said, I have somewhat come to terms with the situation as it is. I cannot change that. I know the doctors and administration want us here, too, for their own selfish, financial reasons. So, everyone has a reason to keep us here, except for us. And while you are resigned to this fact and can see yourself living the rest of your life here, my situation is different." I exhaled before continuing.

"I no longer have a car, and in a few months, I will no longer have a house. My freedom is severely curtailed in a way that yours is not. Am I willing to accept this the way you have? After many days and nights pondering this question, I have to say the answer is a resounding *no*. Okay, so this begs the question, what do I do about it? I feel like a prisoner, looking for a way out. The other night I watched *Shawshank Redemption*. Remember that movie? It opened my eyes because I realized I am not the first person to be faced with this dilemma. Yeah, Tim Robbins had to dig himself out of jail, but my situation is a little trickier.

I can probably get out of here undetected, but where I go and how I stay hidden is another question. So far, I've come up with some ideas. Interested?"

Ben was watching me, fascinated. His mouth was now hanging half open. I certainly had his attention. "Of course, Angie, I am all ears." He laughed and leaned forward eagerly.

"When I was working in real estate, I was successful. I always handled the finances in our house. Tony didn't care about money, and I always had the bills paid. What he didn't know was that I managed to save some of my own money. I skimmed money off the top of my own earnings and hid it away for a rainy day, as they say. I didn't put it in the bank. My mother always taught me that. As a child of the Depression and a young widow with four kids, she was an expert in managing money. So, after I left real estate, I worked at Apex Department Store and kept saving some of that money as well. Retail jobs seemed to fall into my lap after that. I worked part time and sometimes on weekends and holidays. I enjoyed sales and liked people. I found they liked and trusted me. So, to make a long story short, I have quite a nest egg hidden that nobody knows about. Up until now, that is." I paused and winked at Ben. He continued to look impressed. "It's well over six figures. I managed to invest it wisely, and it should give me the start I need for a new life.

"My kids have control of all my bank accounts and CDs. I also gave them all the savings bonds I had saved up, mostly for them and their kids. But they don't know about my stash. It's still hidden in the house. I never got a chance to bring it here because I haven't been home since the accident. So, the first step in my plan is to find a way to visit my house when Gina is not around so I can get my money out. I know Gina is planning to sell my house in the next few months, so it's important that I do this soon."

"Angie, I can certainly help you with that." Ben started out slowly but became positive as he thought things through. "I have my car, and I can find a good time to drive you to your house. You still have the key?" He looked at me quizzically.

"Sure, I even have my old car keys. Of course, the kids don't know that either. But I was careful to keep certain things secret. And I'm sure glad I did." I smiled at Ben as I continued. "I know it's expensive to stay in this place. The kids think I don't realize that they're draining my bank accounts to pay for this dump. My income does not cover the expenses here. I know their plan is to use up most of the cash I have and then sell the house. I only have enough cash to stay here for about a year at this point, so that's why they're planning to sell the house soon. I am not at all happy about having my house sold out from under me. But frankly, I could no longer keep it up, and I couldn't keep going up and down those damn stairs. I slept on the couch downstairs many times because I couldn't climb the stairs to bed. I never told Gina that, but I think she figured it out. Same thing goes for the basement. I like clean clothes, but I wasn't washing my clothes as much because I couldn't keep lugging laundry baskets up and down, up, and down, several times a week. It got to the point where I was rinsing out my undies in the sink." I hadn't admitted that to anyone, so it felt good to unburden all my secrets. Ben was the perfect one to tell all this to. He nodded in agreement, understanding my predicament all at once.

"Well, Angie, you're preaching to the choir," Ben said simply. "I didn't even have a functioning washer or dryer, so what do you think it was like to get a whiff of me after a few weeks? I must admit I don't miss my house much at all."

"You're right. I miss my independence, but I don't miss that feeling of dread when I would wake in the morning and wasn't sure how I could cope with my limitations and that big house anymore. I'm ready to say goodbye to all that but on my terms. I don't like all these decisions being made for me as if I'm an imbecile. I wish my kids would sit down and we could all share ideas like adults. But I've realized it's fruitless. I think they're fine with me having 'diminished capacity' so they can make decisions without me. I have always been headstrong, and they know I wouldn't go along with their self-serving plans at this point. But I am not going to struggle with all that right now. First order of business: Get my money. Second: Plan my escape." At the mention of escape, Ben's eyes lit up in anticipation.

My fantasy so far consisted of thinking of the steps leading up to an escape from Peaceful Havens. I knew I had to have the money to pull it off, and with some help, I could get it undetected. But I confess I had not really thought the rest of the plan through. That's what I needed Ben for.

"Okay, I leave here. Let's say I can get a ride to someplace. I can take a plane, bus, or train somewhere. It must be a place where I am familiar with the neighborhood, but obviously cannot be in Rhode Island. I will set up a new life in a small apartment I can manage. I will hire people to help me when I need it. I can have a small car or manage by walking around. I can always take a taxi if I need to. My secret savings should last for a few years, at least until I am six feet under, so to speak." I winked at Ben.

Ben looked determined. "I can certainly help you get to a train station, and I know all the conductors in the Northeast. With just a phone call, I can ask that they put you on whatever train you want. I can even go with you to help until you want to tell me to get lost." Ben smiled slowly, choosing the rest of his words carefully. "Have you thought about what your kids will say? Do you have a plan for telling them at some point? And what point? Knowing Gina, she will have the FBI on your tail in no time."

We both laughed. I knew he was right. This was the sticky part of my plan so far.

"I haven't been able to figure that part out yet," I admitted. The ideal scenario would be for me to move in with someone else they approve of. "If I had a relative somewhere..." My voice trailed off.

I knew that my destination had to be someplace warm but not too hot. I hate humidity. And bugs. But the winters here were too long for me now, and any place that had snow created lots of problems, the least being falling. I had to be extra careful now and avoid any chance of accidents. A fall would land me back in here for sure, or even someplace worse. I felt like a felon who needed to stay out of trouble, or else he would be thrown back in jail. Now I knew how Tim Robbins felt.

But suddenly I remembered Uncle Nicky.

A few years before Tony's heart attack, we traveled to California with Tony's sister Albina and her husband Henry. Albina was always up for adventures with a huge smile and a martini in her hand, even before five o'clock. It was a great adventure. Henry did all the driving so we didn't have to worry about a thing. Henry was a mechanic for Delta Air Lines. If anything broke down, he could fix it on the spot. I always envied Albina because Henry was extremely handy to have around the house. If I asked Tony to change a lightbulb, he would agree to do it cheerfully. But three months later, the bulb would still be out—and of course, it was up to me to buy the damn bulbs.

We drove out to San Francisco and visited Alcatraz. On the way back, we stopped in to see Uncle Nicky.

Uncle Nicky was not my uncle. In fact, he was not anyone's uncle, since he had been an only child and never had any kids. The reason I got to know Uncle Nicky was that he was Tony's best friend growing up, and he introduced us. He was a quiet guy, and I felt comfortable with him right away. Later on, he became godfather to Gina and Mario. Nicky ended up marrying right after we did and moved to California where he became a professor of Italian at a university. He lived somewhere "up in the hills," as Albina would say. After that, we never saw him, but occasionally we would exchange letters. He went on to write several books about the Italian language and became a rather accomplished author. His first wife died, and shortly after, he was remarried to Vivian, a skinny spinster who always had a million health problems. Her only redeeming quality was that she was an only child with a huge inheritance; her parents died young and rich. Uncle Nicky took care of Vivian, although I suspected he was not happy with her chronic hypochondria. I often told Tony she was healthier than I was. But her medical condition must have taken a turn for the worse because last year I heard she'd died. Her death was rather mysterious. Albina gave a vague explanation of her demise, saying she just got tired of living. So, Uncle Nicky was now a single bachelor again, and he was alone, living in the hills of northern California. That was why I suddenly thought of Uncle Nicky.

I mentioned Uncle Nicky to Ben. I explained to him that maybe Uncle Nicky could be the perfect hideaway friend. I had a feeling Uncle Nicky would not really mind my company. Compared to Vivian, I looked pretty good, especially since I could cook. Uncle Nicky loved Italian food but was always too busy writing to learn the art of making raviolis.

Ben pondered this news for a few minutes. I could tell from the expression on his face that he was a little overwhelmed with this recent turn of events. Surely when he ambled over to my room on a Sunday morning with his box of chocolates, he had no idea what he was getting into.

"Are you thinking of a romantic relationship with Nicky?" Ben finally asked. "If so, it might complicate things. Or perhaps not..."

Ben's question startled me. I hadn't even thought of that. Of course. Uncle Nicky and me? Living together after both spouses have died? Knowing how tongues wagged, especially in my family, I could see the red flags everywhere.

"Wow, Ben, I guess that didn't occur to me. I wonder if it would be possible for us to live in the same house with the understanding it would be totally platonic. Speaking for myself, I am not romantically attracted to Uncle Nicky. I doubt if I ever could be, especially now that we are so much older. I guess I was looking at this whole scenario from a very selfish viewpoint. Here is Uncle Nicky, living happily in his beautiful house in California. Why in the world would he want to harbor a fugitive?" I felt rather crestfallen.

"Why, Angie, that is not necessarily true." Ben sat back in the corner of the couch for a minute, thinking. "The first order of business is to call or write to Nicky. See how he's doing, kind of feel him out. If things are good, maybe you could mention you're thinking of visiting California and would like to see him. Depending on his response, you could then call him and find out how much help he wanted to give you. He might surprise you."

I could envision a phone call to Uncle Nicky, telling him I'm planning to escape and hop a train to California.

What planet was I living on?

Suddenly I felt tired and overwhelmed.

Ben could see my shoulders slump in despair. We both sat there for a few minutes. Suddenly there was a knock at the door, startling both of us out of our reveries. A few seconds later, Ellie, the morning nurse (actually, she was a CNA) came barging in. That was another annoying thing about this place: no privacy. Anyone could come by at any time and barge in with a quick knock to announce themselves. What if I had been on the john?

"Angie, we're having a Sunday sing-along downstairs in a half hour. There will be coffee and goodies and a garden theme to welcome spring! So please join us. You too, Ben! It will be a lot of fun! Do you want me to put your shoes and makeup on for you?" Ellie was out of breath and beads of sweat were collecting on her upper lip. She had that forced smile the staff are all taught to present to the residents, designed as an attempt to appear to be one big happy family.

"Thanks, Ellie, but I'm going to pass. Ben and I are having a visit, and we're not done yet." I was trying to be polite, but my patience had long since worn thin. Even Sunday mornings were not sacred around here.

"You can resume your little visit at another time. This will be much more fun! And we're trying to get Emma to join us too. You haven't seen her in a while, right?" Ellie was not going to give up easily.

Ben spoke up, his voice taking on an air of authority. I was proud of the way he stood his ground when it was needed. "No, Ellie, we are reminiscing about our families right now and don't want to be disturbed. We both ate already. Thanks for thinking of us, but please close the door on your way out."

Ellie was taken aback but retreated reluctantly. "Okay, your call. Have a nice day!" She lumbered out of the room and slammed the door behind her.

We both burst out laughing. "Good job, Ben!" I raised my hand for a high five as we celebrated the small victory. "You know, I was having second thoughts about my little plan, but now that I'm reminded of the situation here, I'm resolved to make this happen." I sat back and noticed Ben looking as determined as I was.

"I'm glad to hear that." Ben looked directly at me; his dark eyes were serious for a change. "You know I came to Peaceful Havens partly because I knew you were here. I always remembered you as a delightful, active, witty lady. Gina always told me how much she admired your strength after your husband died. My first thought, though, when she told me you were here, was dismay. I had hoped you hadn't deteriorated after your accident to the point where you needed to be here. I was afraid you had fallen to the level of these other residents and your mind had become feeble, so to speak. But now I can see that is not true at all. The truth is, Angie, you do *not* belong here. I don't either, but my situation is different. I am okay here for now, but it would make my life so much richer if I could help you with your plan. I want to help you escape!" Ben finished with a grin and waved his hands around in happiness. I hadn't remembered seeing him this excited since he rode in the engineer's cabin on the Santa train four years ago. It was like he had gotten his second wind.

I felt happier than I had in a long time, certainly since I began to have scary thoughts about my house. Now, for the first time, I could feel a definite plan taking shape. I now had help, and my plan was not just in my head anymore.

"Ben, you don't know what this means to me, to be able to talk honestly with you. Up to now, I have had a vague fantasy about my plan to escape, but I knew that it was just that, a fantasy. I never dreamed I could make it a reality, probably because I would be doing it alone. But now I see that it is a real possibility, and that is because of you. I feel a real connection to Tim Robbins!" I smiled at Ben and winked.

"I love that movie. It's one of my favorites! In fact, I know I got the DVD someplace in my room..." Ben's voice trailed off. "But I think your plan is great, and we can firm up all the details as soon as we take care of the first order of business, which is to get the money that is hidden in your house. What is a good time to do this, do you think?"

"The sooner the better." I looked around nervously, suddenly remembering my carefully guarded secret. But we had been speaking in hushed tones, as if we were talking about a dream we once had. "How about sometime this week? I think Gina is working every day except Friday, so tell me what works for you."

Ben thought for a minute. He had a faraway look that amused me. I had a feeling he was living vicariously through what I hoped was going to be Angie's Excellent Adventure.

"I think I have an eye doctor's appointment on Tuesday, but I should be free any other day," Ben said slowly. "It's not as if I have friends or family beating down the doors here to visit me, so to speak." I sensed a real sadness in him for the first time since I have known him. It did occur to me that except for one time when we had his seventy-fifth birthday celebration at Bill's house almost ten years ago, I had never seen any member of his family with him. Ben seemed happy alone, and I wondered if it was because he was so used to it or he really relished the idea of being by himself. Ben took a while to warm up to someone. When he did, he became more than warm, almost hot, but it certainly took him a long time to get there. It wasn't surprising. It took Ben a long time to do anything.

"I'm free tomorrow. My hairdresser here only comes in on Thursdays and Fridays. Mondays are slow, and I know Gina is working, so we should be able to get my money out of the house without anyone in my family seeing us. How about around eleven o'clock? Afterwards I can take you to the Smith Hill Creamery? I know you love the milkshakes there, and I really like their BLTs with fries." I smiled at him, knowing food was the way to convince Ben to agree to anything.

His face lit up. "Wow, that sounds great, but you don't have to treat me. Just being with you, Angie, is enough of a treat. How do we get out of here without someone making a fuss about where we're going?"

"Good question." I pictured all the nosy residents and CNAs

watching me get into Ben's car. I'm sure that would be enough to put all of them into a frenzy of pointless gossip. "You know that when a resident leaves the building they are required to sign out at the front desk. Sharon, who sits at the front desk, usually watches over everyone." I hesitated for a minute as I formulated a strategy. "When she isn't around, though, we can leave without signing out. I could just meet you at your car in the parking lot. I will try, although it might not be possible, to leave without being detected if I can slip out when Sharon is distracted." I sighed, knowing this was only the first of many barriers I would have to overcome to carry out my plan.

"Why don't we just leave together? Tell them we're going across the street to lunch?" Ben spoke slowly but his voice became more confident. "We might as well be open about going out together. It would arouse less suspicion. Everyone here knows we're connected through Gina, so it wouldn't be a big surprise for me to drive you across the street to lunch. If they have a problem with that, I will deal with them!"

I smiled. "Good idea, Ben! We need to stop acting as if we're doing something wrong, until we are!" We both laughed at that one, and Ben got up to leave.

As we got to the doorway, I gave him an impulsive hug. "You don't know how much hope your visit this morning has given me, Ben. For the first time since I came here, I feel as if my life is not in ruins. It's as if a ray of sunshine popped out of my gloom and gave me hope, a hope I didn't think I would have ever again. Thank you." I looked at him somberly and he smiled and hugged me too.

"You are the ray of sunshine, Angie. Don't forget that." He turned and walked resolutely back down the corridor to his room.

Four

It was after one o'clock and I knew I was late for Sunday luncheon. Rules here were rigid and the staff frowned if you showed up late or didn't eat fast enough for the next shift to arrive. I was on the early shift. This meant I had to be at breakfast by eight o'clock, lunch at noon, and dinner at five o'clock. The second shift arrived an hour and a half later. I didn't know who came up with these rules, but they were not at all geared towards the residents that lived here.

To be on a schedule and adhere to a time frame was, for most of the residents, totally unrealistic. When I first came here, my watch was broken, so I didn't know what time it was—and frankly, I didn't care anyway. Nevertheless, if I wasn't down in the dining room on time, someone would pound on my door to remind me. And, of course, if the knock was not answered within five seconds, the door was opened. I had begun locking my door at night. Pretty soon I might start locking it all the time, even knowing that it was against the rules here to lock doors. The head nurse, Kim, explained this to me the very first day: Locked doors were not allowed.

"It is to keep you safe," she said sternly.

I just stared at her in disbelief.

Kim was not her real name. I called her that because she looked just like one of the Kardashians. Her hair, which never moved, was waist length and stiffly curled in high-gloss waves. I imagined she spent a fortune on hair products, but not nearly as much as she must shell out for makeup. Although she was only in her thirties, she wore enough foundation on her face to cover the wrinkles on the faces of everyone here. "Pancake makeup" was how we used to refer to that stuff, but I had no idea what it was called now. Her eyelashes were either fake or extensions. (I found out what extensions were from the *National Enquirer*.) Anyway, they were long and very thick, defining her electric blue eyes rimmed in thick black liner. The corners of her eyes curled up a bit, giving her the appearance of Lily from *The Munsters*. Her eyebrows were shaved and then penciled in above the place where her real eyebrows should have been, making her look permanently surprised. She completed this ensemble with blood-red lipstick carefully applied to her plump lips, which I suspected had been injected with collagen. All in all, her makeup resembled Lily, but her clothes and hair were Kim. Her nurse's jacket was never buttoned, revealing a thin blouse cut low enough to attract the attention of most of the men here, even the ones who were half blind. Her outfit was usually completed with a pencil skirt, short enough to slide up towards her thighs when she sat down. How she could be comfortable enough to work a shift here dressed this way was beyond me, especially since her shoes were not the white, soft-soled nursing shoes all the CNAs wore. Instead, they were pointy, shiny black patent leather stilettos with four-inch heels. Her presence was announced by the clacking of her heels on the linoleum floors, giving her an air of menacing authority that I guessed she was looking for. I could always tell when Kim would appear. Along with the annoying sound of her heels came the telltale whiff of her perfume. It was not dabbed discreetly behind her ears as we were all taught. Like all of Kim's extravagances, it was applied with a very heavy hand. I thought it was Chanel, but Gina said it was only a cheap Victoria's Secret knock off. I suspected her makeup was probably Maybelline as well.

Locking my door behind me, I headed down to the dining room

which as just down the hall. As I passed the nurses' station, Linda, one of the CNAs, frowned at me.

"Good morning," I said brightly. I knew she was unhappy with my tardiness, but who cared. Now that I had an escape plan, things looked a lot brighter for me. I no longer cared about following their dumb rules. Soon, I wouldn't have to worry about these rules anymore. Linda mumbled a greeting and went back to rifling through the file cabinet in the corner of the nurses' station. Across the hall, I could see another nurse, Becky, throw some dirty laundry in the washing machine. I shuddered, remembering I needed to wash some clothes later. I guessed I would be washing them out in my sink. No way would I put them into that germy washing machine now.

As I approached the dining room, I could see John up ahead. John was one of the wait staff here. I didn't know what John's real role was, as he usually spent most of his time gossiping. He was supposed to maintain the cleanliness of the dining room. If the dining room was clean, it certainly didn't smell like it. The rug was disgusting. You would think they would either pull up the rug and put down cheap tile or replace it. It was stained with many years' worth of accumulated bodily fluids and spilled food. The thought of that usually made me lose my appetite so I tried not to think of it.

John was always sneaking around late at night, and so was I. It was no secret that I loved my late-night snacks. When I first came here and could not walk easily, I would indulge myself with chocolates in my room, but now that I had become more mobile, I took a trip to the dining room in the wee hours of the morning after I watched the late show. There were oranges in a large bowl next to the coffee station. I loved oranges. I would always be the designated peeler in my house. My kids and Tony loved oranges, too, but were too lazy to peel them, which was where I came in. It didn't bother me to dig my nails into the soft flesh. Usually, I could peel an orange in a quick flourish, sometimes in one long peel if I was having a good day. Everyone was always amazed at the long peels I could produce in record time. So, most nights (or early mornings) would find me by the orange bowl, grabbing an orange or two.

John didn't like the fact I wandered the halls late at night. Residents should all be sleeping at that time, although I knew from the sounds coming from closed the TV on, reaching decibels that would make my ears ring. I knew my hearing was not what it used to be, especially on the right side, but walking down the hallways, I could hear most TVs loud and clear. So, I guessed I may not have been as deaf as I thought.

"Hi, Angie!" John's deep voice resonated in the dining hall. "Get much sleep last night?" He grinned foolishly, revealing a mouthful of decay.

"Just fine, John," I answered curtly. I knew he was referring to my orange snatching. I had two juicy ones late last night. I knew he wanted to talk about my late-night habits, so I kept walking as fast as this rickety walker would allow me.

"I saw you last night roaming around again," John proudly announced. I ignored him now, sidestepping him to enter the dining room. "You know you're not supposed to wander around at that time of night. I might have to give Gina a report of how her mother never sleeps."

"Gina already knows," I replied stiffly. "So, remind me again what your job is here? Are you the late-night police, patrolling the halls for burglars?"

"I am supposed to keep people safe," John declared. Apparently, he really believed that the staff wants him to keep the residents safe from orange-peeling old ladies who needed a bit of sweetness before bedtime.

"I would worry more about you getting enough sleep to do your job properly," I answered, "whatever that is. Seems like there are a lot more important tasks to accomplish around here than watching my comings and goings." I managed to speed up so he had fallen behind me. I really had had enough of his inane chatter. My focus now was on dinner.

My assigned dinner table was at the end of the room. The only bright spot about coming here, I had thought, was that I could spend meals with my longtime friend Emma. We used to spend many hours sharing drinks at Pine Tree Grille, starting out with wine and ending with coffee and dessert (always their luscious coconut cake with buttercream frosting). I anticipated lots of hours in the dining room with her, gossiping shamelessly and laughing like old times. It soon became apparent that I was in for a rude awakening. Like everything else, my meal buddies were assigned to me. Peaceful Havens apparently decided I would be more suited to sharing meals with Betty and Evelyn, two ladies I had never met and had nothing in common with whatsoever.

Betty was in her eighties and was deaf as a doornail. She was also very skinny and barely ate. In her defense, her appetite had most likely disappeared after she tried out the food here. I told Gina that Peaceful Havens would be the perfect "fat farm." Spend a couple months here and you would shed any unwanted pounds and more. I thought Betty was Jewish. I saw her name tag one day (they insist we wear cheap stick-on name tags during the sing-alongs and parties), and she was a Rosenstein, or maybe it was Rosenblatt. Anyway, it was obvious she used to live a good life, because she still wore all her jewelry—all at the same time. The first day I sat with her, my jaw dropped open at the sight of her platinum rings adorned with several karats of diamonds that twisted around her bony fingers. Her wrists and neck were draped with dozens of gold chains, all different sizes. I nervously watched her stumble through the dining room with her cane, wondering who dressed her in the morning. Surely, she must have had a personal assistant paid very well by the family. If one of the CNAs working here were allowed in her room, that jewelry would disappear faster than an ice cream cone on a hot summer day. I could count on it to show up on eBay within hours.

Betty and I have had two conversations, and I knew she never heard a word I said. From what I could understand (Betty was not the most engaging conversationalist, but who was in this place?), she was a widow and had one son, Jacob. He breezed in and out on family day, usually accompanied by his blonde wife who usually sported a large Chanel bag on her shoulder. They fussed over Betty for about fifteen minutes and then hastily escaped in their white Beemer that was parked in one of the handicapped spots in the front of the parking lot.

Evelyn was plump and smiles all the time. I was happy to see that I might be able to have a conversation with someone on the first day here, but my hopes were soon dashed. Evelyn smiled a lot and ate a lot but was apparently too heavily medicated to string two words together. Either that or she just didn't remember who she was or where she was. After our introductions, Evelyn kept repeating the fact that she thought she knew me from somewhere. She didn't look familiar to me, but I did attempt to find out a little bit about her background because it was possible we had met before. Everybody knew everybody in this town. I asked her a few questions about where she lived and where she grew up, being careful not to pry too much.

Every answer was the same: "Angie, you look so familiar! I am sure I know you from somewhere!"

She repeated the same phrase over and over until I was ready to scream. After that, I did not even try to speak to Evelyn or Betty. What twisted Peaceful Havens staff member thought we all would be a good match? I suspected no one else would sit with these two, so I had to, being the new kid on the block.

So far, I had not asked to have my seat changed. From the look of the rest of the residents in the dining room, a change would not result in any improvement. Most of the residents spent the hour here picking at their food, staring into space, or drooling. It must be easy to be a chef in this place. Except for me and probably Ben, no one was going to complain about the temperature, quality, or taste of the food they dished out here. Their signature dish looked like the one Tony used to make all the time: hash browns. I always called it shit on a shingle. Now even shit looked better than my daily breakfast here.

Last week, I noticed a skinny man in the corner had fallen asleep at his table. He was alone, and his head was drooping towards his chin. I was about to alert the waiter, but it was too late. Horrified, I watched him slowly topple to the floor as if in slow motion. After the EMT guys came, he woke up and became rather annoyed. That night, he was back in the same chair eating his soup.

Today the special was roast turkey with all the fixings. Sounds good, right? Wrong! There had never been real roast turkey here, at least since I arrived. During my first week here, I ordered it happily, thinking it was real roast turkey. Instead, what I got was one of those turkey breasts from the deli department. God knows how long it had been there. It tasted exactly like pressed turkey cold cuts, which is what it was. It was dry as a bone and the gravy over it was clumpy and cold. It had congealed from sitting around in the kitchen for too long. It was the same with the mashed potatoes and the mashed squash, which looked like someone had already eaten it. The only saving grace was the cranberry sauce, which came out of a can but was at least edible and familiar. I should have ordered just cranberry sauce and bread because that was all I ate.

Nothing here was ever served hot, or even lukewarm. All the food was cold, even the coffee. Don't even get me started on the coffee. It tasted like instant coffee probably because it was. I guessed they didn't want to be sued if a resident was burned, and since most of the residents here lacked taste buds, it didn't really matter. I was going to ask Ben to order me a coffee machine on Amazon. Then I could have good hot coffee in the morning. Of course, I would have to hide it since any plug-in appliances in our rooms were banned, including irons. But now that my days here were numbered, I didn't really care anymore. I felt smug and happy to have a secret I could savor.

Evelyn and Betty were not at the table yet. Or maybe they were not coming to dinner today. Betty probably begged Jacob to take her somewhere in his Beemer, and Evelyn was probably still in her room, babbling at her TV set. I saw Ben across the room, eating with his table mates Ester and Ralph. He looked as uncomfortable as I was as he tried to enjoy a meal with two strangers. He looked up and caught my eye and smiled. Tomorrow with his help, I would begin carrying out part one of my adventure.

I smiled back at him, but I had butterflies in my stomach. On my mind was Nicky. Somewhere in California, he was going along with his life, unaware of me. But he was on my mind, more than I cared to admit. I wasn't even sure what he looked like now. I had forgotten what his voice sounded like. Yet I had already begun to picture myself spending time with him. I had imaginary conversations with him where we would laugh at foolish antics from our old days in Boston way back when. What would our first meeting be like? Maybe Nicky already had someone in his life and would not welcome an intrusive old friend from Boston. Or maybe he was feeble and had lost some or most of his marbles. Hoping my fears were unfounded, I still felt a giddy anticipation bubbling up inside of me when I allowed myself to indulge in Nicky daydreams.

Stop it, I told myself. *Don't be silly. Remember to take all this one step at a time.*

That's what Ben said, and it was solid advice. Still, I couldn't help wondering, a great deal of the time now, *What would Nicky think?*

Five

It was cocktail hour, at least for Nicky. It wasn't quite five o'clock, but the gin and vermouth were waiting on his side table, along with a few plump green olives. This was Nicky's daily ritual now, and he must admit it was a good one. Since Vivian died last year, he'd been free to do whatever he wanted. No longer did he have to listen to her incessant nagging whenever five o'clock approached and he began to prepare his martini. Vivian didn't drink. All in all, Vivian didn't do much of anything except comment negatively on everything he did.

When Nicky first met her, Vivian was cute and dressed like a China doll. At first, Nicky was impressed with her many matching outfits. Her clothes and handbags sported every designer label known to mankind. At the time, Nicky admitted he was easily dazzled. He knew she didn't have much in the brains department, but Nicky had been alone too long and wanted some company. He ignored the warning signs: Vivian had no friends, no interests, and mostly nothing to do at all—except give him advice about what not to do. Vivian moved into Nicky's large California ranch overlooking the San Bernardino Mountains and immediately made herself at home. Nicky's life soon became immersed in keeping Vivian occupied, like taking daily drives around the mountains because she was bored. But Nicky was never bored. He loved writing and joyfully embraced every day, which usually consisted of sitting by his laptop in his study. Nicky was an accomplished Italian scholar who enjoyed languages and wrote several well received novels and numerous translations.

Vivian's only interest was shopping. When she couldn't get out to Rodeo Drive as often as she wanted, she resorted to the Home Shopping Network. Soon, she became preoccupied with the TV set and the phone, where she would happily order everything HSN had on special that day.

She was on a first name basis with all the TV personalities on HSN. The house began to fill with boxes and bags of clothes and makeup. Later, her purchases expanded to cookware and kitchen gadgets of all kinds even though she never set foot in the kitchen. Nicky's garage piled up with unopened boxes, spilling over into the shed in the back. At first, Nicky balked at her behavior, but soon he realized his nagging was not going to change a thing. Vivian had a bottomless trust fund which did not appear to be in danger of being depleted by her obsession with spending money all day. So, Nicky called Goodwill and the Salvation Army while Vivian was asleep (she slept until noon most days), and then quietly began removing the stuff she never opened. Apparently, they were used to getting desperate phone calls from the spouses of hoarders and were happy to oblige. Nicky was happy to see the boxes slowly disappear from his house, but Vivian became even more obsessed with buying things. She discovered QVC shopping network. That's when the wheels fell off the bus. Nicky became used to seeing white vans of every size and shape stop at his driveway with large packages. Because his driveway was set back away from the front door, some of the guys didn't bother getting out of their truck. They simply left the boxes next to his mailbox. It was embarrassing for Nicky, who always led a simple and quiet life. He prided himself on being sort of an egghead and isolating himself with his writing, which took up most of his time.

Along with Vivian's obsessive behavior came a change in her mental status. Gradually, she became even more belligerent and confused. She stopped changing her clothes and stopped showering. One night, instead of sleeping, she wandered out of the house. Apparently, she had confused the bathroom door with the front door of the house, and when Nicky woke the next day, he found that she was gone. It took him a while to realize her absence. Vivian occupied the large corner room with the attached bathroom, which was on the front side of the house away from his bedroom. It was about one thirty in the afternoon when Nicky decided it was time to wake Vivian. That's when he saw her empty bed and her slippers still on her bedside rug. Evidently, she didn't even bother with shoes. Nicky realized she probably had left the house barefoot in her flimsy nightgown. Nicky struggled to remember what she had worn to bed and couldn't even give the cops a good description of her clothing. To his chagrin, he worried that she might have left the house naked. Nicky's home was in Sky Forest, located on a ridge surrounded by acres of steep forestlands that were too near the coast to be afflicted by the inland fires that had become all too common in California. Four days later, the rangers found Vivian. She must have stumbled and fallen into one of the many ravines located near his property. Nicky numbly went through the funeral arrangements for her, waiting to feel the debilitating sadness he assumed would follow—but it never came.

It was kind of scary how normal Nicky felt afterwards. He managed to slip right back into his old life after her trust fund transferred to his bank account. He began writing again without skipping a beat. Nicky had no trouble disposing of the rest of the boxes stacked all over the house and cancelling Vivian's Amazon Prime account. He donated her unused and slightly used clothing to a local consignment shop and had his cleaning service turn her bedroom back into a guest room.

The only problem Nicky had was the persistent feeling of guilt that nagged at him all the time. Nicky was always a religious guy. Not in a fanatical way, but he had a strong sense of spiritual faith and kept a crucifix on his bedroom wall to which he prayed every morning. He was not religious enough to use his mother's old rosary beads, having forgotten his Hail Marys many years ago, but still he prayed in his own words. His father always told him that God didn't care how you communicated if you kept up a daily conversation with him. He always found it easy to feel connected to God living in such a beautiful place with a view of mountains from every window. Nicky felt extremely blessed to live a life surrounded by beauty spending most of his time doing what he loved. For this reason, Nicky felt guilty that he was relieved by Vivian's death. That may have been as God intended, but he couldn't help but feel that he should be suffering somehow.

Nicky didn't go to church. He didn't socialize much, though he kept in touch with some of his college friends who had also been on the staff where he had taught. There were only a handful left, but they provided all the stimulation he needed once or twice a year when they all got together for a reunion. There were no more women in his life now. After his disastrous experience with Vivian, he felt extremely fearful of pursuing another romantic relationship.

That ship has sailed, he thought ruefully.

Still, he kind of longed for human touch. It would be nice to hug someone. Not that Vivian ever hugged him either. Sometimes he thought he should just get a cat.

The light was beginning to fade across the hills when his phone rang. He looked at it quizzically. It seldom rang. Most of his friends from college emailed or texted. He really didn't like talking on the phone. Usually, telemarketers would not call at this time of the day, so out of curiosity, he picked it up.

"Hello?" he began cautiously. His voice cracked since he hadn't used it all day.

"Hi, is this Nicky? Uncle Nicky?" Angie began her phone conversations quickly and to the point like she did everything else.

"Yes, is this Angie?" Nicky immediately recognized her voice. She still sounded like she was sixteen.

"Of course, Nick. I hope you don't mind me calling you out of the blue like this. I'm not sure what time it is there. It's not the middle of the night, is it?"

"No." Nicky laughed and relaxed while he poured his martini. "It is a little past five in the afternoon, and I am fixing myself a well-deserved drink. Want to join me?" Nicky always enjoyed joking with Angie. He and Tony used to tease her, but she liked it too.

"Sure, I'll be right there!" Angie laughed too, playing along.

"It's good to hear from you." Nicky sat by his windows watching the mountain light slowly disappear. "You know, I don't get many phone calls these days. Quite truthfully, that is okay with me. I am not a social animal. Peace and quiet suits me fine. But I have been thinking of you. Albina told me last week that you had moved, and I was wondering how that is working out for you."

"Thanks, Nicky. I have been thinking of you too. I am so sorry about Vivian. I'm afraid I haven't expressed my condolences properly, but things have been hectic here." Her voice became quieter, and Nicky paused.

"That's nice of you to say, Angie. The truth is Vivian's condition had deteriorated. I can give you more details but suffice to say, it was kind of a blessing when she passed. I only hope she didn't suffer much, but I suspect her death was quick. I don't think she was aware of what was happening anyway." Nicky's tone changed. "It is sad to watch someone you used to love become a different person. I never thought it was possible that someone could change so drastically. I prayed a lot during those times." Nicky cleared his throat and continued. "I feel guilty now that my prayers were answered."

"Oh, Nicky, it's so refreshing to hear such honesty. Don't feel guilty. Things happened the way they were meant to. I know it's hard to recognize that at first. When Tony died suddenly, I thought it was my fault because I wasn't in the room when he collapsed. I agonized about how he would have lived if he'd had medical attention sooner. It took the EMTs a half hour to arrive, and by that time, it was too late. It was a long time before I understood Tony would have wanted it that way. If he had lived, he would have had brain damage. Then he would have ended up in a place like the one I'm in now... and it would have killed him for sure. Now I'll stop talking before I turn into a babbling idiot."

Nicky took a sip of his martini as he listened to Angie's outpouring of grief. It only made him feel guiltier that he hadn't felt any sadness about Vivian. He only felt relief and a kind of strange giddiness. But then he remembered Angie's situation and curiosity got the better of him.

"So, Ang, are you in a nursing facility of some kind?" Nicky asked.

"Well, that is a kind way of describing where I am," Angie began forcefully. "It's called 'assisted living,' but I can't say I ever see anyone here living, assisted or otherwise. Maybe all assisted living places are not like this, but I suspect they are." Angie's voice was full of frustration.

"People who have outlived their usefulness are placed here by their kids or spouses who have the means to do it. While we're here, we are subjected to the repeated attempts of the staff to pretend we're all a big happy family. But our 'loved ones' are just waiting for us to croak and hope that we will still have enough money left for them to enjoy our inheritance, for what that's worth."

"I'm sorry to hear that," Nicky said sympathetically. He felt a sudden compassion for Angie and could understand how she felt abandoned. It had always been a deep-rooted fear of his that he would end up the same way. But she certainly sounded like she didn't belong there.

"How did this happen? I hope you don't mind me asking, but you were always a woman full of strength, hope, and beauty. I think I told Tony many times he was lucky to find a woman as perfect as you are! I remember you sewed, cooked, baked, and took care of everyone as if it were the easiest thing in the world." Nicky sipped his martini thoughtfully as the skies darkened outside his window.

"Well, I admit I had declined a bit at home because I wasn't eating right. I think it started with a virus. My doctor said I had a beginning case of shingles, and I lost my appetite. I became weak, didn't tell anyone." Angie paused and chuckled. "I always was so stubborn! Then I had a little car accident that totaled my car. That was the beginning of the end. It was a perfect excuse for my kids to put me here after exhaustive tests confirming what they wanted to believe: that my mental health had declined." Angie stopped to catch her breath while Nicky waited patiently for her to continue. "Nicky, the truth is that my mental health is fine, but once you are stuck in a place like this, you can never leave."

"Yeah, sort of like 'Hotel California'!" Nicky chimed in, and then they burst out laughing together.

Nicky put his drink down for a moment and reached over to turn on a lamp next to his desk by the window.

"All kidding aside, Angie, I am worried about you. You have a lot of productive years left to enjoy. Somehow you must convince your kids to release you from the shackles of your prison walls!" Nicky spoke frankly. He knew Angie, and he knew she was the kind of woman who appreciated the fact he was not going to mince words.

He heard her sigh softly on the other end. "My daughter Gina is getting ready to sell my house, so as Thomas Wolfe would say, 'I can't go home again.' I am not fighting her on that because returning to my big house has little appeal to me now. With the help of a dear friend, however, I am beginning to formulate an escape plan."

Nicky sat up straight. Now she had his full attention. "Wow, Angie, what do you have in mind? I hope you don't mind me asking because you know everything you tell me is strictly confidential." Nicky paused for a minute, then continued. "You are a strong woman with a mind of your own, and I admire your determination to take hold of your life no matter what the cost. Please tell me what you're thinking, and I'll try to help you any way I can. Listening to you makes me realize there are probably many people in your situation. I could easily have been one of them myself."

"I appreciate you saying that", Angie continued. "Even though you are, what, three thousand miles away? I feel you are right here beside me.

"Okay, here's the plan so far. My friend Ben is one of the very few residents living here who's still thinking clearly. In fact, he's as sharp as a tack. He was an Amtrak dispatcher and supervisor for years before he retired. For that reason, he can contact his friends who still work there and get first-class seats for any train in the country. So, he will help me leave as soon as I know my destination. Thanks to Ben, I can travel by train undetected to almost any part of the country, no ticket needed. My destination? Well, I would prefer a warm quiet spot, probably on the West Coast. Money is not a problem for me; I have managed to hide a considerable sum of money away from the prying eyes of my family. Tomorrow, I'll pick up my little stash, and then I'll be ready to plan the rest of my adventure. As you can see, there are still gaping holes in my plan, like mainly, where will I end up?" Angie asked with a nervous chuckle.

Nicky thoughtfully sipped the last of his martini. "Not too many holes, Angie, you have given careful thought to your plan so far. You were able to determine how and when. Now all you need to do is figure out where. Am I correct in concluding that your phone call to me today is part of the where?" Nicky almost laughed as the entire picture began to come together in his mind.

"Yes," she said quietly.

Six

I spent most of my life, even after the kids left home, actively on the move. Except for the last year at home, I had boundless energy to accomplish the many things on my daily to-do list: cooking, shopping, lunches or dinners with friends, and my ever-present stash of crossword puzzles to work on once I finally sat down for the evening. Since I came to Peaceful Havens, though, all my activities had come to a screeching halt. Monday mornings would usually find me staring out the window feeling useless. But today was different.

The sun hadn't even peeked through the window yet as I got out of bed. Strangely enough, I didn't have the aches and pains I usually felt as I sat up and hung my legs over the bed to reach my slippers on the floor below. My body felt strangely energetic, filling me with purposeful resolve. I reached for my rosary beads to start my morning prayers and realized with a start that I knew exactly what was missing. Dread. Yes, that awful feeling of dread I had woken to every morning since I came here was now gone.

After I showered and dressed, I heard the nurse of the day knocking on my door. Sighing, I turned the TV louder to drown her out. The knocking continued anyway. I sat on the bed and waited for the inevitable appearance of the Monday morning nurse. Immediately, Linda appeared. Linda was a new CNA, so she hadn't had time to acquire the obnoxious attitude of the seasoned CNAs here. She was kind and personable as she approached me with a nervous smile.

"Good morning, Angie, how are we this morning?" Linda asked brightly.

I looked at her with disgust. I never could become comfortable with the plague of improper pronouns the staff here used. How were *we* supposed to answer that question, I wondered? Along with the annoying pronoun problem, all the staff here had the insufferable habit of addressing the residents in a condescending manner that was way too familiar. Whatever happened to addressing the elderly by their surnames? Tony was always a stickler for that, insisting that the younger generation call him Mr. Martini instead of Tony. Inevitably, his request would be ignored after about five minutes.

That's how long the attention span is of most of these millennials nowadays, I thought ruefully.

I knew if I corrected Linda and asked her not to call me Angie or refer to me in the plural form, she would think I was just making trouble. And I was positive she had no idea what a pronoun was. Don't they teach anyone grammar anymore?

"I'm fine, Linda, how are you?" I knew from experience to play up my role as the nice old lady in room 323. "Can you do me one favor, though, and help me with my shoes this morning?" The one activity I still struggled with was my shoes and socks. In the last few days, however, I had been stretching more to allow myself to reach down. I knew once I no longer had any assistance, I would have to take care of these things alone. Living independently never fazed me, but I admit I felt a little apprehensive about my inability to put my shoes on without help. But I was determined to clear that hurdle soon. It would take some arduous daily exercise, which I loathed, but I would do it. I had to keep my eyes on the prize here, I reminded myself.

Linda fastened the Velcro straps on my sneakers. I suddenly remembered an infomercial I saw on TV last week before the *Today* show. It showed an old man using a long shoehorn to get his shoes on unassisted. I wished I had written the phone number down to buy that long shoehorn. I knew if I asked Ben, he could find it on Amazon and get it for me. Another problem solved! I mentally checked that off my list of tasks to accomplish before I put my plan into action. But first, I needed to get my cash.

Ben was not at breakfast, but I knew he had probably already grabbed a coffee. He preferred to have an English muffin in his room topped with some fancy gourmet jams he always ordered from Stonewall Kitchen. Ben was an expert on all kinds of jams and condiments, as well as maple syrup. His syrup had to be authentic grade B. One day he explained to me at length the differences between the grades of syrup as my eyes glazed over. Ben had many interests and never got tired of explaining them in detail to anyone who would listen. I quickly learned not to get Ben started on the topics on which he loved to preach. There were many: coffee, ocean liners, trains (of course), milkshakes, ice cream... the list was endless. I didn't mind his stories, probably because I lapsed into my Walter Mitty mode while he prattled on happily. But his brother-in-law Alan became visibly disturbed when Ben would not stop talking. I knew Alan's lack of patience was something that bothered Ben although he seldom mentioned it. The truth was, I found Ben's aimless chatting kind of endearing. Certainly, it was a comfort for me to have a comrade in my corner. I felt eternally grateful to Ben.

I ordered a bowl of Cheerios and side of fruit with coffee. The coffee came in a tiny chipped teacup. I thought longingly of my big coffee mugs back home. These cups only held enough coffee for a couple of small gulps. I looked at the brown sludge they called coffee with disdain and took a couple of sips out of desperation. Cold again. But I still needed my morning caffeine fix. Coffee worked any time of the day for me. I didn't sleep anyway, so who cared how much caffeine I drank? By the time my Cheerios arrived, I was hungry and poured the thin milk over them quickly. They were stale, though there was no surprise there. I picked out the fruit that wasn't rubbery and slimy, which basically ruled out anything but the grapes and pineapple. The peaches were from a can, and I couldn't imagine where they got the cantaloupe. It certainly had seen better days. I so longed for the time, soon I hoped, when I could pick out my own fruit from a farmer's market like I used to.

I managed to get back to my room without any confrontations with Kim or other staff members harassing me. I warily scanned the corridors for a Barbara sighting. I cringed at the thought of bumping into her more than anyone else.

Barbara was an imposing character, even though she was probably only five feet four. She barged into rooms without warning, clumping along with her huge legs and feet, which were swollen with neuropathy. She made no secret of the fact she was dependent on insulin for her uncontrolled diabetes. It soon became obvious to even the most casual observer, however, that her diabetes was uncontrolled because she ate sugary sweets constantly. Her sugar of choice, at least in here, was a glazed Krispy Kreme donut smothered in chocolate. God knows what she ate when she was alone in her room. Barbara was no picky eater. Every month or so, the staff took a busload of residents to a family restaurant. All the trips involved lunch or dinner, since any other destination would involve actual physical activity. Forget museums, zoos, lectures, or plays. Any activity where any degree of thought was required was eliminated too, for obvious reasons. Barbara was the first one to sign up for any trips where food was involved. She pushed herself to the front of the line and filled the largest plate at a buffet, spilling half the contents as she lumbered back to her seat. Sometimes she would pretend she needed a wheelchair just to have someone push her around. She inevitably ordered the poor shmuck to rush her to the front of any line while grabbing food along the way.

As if Barbara's gluttony was not bad enough, her personality was even worse. Any filter she might have had vanished a long time ago. She had an opinion on everything, loudly interrupting anyone within earshot. She never had to be prompted to get on her soapbox and proceeded to dominate any conversation. Most of the residents who could backed away from her and retreated in a hurry. Others who couldn't move fast enough (the majority, I'm afraid) were held captive to her incessant rants. Barbara never married and never had a family, so she depended on her own voice to provide the stimulating conversation she apparently craved. She was a miserable old spinster, full of venom and hate. Her features were coarse, her clothes always rumpled and stained, and she always stank to high heaven. Normally I would pray for her soul, but Barbara did not inspire any charitable feelings for me.

Barbara's worst trait was that she was a constant gossip. She had nothing to do all day but sit in the lobby and watch everyone with her hawk eyes. She didn't feel the slightest bit shy about prying. Her favorite question was "Where are you off to?" hollered in a shrill voice that could be heard throughout the building. I knew right now Barbara had to be avoided at all costs. If she was on the prowl, she would not miss seeing me go off to lunch with Ben in his car. Although Ben and I had already discussed the possibility of this happening, I did not relish the idea of being the subject of Barbara's latest rumor mill.

It was ten thirty, and I was already dressed to meet Ben. I thought of calling him on my house phone to confirm, and then remembered my cell phone.

Gina got me a cell phone years ago, after Tony died. She put me on her Verizon cellular plan (she said it was only $10.00 a month, but I knew it was more). It was a small flip phone, and I instantly disliked it. First, I could hardly see the numbers. Gina programmed it so all I had to do was ask the phone to call people. That never worked. The lady listening to me never knew who I wanted her to call. Once she called someone in Peoria, Illinois. Gina was upset with me after that. I also could never hear the phone ringing, especially if it was buried in the bottom of my pocketbook, which it usually was. I lost it several times. Sometimes I just pretended I had lost it. When I came to Peaceful Havens, though, Gina got me another one. She gave me a charger so I could plug it in every night to charge it. What a giant pain. Another thing to remember to do! On the nights where I collapsed into bed with exhaustion, do you think

I remembered to plug my phone in? If I could even find it. Gina had been trying to find a good solution to this problem. It was a continual source of frustration for her because she wanted to make sure she could always reach me. Well, short of implanting a GPS under my skin, there was no way she was going to track me now. I smiled as I thought of how that damn phone would keep ringing under my bed a few weeks from now. That was where it would be when I made my escape! How clever I was.

I heard a knock on the door and dreaded the inevitable appearance of whatever nurse was on duty. But instead, I heard a soft voice calling me.

"Angie?" Ben's voice was quieter than usual, his first of many attempts to be discreet.

"Just a minute," I answered, reaching for my walker.

I hastened to the door and flung it open to find Ben standing there dressed in fresh shirt and trousers. He even smelled good. I recognized the familiar scent of Old Spice. How nice that he took the time to clean himself up. I felt a sudden surge of affection for the fact Ben was directing all his energy right now to make me happy. How I wished my family felt the same way.

Ben smiled. "Hi, there, ready for lunch?" He winked and we both chuckled, feeling very wicked.

I walked out with him and locked my door behind me. Ben walked slowly and I matched his pace with my walker. I vowed to start exercising later in the day so I could ditch the walker by the following week. I had a sturdy cane that would suit me just fine as soon as I got my balance back. Buoyed by the possibility of freedom, I already felt stronger as I wheeled my walker down the corridor towards the elevator.

Thankfully, we encountered no one until we were almost at the front door. I knew Ben had already signed us out, so we didn't have to stop and chat with Sharon, the receptionist. I looked over to the desk and didn't even see Sharon, so the coast was clear. Just as we approached the door, however, I heard the familiar shrill voice of Barbara, who, in her usual devious manner, had positioned herself out of sight in the corner of the lobby.

"Hey, where are you two headed out to today?" Her voice resonated across the lobby and ended in a whiny demand. I knew the only way to deal with Barbara was to exit her space as soon as possible.

"Good morning, Barbara." I smiled stiffly. "Have a nice day!"

Ben quickened his pace and the automatic doors opened for both of us.

"Going to lunch? Where are you going, anyway?" Barbara's voice grew louder, as she didn't appreciate being ignored. "Any place nice?"

She kept probing as we exited the building and headed as quickly as we could to Ben's car in the front handicapped spot.

"Whew," Ben sighed loudly. "What a giant pain she is. I should have known we couldn't make an escape without being detected by the infamous Barbara. We should call her Barbara Bullhorn, because that's what she is!"

I laughed. "Okay, Ben, from now on we will refer to her as the Bullhorn. Good name for her! We both know it's inevitable that she was lurking around somewhere. We have faced the first hurdle. There will be others, probably more daunting than that. Let's approach each roadblock one at a time and then we can get through them all!" I was surprised at how calm I felt.

"Sure, Angie." Ben approached his car and held open the door for me. "It's not a big deal if we don't let it be." Ben took my walker from me and folded it into the back seat. "Let's head over to your house now, okay?"

I settled into Ben's passenger seat, still littered with napkins and scraps of paper. I noticed he had the same obsession with sticky notes that I had, but most of his were limited to the dashboard except for the few that had fallen on the floor. Whoever invented those little notes should have made the glue stronger, I thought. Gina always expressed her frustration at me when she saw the little yellow and pink flags everywhere in my kitchen.

"Mom," she would say, heaving an exasperated sigh, "do you have to write a sticky note for everything you do? Why not your bowel movements as well?" Apparently, Gina inherited her lack of patience from me.

I didn't make a comment on the messy state of Ben's car. I knew the back seat was even worse, but today it didn't matter. I was just grateful to get to my house and my stash of cash. I'd had a restless night thinking of returning to my house. I hadn't been inside since that fateful day when I had my accident.

What would it look like? I wondered nervously.

I had visions of an empty house, all my stuff disappeared to parts unknown. It was a scary thought. I didn't share my feelings with Ben, who proceeded to drive at a snail's pace along the five blocks to my house. He seemed oblivious to a tailgater who impatiently honked behind him.

It was a short ride to my house located on a shady street in my old neighborhood. I was friendly with all my neighbors when we moved in.

That was almost fifty years ago, I reflected ruefully.

The neighbors on either side of me had been gone for years and replaced with unfamiliar renters. Their dogs yapped incessantly. The Montis had lived across the street until about six years ago. They both died, and their daughter decided to rent their house out. The current occupants of that household held weekly yard sales, during which they hauled out the piles of junk they'd scarfed up from the curbside on trash day. Every Saturday, cars were parked every which way in front of my house, full of carloads of people who would pick through the same old stuff. One day I went over there and found a worn little Cuisinart chopper like the one I had. Gina has one too. I could have used another one, but on closer examination, I noticed the cord was badly frayed. I passed on that, thinking of electrical fires.

Who buys this trash? I wondered.

The renters were not friendly and never even said hello.

Across the street on the other side lived the Carnevales. They had been living in their big farmhouse since the neighborhood was first developed back in the late '40s. Originally there was the elder Carnevale and their ten kids, seven girls and three boys. The patriarch of the family, Joe, was an old-fashioned Italian from Sicily. He owned the Imperial Knife Company and insisted everyone in the family work in his shop making jewelry. All the girls complied. They were never allowed to date, obeying Joe's strict rules. They all became sad spinsters, spending their days waiting on their brothers, who were of course treated much differently. All the boys went on to marry, and two of them started their own businesses. Now there were three girls left in the house. Everyone else was dead. Vicky was the oldest, and I could see her now in her garden. She was approaching ninety, and she stooped over, weeding her tulip beds. She had a big hump on her back and was wearing the worn apron with the big, frayed pockets that I remembered so well. She always had a rumpled Kleenex stuffed into the sleeve of whatever blouse she was wearing.

She didn't notice us as we pulled up.

"Ben, can you park in my driveway and pull way up?" I asked, knowing that we should be as unobtrusive as possible. I didn't care if the neighbors on my driveway side of the house saw me. I doubted they would remember me or even care if they did, but the Carnevales were like the neighborhood police.

Tony and I always felt safe when we went away on vacation. A quick call to the Carnevales was all it took to put their daily surveillance in place. Any mysterious activity across the street was looked upon with extreme suspicion by the Carnevale family when they knew we were away. Hell, even if we weren't away, we knew they watched our house like hawks. One day, Vicky called the cops (I swear the local police number was on their speed dial) because she saw Gina's car in my driveway and didn't recognize it. Gina had had a rental car that day because her car was in the shop. It was apparent that Vicky kept a list somewhere, probably in her head, of everyone's license plates. When a car pulled up or into my driveway, Vicky would mentally check off that plate number; good luck to the poor owner of that car if their plate was not recognized by her. Now, however, Vicky had lost a lot of her mental capacity due to a couple of strokes. She puttered around the house carefully watched over by her other two sisters, who were frankly not much better off than she was in the mental health department. Still, I didn't want to take a chance that Vicky would spot us and call the cops. That would be just what I needed right now. I nervously wondered if I had remembered to bring my driver's license in case I had to prove who I was.

Ben got out of the car and came around to me to help me get my walker set up. I glanced anxiously across the street again but thankfully Vicky was not in sight. Ben held the gate open for me and I reached for my keys carefully hidden in my purse.

"No alarm, Angie?" I noticed his voice kind of squeaked. Ben seemed a little unsettled too.

"No, Ben, never needed one. Our neighborhood was always protected by nosy neighbors. That might work against us if we are spotted, so I'd like to complete this little adventure as quick as possible." The key went into the lock, and I stepped onto my porch. A second key was needed for the main house.

I noted with relief, that the porch looked the same. All my worn furniture was still there, including the little embroidered stepstool that Gina had given me years ago to prop up my legs while I sat and read the morning newspaper. Ben followed me as I unlocked the main door and entered my house. Immediately, I was overwhelmed with sadness. There was a musty odor that I recognized from when I cleaned out my own mother's house twenty years ago. Her house had been unused for a year, and this was the same smell I had noticed then. It was so alien to me to recognize it here. This house had always been filled with the delicious aromas of fresh pies and Sunday sauce with meatballs. But I was on a mission, and it was not helpful to wallow in pity. So, I pushed the thoughts from my mind impatiently.

"Focus," I muttered to myself.

The mahogany cedar chest Tony gave me for our engagement still stood in my dining room. I breathed a sigh of relief when I made my way through the kitchen to the front of the house. Gina had opened my hutch and had removed my Waterford crystal, which was placed on a tablecloth on the dining room table.

Looks like she also had begun taking the bar items out of the bottom of the China cabinet, I thought.

But I knew she had ignored the cedar chest, probably because she had no idea where the key was. More importantly, Gina did not know it was my secret hiding place.

I stood in front of my cedar chest, not quite believing I had made it this far. Ben stood patiently behind me, taking the whole scene in silently.

"This is where my hidden treasure is," I began slowly as I reached for my purse. "I have my key with me. For some reason, I've always kept it on my key ring with my house key and car key." Even when Gina took my keys from me for a while, she never noticed the little skeleton key dangling from the small ring on the side. Quite frankly, I also forgot about it for a while during my "black out period." That was what I called that dreadful month when I was in rehab. My memories of those days were still blurred in my mind, probably because they were still too painful to think about and the doctors kept me too doped up to come to my senses.

I fit the little key in the lock on the button that opened the latch and turned it. It slid in easily and allowed me to push the button. The cedar chest popped open. I looked up at Ben and he smiled at me.

"I feel so wicked!"

Ben laughed and replied, "Yes, it's a good feeling! You are taking back control of your life, Angie, so feel as wicked as you like!"

I pulled the top open and gazed inside. All my linens were still intact and folded meticulously the way I had left them. In the corner were the crocheted doilies I had collected through the years. Some were ones I made (*how the hell did I have time to do that*, I marveled), along with my mother's and mother-in-law's creations.

That's what women did at night back then instead of watching Wheel of Fortune, I thought ruefully.

I knew that way underneath the doilies was where I hid my money. I used two of Tony's old Garcia Vega cigar boxes. When Tony had his heart attack, Dr. Wilson told him to stop smoking. After a few failed attempts, he took up smoking the thin cigars, which smelled horrible. Tony thought it made him look debonair like Ricky Ricardo. I would have preferred he started smoking pipes, but he always said he didn't want to look like Sherlock Holmes. I never threw out any of the large cigar boxes that held a few dozen of the long, thin cigars Tony loved. Now two of the large ones held my stash of cash.

I reached down, way down, underneath all the doilies and linens, to the very bottom of the cedar chest. It was deep, deeper than I remembered it was. I had to stretch far to do it, but I was positive I knew where I had hidden it. I waved off Ben's offer to help, excited to finally get my tired old hands on my hidden treasure. Finally, I felt the two large boxes under my fingers and lifted them, disturbing all the assorted piles of material covering it. I silently praised myself for having the foresight, years ago, to come up with such an ingenious hiding place!

Ben stood there, his expression was one of astonishment and bewildered amusement. I knew he was probably wondering how the hell he had ever gotten himself mixed up in this situation. I looked up at him and smiled impishly.

"Here it is." I took the two boxes and cradled them in my arms for over a minute. I was breathless, and my usual anxiety kicked in. What if I had a heart attack just as I finally got my hands on my escape route? But then I stood up straight and remembered why I was there.

I shut the lid of the cedar chest and relocked it. Ben and I stared at each other in relief.

"Okay, let's sit for a minute so you can check over everything in the boxes. Are you going to take both boxes with you?" Ben stood quietly beside me, but I had the feeling he was anxious to finish up and get to lunch. For that matter, so was I.

"Yes, let's have a seat at the kitchen table," I spoke. "I'll take everything with me, but I do want to check and make sure everything inside is the same as I left it." I slowly turned and headed into the kitchen. Ben took the boxes for me because I needed both hands for the walker. I silently resolved that I would have to work hard and ditch the damn walker in the next couple of weeks. It was too much of a hindrance if I really wanted to get around quickly like I used to.

We sat down and I opened the first box. It was filled with the neatly piled stacks of fresh $100 bills bound with large rubber bands, the kind that the daily newspapers were wrapped in every day. In fact, that was where I got them. It never occurred to me to toss them in the trash so here they were. Waste nothing! That was my motto.

We both looked at each other as I pulled out the stacks of bills. Each box had $75,000 in it—three tall stacks of $100 bills in one box and four stacks in the other box, carefully accumulated through the years.

I gulped. I was feeling overwhelmed at the sight before me. Never had I dreamed I would use this money. Like all the savings I had hoarded over the years, I enjoyed seeing it pile up, but it wasn't real in my mind. It was like Monopoly money, and it was fun to collect. Now I was beginning to understand what was in front of me. I wondered how it would feel to spend some of it. Ben just stared at the stacks of cash and let out a low whistle.

"Well, Ben, it looks like it's all here, just as I left it..." My voice trailed off. I was waiting for him to comment, but it appeared he was at a loss for words. "I'm relieved all of this is still here." I swallowed. "Still, I must admit it's going to make me nervous carrying all this around."

Ben smiled and found his voice. "Maybe we should get a Brink's truck." Leave it to Ben to see the humor at any moment.

"You think that might arouse suspicion in my neighborhood?" I chuckled, relieved that we could joke about it. "So, this stash of mine comes to $150,000, all in crisp $100 bills. They don't make bills larger than that anymore."

"Wow," was all Ben could say. His eyes were wide as he stared at the bag in front of him. We both were silent for a few minutes. The reality of my situation was just beginning to sink in. "Those boxes are big; maybe we could put them in a large shopping bag to take it out of here?" Ben looked around the kitchen as if expecting a bag to materialize out of thin air. He turned to me. "Do you remember if you saved any bags?"

I laughed. "Bags? You're talking to the queen of bags... and scraps of aluminum foil, wax paper, you name it!" I knew the storage place for all my bags was in the drawer under my stove. It was an unlikely place for bags, so few people knew what was in the drawer. I reached over to the stove and opened the drawer. There, in a large messy jumble, were bags of all kinds. We both stared at the pile and then burst out laughing.

"Angie, even though you think that's unusual, you wouldn't believe what my stash of bags looked like. It certainly wouldn't have been contained in one drawer!" Ben joked but his thoughts seemed to be elsewhere. Perhaps he was thinking dejectedly of the house he left behind with closets full of trash. "And your drawer is so nice and neat compared to mine..." His voice trailed off wistfully.

"Well, Gina didn't think so." I remembered Gina chiding me more than once that the drawer was a death trap. "Gina said all those damn bags would catch fire some day and the house would go up in flames." I smiled sheepishly. "She was probably right about leaving them under the stove, but here we are, and so far, we are intact and so is the house. The things we worry about, right?"

Ben nodded slowly. He was beginning to look nostalgic, so I closed the drawer after grabbing an old Almacs grocery bag with handles.

Ben's eyes lit up. "I had a few of those myself," he admitted sheepishly. "I think they are collectible..."

I remembered the old supermarket fondly. "I think they closed sometime around 1995," I murmured vaguely. Truth was, I was beginning to feel overwhelmed and hungry. "Well..." I looked at Ben. "I think we're ready. We'll have to lock this bag in your car while we're having lunch. I think it'll be fine unless we're being watched." I nervously glanced out the back window expecting Vicky Carnevale to appear any minute.

"Don't worry, I'm sure it will be fine. I'll put it in the trunk. Is there anything else you want to grab from the house before we leave?" Ben stood up slowly and looked around. "I know you mentioned you didn't have any of your nice clothes. Do you want to take some of them also?"

I thought for a minute. The idea of having some of my favorite clothes was tempting, but I didn't want to spend any more time in the house than necessary. I knew Vicky was still lurking outside, and there was always the possibility Gina would get out of work early.

"I think I'll wait, Ben. Before I make my escape, I might come back and take the clothes that I really want. I might also find a suitcase or small duffel that I'll need. But right now, I'm not sure what I want. Can I ask you to come back with me another time to get the rest of the stuff I want?" I looked at Ben, who looked relieved to be leaving.

Ben chuckled softly. "Sure, Angie. As many times as you want. Before you leave you will probably think of a lot of stuff you want. Sometimes it's not easy to even remember what you have unless you look in your closet. At least that's true for me.... Sorry Angie, but I was thinking about my old bedroom with clothes heaped all over the place. Seeing your home makes be miss all the things I've given up living in Peaceful Havens."

As I locked the house back up, I was careful to cover my tracks. I made sure there were no signs that I had been there in case Gina was worried about robbers. Now that I had taken my stash of cash, however, the only things left to steal were the crystal and silver that were underneath the hutch. I tried to remember if my candlesticks were silver or silver plate. To my knowledge, Gina had already received my silver flatware. I had given it to her years ago having gotten tired of polishing it after every holiday meal.

I doubt she has even opened it since I gave it to her, I thought sadly.

I remembered all the lovely praise I received over the years when I had set my tables with holiday China and real silver. No one did that anymore.

We sped away, at least according to Ben's definition of speeding, which did not involve approaching the speed limit. Vicky did not even look up from her flowerbeds. I felt sad observing another sign of change in my old neighborhood. I looked wistfully at my church, too, as we turned a corner to the Smith Hill Creamery. How I longed to sit in a quiet pew with my rosary beads. I could have really used some divine intervention.

Ben pulled into a handicapped spot close to the door of the restaurant.

"I'm going to lock the bag in the trunk, Angie, and then I will set the car alarm, okay?" Ben looked over at me quietly. "I think we can see the car from our table, so it will be perfectly safe."

"Sure, Ben, thanks for doing that. I'm not worried about the cash right now. No one suspects that an old bag contains all this money. At least I hope they don't!"

We slowly walked into the restaurant, my walker making faint scraping sounds on the tile floor. We took a small booth at the back, away from the counter and a couple of screaming kids who were having a meltdown near the ice cream counter. I had not been inside the restaurant for about a year, but it looked the same as I remembered it. Smith Hill Creamery was famous for its ice cream. Back when Tony and I were younger, we would go on hot summer nights for an ice cream cone. I found myself longing for a small dish of vanilla. I wondered if Ben was thinking the same thing even though dessert was a long way off. Finally, we could have some decent food in a place that didn't stink like a hospital.

"What would you like?" Ben had already looked over the menu. I suspected he had memorized it. This was his go-to place now. I was sure he went there more than he wanted to admit.

"I know what I want. A BLT, fries, milkshake, the works!" I settled back in the booth happily.

"Me too. If it were Friday, their fish and chips would be good. Had them last Friday." Ben looked up sheepishly. "Maybe we can share ice cream for dessert."

"You read my thoughts! I've been craving ice cream. I have been craving anything other than the slop they serve down the street. I can't believe the Department of Health hasn't shut Peaceful Havens down by now." I shook my head in disbelief.

"Well, the answer to that is to consider the clientele they serve. Look at them! Do you think there are any discriminating palates there?" Ben smiled and we both relaxed in our seats, so glad to be out of there.

"Ben, I can't thank you enough for your help. A month ago, I was in such a state of despair I didn't think I could go on. You have given me hope that I can get my life back, and now that is becoming a reality. I feel happy for the first time since I can remember," I ended quietly, afraid I would get tearful. No way did I want to start blubbering before lunch.

"Angie, I am happy to help. You also have given me a new lease on life, so to speak." Ben looked at me with a steady gaze. "Now, let's talk about the trains that can get you to your destination. I have already looked up schedules, times, and have even spoken to my conductor friends who can help you along the way. Are you ready?"

Our food arrived, hot and delicious, as I looked up at Ben and grinned.

"As ready as I'll ever be! Let's get started!"

Seven

It was a Tuesday morning, and Gina was running late. Normally she worked on Tuesday, but today she rearranged her schedule to meet with the realtor. Knowing she had to put on a happy face to greet the lady who was going to sell Mom's house made her stomach hurt. Lately, Gina had been going over to the house less and less to avoid the pain and sadness she experienced every time she saw the house looming empty and quiet.

As Angie's house came into view, Gina chided herself once again. She had taken to giving herself pep talks whenever disturbing thoughts crowded her mind. Wouldn't it have been nice for one or both of her siblings to share her frustration? But how useful would they be? Maria would matter-of-factly tell her that it had to be done and "it's for the best." Mario would probably just not say anything. Talk about denial!

She pulled into the driveway and stared at the small cherry tree in the backyard. Remembering how much fun it was to plant it fifteen years ago made her stomach churn again. Those were the happy times when everyone was alive and healthy. Relatively healthy, sure, but still able to walk, talk, eat, and plan for tomorrow. That all came to a screeching halt when Dad died. After that, it was up to Gina to keep Mom busy. It didn't always work out because Gina worked a lot. Still, she managed to take her to Boston and Foxwoods and out to dinner every Tuesday. At first, it was okay, and Mom was able to enjoy herself despite slowing down. But it had become obvious in the last couple of years that she was struggling to keep up the house the way she always did. Forget hiring someone. Mom was old school.

"*No way*," she'd said stubbornly when Gina gave her the number of her cleaning lady. "I will *not* have someone scrubbing my tub for me!"

Gina sighed. Thinking back, she wondered if she could have handled things better.

Sometimes she forgot Mom was in Peaceful Havens. She cringed whenever she remembered the icy silence on the other end of the phone when she called her aunts to tell them where Mom was. The unspoken question was "How could you?" Her oldest aunt, who was known for her candid retorts, always proudly stated that her kids would *never* let her go into one of "those places." Well, Mom was now in one of those places. But what choice did she have? All the nurses and psych doctors at the rehab place told her mom could not go home. And if she ever had convinced Mom to live with her, which was extremely doubtful due to the mutual stubbornness involved, they would have killed each other within a week. It was admittedly a hasty decision, one that led to many agonizing second thoughts and sleepless nights.

Gina sighed again. She just hoped and prayed Mom would grow to love Peaceful Havens and make many friends there. But deep down— hell, not even *that* deep—she knew that Peaceful Havens would not grow on her mother. Especially since it appeared that her earlier signs of dementia were a thing of the past. Lately it even seemed as if Mom's brain cells had somehow rejuvenated themselves. She would sharply take Gina to task when Gina tried to lamely point out the benefits of having everything done for her.

"What am I, an invalid?" Mom would retort haughtily. "Just because I'm unsteady on my feet doesn't mean I'm ready for the glue factory. But that's how I feel I'm treated in this godforsaken place."

Mom was never one to mince words. And although her expressions like "glue factory" would usually make Gina laugh, she guiltily admitted to herself that Mom was right. Peaceful Havens was, at first glance, a nice haven for old senile people, but the underbelly of Peaceful Havens was a sad, smelly rest stop on the way to the grave. And Mom was not senile. Gina realized now that she never really was. Everyone had panicked when she exhibited all the signs, including herself. That was why Mom was now in Peaceful Havens. It was heartbreaking to realize that now, there really was no way out.

Gina walked into the house and tried to ignore the musty smell that greeted her.

Maybe I should buy one of those Glade air freshener things that you plug in, she thought, or a diffuser like the one she saw on a TV ad that made the air smell sweet. But usually, those artificial gadgets made her gag, like the ones you hang from your car's rearview mirror. There was nothing like the aroma of a good meal baking in the oven. Gina vowed that before she showed the house to any prospective buyer, she would bake an apple pie. That would certainly help the situation! She mentally made a note to look for the recipe she knew was stuffed inside her mother's copy of *The Betty Crocker Cookbook* downstairs in the bookcase.

The doorbell rang, startling Gina. She glanced at her watch. It was nine thirty, and the realtor was scheduled to arrive at ten. A quick look outside revealed no car, so she peeked out the dining room window. On the doorstep was Vicky Carnevale, stooped slightly, dressed in her old housedress with an apron tied lopsidedly around her waist.

Gina opened the door to see Vicky staring at her with a questioning look.

It was as if Vicky had never laid eyes on her before. Gina knew she was not Vicky's favorite of the Martini children. Vicky loved Maria the best. Maria always fawned over the Carnevales and chatted them up when she saw them in the neighborhood. Gina's inclination was to run in the other direction. When it came time to sell Girl Scout cookies, Maria got all the Carnevales to buy her cookies. Gina's sales came mostly from her aunts, who felt obligated to buy them for Gina to go camping in the summer. Gina always wished she didn't have enough sales to go camping. She would have preferred to stay home playing with her Barbie dolls and reading her Nancy Drew books.

"Well, hello, Vicky." Gina forced a smile and held the door open. "It's great to see you. Would you like to come in?"

Vicky looked at her suspiciously. "No, that's fine. I wasn't sure if you were home. Lately I have no idea who is living here anymore."

Gina stared at her, trying to hide her annoyance. "You know my mother is now in Peaceful Havens, right? She had a car accident and needed rehab and now is being taken care of by the folks at the assisted living place." Gina's tone was polite but had a slight edge to it. How many times did she have to explain to the neighbors that her mother was not living here anymore?

"Well, that's what I thought you told me," Vicky said defiantly. "But I got confused because I saw her here yesterday with a strange man. They both went into her house and spent about an hour together. Then they both left the house, laughing, holding a large bag, and sped off. At first, I couldn't believe my eyes. But I timed it. They were in the house together for forty-six minutes." Vicky dabbed her dripping nose with a crumpled Kleenex that had been stuffed in her sleeve. "So, you can imagine my perplexed state of mind right now! I almost called the police, but decided it was not my place to do that. So, I am glad I had the chance to talk to you now rather than taking further action." Vicky finished her last sentence in a huff, obviously pleased with herself.

Gina looked at Vicky with both annoyance and bewilderment.

What the hell is she babbling about? she wondered. Mom, here yesterday? With another man? Leaving the house with a large bag? Obviously, Vicky was hallucinating. Maybe she was taking some kind of weird medication for the strokes she'd had. That would explain it. Gina vaguely remembered the side effects of those drugs on the TV commercials that ran all the time. Didn't they say they could cause memory loss and confusion?

"I'm sure that couldn't be," Gina began slowly. She wasn't quite sure how to tell Vicky that she had lost her mind. "Mom is not allowed to leave Peaceful Havens without signing out, and I am the only one who takes her out. The staff knows that. It's not like Mom can just walk out the door with a strange man..." Gina's voice tapered off. She could see Vicky was not convinced that she had seen a ghost.

"Are you saying I did not see your mother and a strange man?" Vicky said huffy. "I may be getting up in years, dearie, but I certainly know what I saw. I have *always* been the eyes and ears of this neighborhood, as you well know, and no one is going to tell *me* that the sight of your mother and her paramour was a figment of my imagination!" Vicky ended abruptly, clearly proud of herself.

Gina stood with her mouth open. She was at a loss as to what to do with this babbling idiot standing at her mother's doorstep. Vicky obviously had been losing track of how many pills she'd taken. Or maybe she'd been dipping into the cooking sherry. Gina just wanted to get rid of her. It was almost time for the realtor to arrive. The last thing she wanted was a scene in front of her. What if the realtor refused to sell the house, convinced the neighborhood is full of nosy, wacked-out ladies?

"Well, Vicky, I certainly appreciate you coming over here and letting me know that." Gina smiled stiffly. "I will check it out and find out what happened, but right now, I'm afraid I have an appointment, so I must let you go." Gina began to close the door, but Vicky stood firm.

"Well, dearie, I hope you get to the bottom of it! This has always been a wonderful house, and I don't want to see it fall into ruin now that your mother has been sent away!" Vicky took another dab at her running nose, glared at Gina once again, and turned and walked away.

Whew, Gina thought as she slammed the door shut, *what a nosy busybody!* Where did she come up with such crazy ideas anyway?

For a moment, Gina paused and thought about what Vicky said. Could she possibly be right? A strange man bringing Mom here? There was no way that it could be possible. The only man in her life was Mario, and, of course, Vicky knew him.

She even knew his name, Gina thought bitterly. *I bet she wouldn't call* him *dearie!*

After thinking for a few minutes, Gina decided that she had to dismiss Vicky's preposterous accusation. Hell, if she was going to start believing the obvious hallucinations of stroke victims, then she might be losing her marbles as well. Gina shook her head and walked back to the dining room to finish packing the crystal.

Time to get focused on selling this house, she thought. No distractions were going to come in the way of all her careful planning!

Eight

B en pulled his car into the handicapped spot he had called his own since he came to Peaceful Havens. So far, no one had noticed that he was parking outside of the lines. As he pulled his key out of the ignition, he felt a pang of sadness and regret.

He knew his doctor was not going to give him good news. Forty years ago, when he lost the sight in his right eye, the doctor who tried to repair it warned him that the left eye would also suffer the same fate. At that time, retina repair was not a simple job. Ben suspected it was botched from the beginning, but time marched on and Ben had no problems until about six months ago. Right after he ended up in the hospital, he noticed the familiar blurriness creeping into his left eye. He ruefully remembered that he expected to be dead by then, so it was no surprise that his retina had finally worn out. True to his stubborn streak of denial, he refused to admit the fact that his eyesight was deteriorating. It was only when he got to rehab that his doctor gently reminded him that he needed to be checked out. Ben ignored it for as long as possible. He knew Angie depended on him now for help with her great escape and there was no way he was going to disappoint her.

But today his doctor read him the riot act. He warned him that in a month's time, he would have to give up his driver's license. His license! How would he ever be able to survive if he couldn't escape from Peaceful Havens whenever he felt the walls closing in on him (which he admitted was more and more frequent nowadays)? He shook his head, not wanting to think about the consequences of his appointment. Maybe he could think of a way to still drive occasionally. After all, no one was going to take his car away, at least not right now. He was lucky, he thought happily, that his relatives did not know or care what was going on. He knew that for the immediate future, his keys were safe. His birthday was not until September. Ben didn't remember if he needed an eye test for his birthday. Maybe he could somehow avoid that test too. It could probably be months before his lack of sight was a real problem. Until then, he could fake it like he had been doing most of his life.

Ben walked slowly towards Peaceful Havens, deep in thought. He pressed the automatic open button for the doorway inside and entered the lobby. Too late, he saw the looming form of Barbara sitting on one of the chairs, ready to pounce on him.

"Hello, stranger!" Barbara's voice boomed out and seemed to echo through the entire first floor. She was dressed in a stained housecoat, her usual attire if she was not finagling a ride to a free lunch somewhere. She had that look on her face that Ben was familiar with. It was the look of someone who had managed to catch her prey unaware. Ben flinched. The last thing he needed right now was to endure the annoying scrutiny of the Bullhorn's twenty questions.

"Morning." Ben briefly nodded in her direction, trying to hurry past her.

No such luck.

"So, where did you and Angie take off to this morning?" Barbara bellowed out her question in an even louder voice.

Ben wondered how it was possible for such an old hag like Barbara to have such a strong voice. God knows she had no strength in any other places in her body where it was really needed.

Guess that was why she was in this godforsaken place, he thought.

"Couple of errands. Why do you need to know?" Ben knew that

was probably the wrong answer, but he didn't want to spend much time even talking to her. While he answered her, he quickened his pace to get past her as soon as possible. Unfortunately, Ben could only go as far as his feeble legs would allow.

"Well, I was just asking. Usually Angie doesn't go out with anyone but her kids, and I know she had you visit her a couple of times in her apartment too. So, is there a budding romance brewing?" Barbara giggled in her obnoxious way. She was obviously pleased with herself.

Ben tried to suppress his growing impatience and annoyance. He knew he had to keep his cool, but it was getting more difficult to ignore the windbag.

"Barbara, I wish I could chat with you right now, but I have a few phone calls to return. Catch you later." Ben had finally reached the elevator. Somehow, the need to get as far away from Barbara gave him the sudden burst of energy he needed. He pushed the button and the elevator popped open. He was grateful he didn't have to waste any more time waiting for it. Fortunately, Barbara was too lazy to follow him all the way to the elevator. As the door shut, he waved to her. Ben happily left her sitting there, spread-eagle, with her mouth open in astonishment. Ruefully, Ben realized her expression was more of a scowl. He knew she was hoping for some juicy gossip to fuel her pathetic need for more aimless blather. She no doubt looked forward to spending the afternoon chatting up the half-deaf ladies who would be held captive by Barbara's latest inane rumors. Ben shook his head slowly, wondering how in the world he ended up spending his last days with someone like Barbara. What a cruel twist of fate.

As he walked down the corridor to the mailboxes outside his room, he soon forgot all about Barbara. His mind focused on Angie and the help she would need from him. Ben knew most of the crew on the trains leaving Providence, so it would be no problem to get her on her way when she was ready. From Providence, his friends could connect her to any other train in the country for no charge. Angie could get first-class accommodation and be comfortable in whatever destination she decided on. Ben knew most of the train routes and would give her the details when she was ready to make her final preparations. Ben felt conflicted. On the one hand, he was sad knowing she would be leaving. At the same time, he felt happy and useful that he could help. This adventure of hers would be his too. Finally, he felt a sense of purpose. It had been a long time since he believed he had a reason to still be on this earth, taking up much needed space, but maybe this mission, if you could call it that, was the reason Ben had been spared the fate of many of his friends who were now, as Ben put it, six feet under.

Ben opened the door of his room and plopped on his bed, feeling comforted in the familiarity despite the extreme messiness that surrounded him. Soon, before he even had time to take out his hearing aids, he was on the other side of wakefulness, and his lips curled up in a smile as he drifted into a young man's dream.

Nine

After Ben dropped me off at the door, I luckily escaped the scrutiny of the Bullhorn and managed to make my way to the elevator undetected. I was nervous about carrying my bag of money into my room and wanted to make sure I accomplished that task with discretion.

When the elevator opened to my floor, however, the first person I encountered was Kim. I heard her before I saw her. The staccato click of her high heels on the linoleum alerted me to her presence. Usually, I tried to avoid her only because I avoided all the staff members here. The only worker I really liked was Sharon, who ran the receptionist desk downstairs. I could tell right away that Sharon was my comrade. She rolled her eyes behind the backs of the directors who marched around the lobby with an air of extreme importance. Whenever there was a real crisis, however, the directors scattered like the wind. Either they were safely locked behind the closed doors of their offices, or they were nowhere to be found at all.

Most of the crises that occur, though, were in the Lodge, which was the building next to ours. The Lodge was where they put the residents who were "memory impaired," which was another name for losing their marbles. Recently, Annie, who was at the table with me in the dining room, disappeared suddenly. This happened occasionally and left everyone in a state of high anxiety, mostly because we all knew the resident left for one of two reasons: either they got pulled out of Peaceful Havens into the Lodge or they died. Either fate was not good. Most of the residents here who were not heavily medicated were always worrying about something, and death and the Lodge were probably high on the list of things to worry about. The Lodge was the closest Peaceful Havens could come to an actual nursing home, with most of the residents locked in their rooms dozing through the day. If you thought this place smelled bad, well, it was a spa compared to the Lodge. When most of the residents were wearing diapers, there was just no way to mask that odor and it hit you right in the face when you walked through the door of the Lodge.

Annie should not have been moved to the Lodge, but I believed it was because she misbehaved. She was always vocal about the atrocious level of care these nurses gave us, pointing fingers at Kim as a prime example, who spent her days strutting around in her high heels and makeup. Annie also was privy to all the local gossip and didn't feel shy about announcing to everyone all the dirt she could find. There was no shortage of dirt at Peaceful Havens, especially concerning the nurses. Last year, Annie found out that one of the nurses, Ceci, was sleeping with one of the ambulance drivers from Speedy Ambulance Service. Ceci convinced the director to switch our ambulance company, Gold Star Ambulance, to Speedy Ambulance, much to the chagrin of the residents. Speedy Ambulance balked at picking up the residents for doctor's appointments for a nominal fee like Gold Star used to. So, the residents began to complain among themselves that their monthly fees for transport were doubled and tripled. Of course, Annie was all too happy to explain to them that the increase was due to Ceci's improved sex life. More tongues wagged, and Annie told her daughter, who complained to the local newspaper. Shortly after that, Ceci mysteriously disappeared, and Gold Star was back. But Ceci apparently got her revenge. The next thing you knew, Annie flunked her mental status exam. Poor Annie. I wondered if she even took a mental status exam or if her results were somehow "mixed up" with another resident who clearly could no longer play with a full deck.

But despite how appalled I was at the Gestapo-like treatment of paying residents, I knew enough to keep my feelings to myself. It was like a prison camp here. If I saw something, I had better not say anything, because I knew it would be my head on the chopping block next. Ben and I talked about this, and we both knew the rules. It was easier for him because he could drive. So far, I had to retreat to my room, the TV, and the world of Chris Matthews to escape. But now it was easier to keep silent because I knew that soon I would not have to see any of these people ever again, God willing.

This sudden appearance of Kim did not make me happy. I glanced in her direction, smiled, and continued to my room as quickly as I could. Kim, however, was not going to let me escape so easily.

"Hi, Angie!" Kim smiled brightly, walking towards me. "Marjorie was looking for you."

I stopped and tried to remember who the hell Marjorie was. Then I remembered that she was the secretary to Dr. Brown. Dr. Brown was now my primary care doctor because she took over the care of everyone in Peaceful Havens.

"Marjorie says you missed your appointment this morning with Dr. Brown. She wants you to call her and set up another one. Today was your physical, so it's important that you don't miss again." It was obvious Kim was pleased to deliver this message to me.

I didn't know that I had an appointment with Dr. Brown, but I couldn't let on that I had forgotten about it. I knew how important it was not to show any signs of forgetfulness. Otherwise, I could also end up in the Lodge.

"Oh, right!" I managed to put on a sheepish smile. "I totally forgot to look at my appointment book this morning." I clutched my bag and walked towards my door. "I'll call her first thing tomorrow to reschedule. Thanks so much for reminding me!" My key slipped into the lock of my door, and I gratefully escaped, shutting the door behind me.

Whew, I thought.

The last thing I needed was to have a nosy nurse notice that I came back with a large shopping bag. Normally that would not arouse suspicion, but everyone knew I didn't drive, and the only person I usually left the building with was Gina. If someone like Kim decided to check the visitor's log, she would see that Gina's name did not appear as a guest.

I should begin to act extra sweet to everyone, so I don't piss anyone off.

Even a simple hint at sarcasm could cause someone to investigate any of my records, including where I had been and who drove me where. The Bullhorn had already made a few comments about Ben and me spending more time together, especially in my apartment. To someone like the Bullhorn, who had no other form of recreation, a sweet piece of gossip like that could cause lots of excitement. I had to remind myself that her audience was also starved for excitement and would welcome a bit of juicy scandal. After all, the high point of their day was usually falling asleep watching *As the World Turns* at one o'clock in the afternoon.

I sighed as I took my shoes off and plopped into my recliner. Now my biggest problem was where to hide my bag of money. It was not a very big bag, and I could probably squeeze it into a smaller bag or even a small box, but where to put it? I looked around my room critically. It was only a studio apartment with one big room and a bathroom. It would not be a smart move to hide it in my bureau. Although I had been doing most of my own laundry, sometimes one of the nurses rifled through my stuff. Under the bed would also be a huge risk because of cleaning staff—although I knew from watching the housekeepers that they rarely did a thorough job of vacuuming under the bed. Still, the best solution would be a place most of the staff would avoid.

During our happy hour chats in the bar, a lot of the residents would talk about this dilemma. Some of the ladies still wore their diamond rings and gold jewelry, and many of the more independent types carried cash with them if they were able to go out and buy something. These types, however, were rare. Most of the residents didn't even remember how much money they had to their name, let alone how much they had on them. That was why they were here in the first place.

Every long-term resident at Peaceful Havens had a tale about theft. I heard many stories about valuables going missing inside apartments even though a perfect hiding place had been found. Annie had kept money under the middle of her mattress. Betty told me how she stashed her gold earrings in the chocolate tin in her freezer. I remembered Evelyn babbling one day about how she stuffed money in her winter boots in the back of her closet (a dumb move since I suspected every CNA within earshot perked up upon hearing that information). None of these solutions appealed to me. I would feel much better knowing the money was right next to me on my person somehow. I knew all that money was just too bulky to keep in my purse. It would also arouse suspicion if I began to keep a purse with me all the time. Right now, I only carried a small beaded bag that Gina bought me in Mexico last year. It was the size of a passport, and I only carried a couple of dollars in it for bingo games and my cell phone when I remembered to take it with me.

There was no hiding place in my room that was beyond scrutiny. I didn't want to have to worry about theft every time I left my room, and I would if the money was not perfectly safe. Even the bathroom would be off limits. I remembered watching a mystery with Tony years ago where the thief hid his stash under the toilet lid hung on some kind of hook so it wouldn't get wet. Although I knew it would be highly unlikely that anyone would want to open my toilet lid, that idea had to be scrapped too. With my luck, the pack of money would fall into the water somehow. The thought of drying out all the bills on my bed or floor filled me with anxiety. So where to put my stash while I plan my escape?

Suddenly I thought of Ben—not his apartment, but his car. The Buick sat in the parking lot day after day undisturbed. It was locked, and no one but Ben used it. I knew Ben's nephew Russell had no interest in it, just as he had little interest in Ben. I could ask Ben if he could give me a key and we could hide it in a small box in the trunk. God knows that, considering the piles of junk inside Ben's car, no one would ever think of breaking into it. I was sure there was stuff in Ben's trunk that hadn't been touched since the day he bought the car. I started laughing. Poor Ben. I could picture him sitting happily in the middle of his messy apartment, probably listening to a ball game on the radio, unaware of all the chaos around him. It would be nice to be Ben, oblivious to his plight and just happy to be alive.

With all the excitement of the day and my money dilemma resolved for now, I felt suddenly tired. It was a good tired, and I sat back in my recliner, putting my feet up for a restful hour before dinner. As I dozed off, I couldn't help feeling elated and somewhat excited about my new life ahead of me, God willing!

Ten

Ben didn't hear the knock on the door. This was not surprising, since he had not yet felt the need to put his hearing aids in. Sometimes it was more pleasant to live in silence, which allowed him to focus on his own thoughts. Today, lots of those thoughts swirled around in his head.

Ben turned and saw his usual nurse, Nancy, standing there. He knew she was talking to him, but he could only see her lips moving. He was frequently surprised by her when he forgot to put in his hearing aids first thing in the morning. Last week, Ben was sitting on the john reading his train magazines only to discover she had walked in and surprised him. Ben knew she was appalled. However, he wasn't that concerned about any of this, having lost most of his modesty years ago. He no longer felt the need to cover up the fact that, most of the time, he slept in his birthday suit. No need to cover that up either, so to speak.

Today, Ben was dressed and sitting on his bed, fumbling with the hearing aids to start his day. Soon his nine o'clock radio program would be on, and he liked hearing *Sports Talk* on WPRO AM. It was so hard for him to see now that he relied more on the radio than the newspaper. Reading the newspaper used to be a favorite morning activity. He felt a momentary pang of sadness as he realized how his daily activities would soon be curtailed, but he quickly dismissed those thoughts as he focused on what he needed to do to help Angie. He looked up and smiled at Nancy.

"Can you help me with my hearing aids?" Ben croaked from his bed. He hated to ask for help, but he had to admit to himself that his failing eyesight had also affected his ability to see the tiny hearing aids and where the batteries went. He wondered for the hundredth time why they made the damn batteries so tiny. Didn't they realize that most of the elderly patients using these things also had diminished eyesight? He sighed in frustration.

"Sure, Ben." Nancy walked over. "Thanks for being dressed," she said with a smirk.

"Ah, yes, you're remembering the day you surprised me while I was still in bed," Ben said.

Now Nancy announced her entry into his apartment. Ben laughed to himself.

"I'm glad to see you're up and dressed, Ben. In the last few weeks, it seemed you had little interest in even getting out of bed. Now I'm happy to see that you seem to have a renewed interest in living. You're smiling more. You're even cracking those corny jokes of yours. It's great, Ben." She gave him a big grin and a thumbs up.

Nancy plopped on his bed and Ben handed his delicate hearing aids to her. She deftly inserted the new batteries. Ben was relieved. As much as he liked silence, right now it was important for him to hear exactly what people were saying to him. He thought ahead to the train reservations he would need to make and all the people he would have to contact to assure a smooth trip for his friend.

"Thanks, Nancy, you are an angel." Ben smiled one of his crooked grins and patted her hand delicately. "I appreciate all your help, even though I might not always say so."

Ben got up slowly and put on his shoes, a task that had caused him difficulty just weeks ago. He had shaved and put on a clean shirt. As he shuffled past her, she sniffed the air.

"Is that Old Spice I smell, Ben? Very nice! You better watch out for the ladies at breakfast. You know they can't resist a dapper looking dude like you!"

Ben smiled distractedly.

"Ben, just a heads up..." Nancy began hesitantly, "Between you and me, the word around here is, well, there might be a strike soon. Not sure when, but the nursing staff is very upset that their medical benefits are being cut. It's kind of up in the air, but if it happens, it will get ugly."

Ben nodded slowly. "Wow, thanks for letting me know, Nanc. I'll keep it under my hat, so to speak."

Nancy nodded and sighed. "Thanks, Ben. I know I can count on you. You're an interesting man. With your sharp mind and keen imagination, you're a breath of fresh air here at Peaceful Havens. And you don't need to hurry off on my account," she added.

"I know I keep you from getting your job done, Nancy. Once I get started, I keep talking as you know. But I have a few things to catch up on before breakfast," Ben said. The truth was, Ben needed to hurry down to breakfast, not to eat, but to talk briefly to Angie on the way. He figured he could knock on her door without the Bullhorn or Kim snooping on their activities. He would be brief, but there were a few loose ends he needed to square away with her. Calling on the phone was frustrating for them both. They preferred face to face conversation even though it was riskier. He hoped she had not left her room yet.

Ben slowly put his jacket on and looked around for his car keys. That was always a problem for him, the keys. Usually, he left the keys in an old mason jar on his desk, but the desk had become so littered with mail, newspapers, receipts, and brochures that it was almost impossible to find the mason jar, which was also partially filled with old marbles. He tried to think back to yesterday when he returned from the doctor. Quite possibly, he left his keys in his jacket pocket. Was he wearing his old Amtrak jacket or his jacket with the Three Stooges on the back? Or maybe he was wearing his Boston Bruins sweatshirt. Wait, it was the Three Stooges. He remembered his doctor's secretary joking with him about it when she helped him remove it before his eye exam.

Thankfully, he found it hanging over his chair in the corner. Reaching inside, he was even more thankful that his keys were there.

"Whew," he said to Nancy, who looked up from the spot where she had gone down on one knee to retrieve a bunch of Amazon receipts that had fallen off the bed. "That was a close call, but I dodged another bullet, so to speak!" Ben happily ambled over to his door. "Thanks again, Nanc. See you later!" Ben called over his shoulder, leaving Nancy to finish collecting the receipts while he closed the door softly behind him.

Eleven

I woke as the sky outside turned to dusty ash before the sun rose above the rooftops over Peaceful Havens. I was not the only one feeling energetic. Outside, I could hear the birds chirping away even though the windows were closed and the air conditioner was on. I shook my head in amazement. It was not going to be a hot day.

Doesn't anyone here believe in fresh air?

Opening a window would probably trigger a silent alarm, causing a flurry of staffers to hurry down the corridor to investigate. I imagined there was more than one escapee who managed to climb out a window. Although I tried to shove those first few weeks out of my mind, I remembered that some old coot had walked all the way to the bakery three blocks away. She was trying to hop onto a bus but didn't bring enough change (what a way to plan an escape, right?), so the bus driver became suspicious and called the police.

I had better make sure my plans are airtight when my turn comes, hopefully soon.

I kicked off the covers of my bedsheets and sat up slowly. I was very happy, an unfamiliar feeling. I tried to remember the last time I felt this way. My guess was when I was home making stuffed artichokes for my kids who were coming down for the day. I struggled to remember exactly when that was. It had to have been at least two years ago. I had been at Peaceful Havens almost exactly a year. I shook my head in amazement. I didn't really allow myself to deeply reflect on what had happened to me to get me here. I knew I didn't really have time for it. Today was an important day to get the rest of my life on the right track, and I needed to focus.

I headed to the bathroom and managed to shower and change by myself before any of the nurses arrived.

There was a definite advantage to getting up early, I thought ruefully.

Most of the staff were not very timely, mostly because the residents rarely went by clocks. As a result, they could show up late—or not at all—and would not be missed. As Tony used to say, they were slow as molasses. I knew there was an Italian expression for that sentiment, but it escaped me. Something about *lenta melassa* but I was sure that wasn't really the "good" Italian.

Unfortunately, when I was growing up in the third floor flat with my three siblings and my mother, we were not taught the kind of Italian anyone would want to speak in this country. Instead, we learned the dialect from the Abruzzi region of Italy where my mother was born. She lived with goats and chickens wandering in and out of their tiny house which indicated how unsophisticated their lifestyle was. My grandmother used to speak her dialect quickly, especially when she was angry, and we kids would scatter when we heard her raised voice. I was sure her expressions would make no sense to Italian students now.

Tony was embarrassed to be an Italian. When he came off the boat at Ellis Island at the age of two, he was an immigrant child with his mother and his older sister, who held his hand for dear life. His father arrived on another boat later and found work as a chef, so they were able to find housing quickly in an old tenement in South Boston. They were looked upon as poor "wops," as they were called then. *Wop* simply meant "without papers." So named, they usually took the kind of jobs that no one else wanted since they were not yet legal. In those days, it was not like you could go get a green card and work legally. For years, Tony grew up feeling like an inferior outsider in a new country where he could not speak the language, but he felt strongly about wanting to fit in, so he studied English and learned quickly. Unlike his parents, he never had an Italian accent, and he would stand up strong and proud in school, speaking perfect English. As a young man, he appeared poised, articulate, and intelligent. No one would ever dream he got off the boat at any age. He had them all fooled. Before he died, though, Tony decided to learn the "proper" Italian we were never taught in Italy.

I must admit I used to nag Tony about going to Italian classes. He would usually take off for a class as soon as I mentioned a chore he had to do. His mother told me before we got married that Tony would always be agreeable, never said no, always a smile on his face, but his intention was to never complete any task on his "honey-do" list. Tony was smart and learned that the word "yes" would always be part of his vocabulary, but no one ever reminded him to follow up on his promises! My constant nagging was unproductive and resulted in a hasty retreat. I was just beginning to realize how pointless my actions had been.

I had plenty of time to reflect on my past, but up until now, I hadn't given it much thought. Lately, however, thoughts kept popping up, interrupting my daydreams. I knew I had to confront some of the demons from my past at some point, but for the present, I shrugged them off. I had to make some real plans that would affect the rest of my life for whatever short time I had left.

There was a timid knock on my door as I finished putting on my lipstick. I had a feeling it was Ben, so I called out right away, "Be right there!" I was excited at the thought of finalizing our plans, but I had to admit I was also edgy.

Ben looked nervous too. He smiled at me, and as soon as the words "Good morning" came out of his mouth, I told him to come in and have a seat. To my amazement, he was all spiffed up and smelled pretty good.

He must have gotten up at four o'clock in the morning, I thought.

Usually, it took him several agonizing minutes to even button up his shirt from what I'd observed so far, but here he was, all set to go, and it wasn't even eight o'clock.

Will wonders never cease, I thought.

I realized I was happy too. We both settled into our seats and looked at each other. Ben spoke slowly, sounding like he had rehearsed his words for a while.

"So, Angie, I have been thinking about how we should proceed." He stopped to clear his throat and then proceeded to speak a little more quietly as we both nervously looked around. "I have just spoken to several of my conductor friends, and they assured me they can have you travel safely on Amtrak all the way through to the station in California nearest to Uncle Nicky. Some of the time, you will be riding on the Acela, which is kind of a first-class Amtrak train. There will be no charge, of course, and you will travel in a nice deluxe sleeper car with all your meals provided. I've traveled that route many times, and it is pretty and very scenic. Aside from being alone, I think you would be very comfortable, but please tell me your concerns, and maybe we can sketch out some kind of timetable as to when we can begin... so to speak." Ben's last words faded as he looked at me anxiously.

I looked at him in amazement. He had done his homework and already mapped out a route with my connections. I felt like hugging him and crying at the same time. I guessed I was beginning to realize that it was a long time since I felt anyone cared about me. Since my accident, and certainly even before that time, I had felt alone—alone in the sense that I no longer felt as if my presence mattered. I had buried all the sadness I felt after Tony's death. At the time, I threw myself into cooking and caring for the rest of my family, but the sad fact was, I had begun to feel more and more like a burden to everyone. No one needed me to make a big Italian Sunday dinner anymore. My kids were consumed with their own families now. Trudging over to drop in every weekend was no longer a priority. Their visits became more like an obligation, and they began to occur less frequently. I pretended I wasn't hurt by their lame excuses, but I was. Still, I buried all my feelings and kept cranking out food that no one was eating. Last year, when autumn rolled into winter and the house became darker, the walls began to close in around me. That was when I began to deteriorate. I now admitted that depression was a big part of my downfall.

I tried to keep tears from springing to my eyes, so I looked down for a few minutes. When I finally met Ben's eyes, I was smiling. His face had a strange mixture of relief and anxiety as he smiled, too. I had a feeling he knew how I felt.

"Ben, that sounds great. You can probably tell I'm overwhelmed right now. What I am feeling is a mixture of happiness, relief, and extreme gratitude for what you have done. But I admit I am afraid too. I have sort of mapped out my plan of departure, especially the part about how to leave. Maybe we can talk about the ideas I have to make this as painless as possible for everyone."

I took a deep breath. "One thing I've decided is that I don't want your involvement in my escape to be a problem for you. I would like to make sure that no one suspects that you've masterminded my escape, so to speak. So, I have some ideas about how we can do that... and maybe you do too?" I looked at Ben and his expression was calm and thoughtful. He nodded as he began to speak slowly but firmly.

"Yes, Angie, I have also been trying to come up with a way I can get you to the train station undetected. There are several ways. I can drive you, of course, but we need to decide how to do this and how to avoid being detected. I'll admit that I have been racking my brains trying to think of the best solution to this problem." Ben shook his head and looked down at his lap.

"Well, Ben, I have also been thinking about this plan, because it is important to do it right. A botched attempt would be disastrous, as you can imagine!" My voice rose in my attempt to be humorous, but I was nervous. This was the part I had planned in my head, and I wanted to present it carefully.

"You probably know that I don't sleep very much, sometimes not at all. I never did. Seems like I could always get by on just a couple of hours of sleep most of my life. This has never been a problem until I moved here. Now, when I wander around the corridors at night, I head to the kitchen where I snatch a couple of oranges for a snack. This is undetected, except when John is patrolling around." I glanced at Ben, and he nodded. Everyone knew who John was. He was generally considered to be a giant pain.

"One night when John was not around, I went into the kitchen to look around. It was empty, of course, but I was curious, and perhaps a little nosy. I'm a stickler for food prep and wanted to make sure everything in the fridge is as cold as it should be." I didn't reveal to Ben that the milk for my coffee frequently curdled, a fact that had made me look in the fridge in the first place. "After I snooped around the appliances, I made my way to the back of the pantry on the other side of the corridor leading up to the countertops. There, next to a pile of large pots and pans, I saw a door leading out to the back of the building—I thought it must have been the delivery door for the trucks unloading food in the morning—and it was unlocked." I swallowed before I continued in a low voice. "Yes, Ben, it seems as if Peaceful Havens doesn't bother locking the kitchen door. I tried the knob and it turned and the door opened out to the back of the building. No alarms went off, except in my head of course!" I couldn't resist grinning at my little joke. Ben stared at me in wide-eyed amazement.

"This was around ten thirty at night. I thought that maybe it was a one-time thing, and someone like John just forgot to lock the door for that one night, but then I remembered John wasn't working that night. So, I concluded that it's John's job to lock the back door, and when he's off duty, it remains unlocked. I tested my theory the next night. I saw he was not working, which was last Sunday night. I made sure to retrace my steps at the exact time as the first night, and the door was again unlocked. The next night, I saw John walking around and casually asked him about his schedule. I'm glad that John blabs a lot because he easily divulged his schedule, so now I know what nights he's not working." My voice trailed off breathlessly.

"Wow, Angie," Ben began, shaking his head. "You should have worked for the FBI! I am very impressed with your powers of observation; you are truly a super sleuth!" He grinned and his eyes shone with excitement. "So, I'm assuming you're suggesting that you leave from the delivery door on one of the nights that John is not working?"

"Yes, Ben, I think it would work. Remember, after eight p.m., the doors here are locked. But instead of both of us leaving at the same time, I have another idea for you. Tell me if you think this is a good one: You can sign out late in the afternoon and mention you're going to a family gathering. You can also mention you will probably be out late and will use your clicker thing to return after hours. I don't think that would arouse suspicion at all because you're independent and use your car frequently."

The clicker thing I was referring to was the little device that was attached to a car key, the part that sounded an alarm. Some of the residents had one in case they came in after hours. Hitting the little button on the clicker would unlock both front doors without sounding an alarm. I gave mine to Gina in case we came in late at night. We had used it a few times for late-night dinners at Gina's house. It was surprisingly easy to use, even for me. I assumed Ben had a couple of them as well,

Ben laughed. "I think it's called a key fob, Angie, and I have no idea why! I know these kinds of ornaments used to be hung from key chains and are given out to people when they buy a car. I remember my dad had one, but we didn't call it a key fob. I think I still have it somewhere..." Ben's voice trailed off, and I suspect he was thinking about all the stuff piled up in his old house. I quickly changed the subject.

"That's right, key fob—fob for short. I remember Gina calling it that while she was desperately looking for it in her purse that night. Now she keeps it in her glove compartment. So, if you get back from the station late, you can use it to come in undetected. I'm suggesting this because once my absence is detected, I don't want anyone to suspect you. We need to avoid the idea of collusion, do you agree?"

Ben nodded slowly. He sat still for a few minutes, and I could almost hear the wheels turning in his head.

"So, what I can do is pick you up by the loading dock behind the building when you leave through the back door of the kitchen. Assuming, of course, that the door is open. Then I will whisk you to the train station, make sure that you get on the train and are settled in, and when I return to Peaceful Havens, I will use my key fob to get back in. It sounds like a good plan. Have I got it right so far?"

I sat back on the couch and let out a big sigh. I needed a minute to stop and think. It was all shaping up; my plan was becoming a reality! I felt nervous and excited at the same time.

"I'm sure I will be okay with it the more I get used to the idea, and that is happening already. For months now, I've been formulating this in my mind and now it is finally taking shape. I talked to Nicky yesterday—we have been speaking every few days—and he is ready when I am. He told me that he has a spare room and is looking very much forward to seeing me. I am okay with that part. The only sticking point left to decide is if should I leave an exit note for my children or wait and call them when I get to my destination."

Ben and I stared at each other. This was the only piece of the puzzle we had left to fit into our crazy scheme for it to work properly. We sat for several minutes deep in thought.

"I'll tell you what, Angie. Let's both think about this and meet later for an early dinner. I'll pick you up around three at the side of the building if you can slip by Sharon... Maybe we can go to the Pine Tree Grille? I know you love that place, and you can relax with a glass of wine while we decide what the best plan is. It's important to plan this so we don't have all kinds of alarm bells going off. Although we both realize some drama is going to be inevitable."

"Sounds great, Ben!" We both got up and hugged nervously. "See you later!"

Six hours later, we were seated at a booth on the outside wall of the giant room in my favorite spot by the window overlooking Spectacle Lake. Pine Tree Grille had always been my favorite restaurant, mostly because it held so many wonderful memories. All our family anniversaries and birthdays had been celebrated there. I was sure we also had someone's wedding or baby shower there at some time in the back banquet room. Through the years, Tony and I got to know the staff well. In our early days, it was impossible to get a table on a weekend night, and they did not take reservations. In true Rhode Island fashion, it was all about who you knew, and we knew everyone there. Upon arrival on a weekend, we were surreptitiously ushered into a back room to be seated ahead of everyone else. This favoritism was frowned upon by unsuspecting patrons who showed up for dinner, but we ceased to care after a while. It was kind of exciting to be treated as if we were special even though we knew we were not. That was the closest we ever got to feeling like real VIPs.

For my dinner with Ben, Raymond was our waiter. He was showing his age, and his step was slower as he approached our table. "Angie! How great to see you! *Come sta?*" All the waiters here knew I spoke Italian and loved to practice their own fractured attempts at the language.

"*Bene! E tu?*" I answered instinctively as Ben looked on in amusement.

After a few minutes of conversation, Ray stepped away to get our drinks and Ben chuckled.

"Well, Angie, I knew you liked this place, but I didn't realize what a celebrity you are here! Getting the royal treatment is not something I am accustomed to; I should hang out with you more often!"

I laughed. "Well, Ben, looks like you will have to do that in the next four days, or you will be out of luck!" The minute I said it, I regretted it because of the crestfallen look on Ben's face, but he quickly recovered and smiled.

"Yes, Angie, I know. I admit I will really miss you, but I'm happy for you also. You really don't belong in Peaceful Havens, and I also think Gina knows it. In the end, everyone will be happy that you have found another more fulfilling life. You really deserve it!"

I felt tears well up in my eyes. I tried not to be sad when I thought of leaving Ben behind in that awful place, but I was consoled when I saw how happy he was for me. I certainly could not move forward with my plan without his help. I felt better knowing this adventure of mine seemed to have given him a new lease on life.

"Thanks, Ben. I'll miss you too, but I promise I will keep in touch using my new cell phone! Maybe we could plan a phone date every week, say on Sunday mornings? Around eleven? I would really look forward to that!"

"Sure, Angie. I would too! It's a date! If Uncle Nicky doesn't mind." Ben beamed at me in delight.

I laughed as our drinks appeared. I had my usual, a glass of Kendall Jackson chardonnay and Ben had a Bud Light. Now came the tough part: the real nitty gritty of my plan.

I outlined to Ben all the details of how I wanted my escape to play out. I had thought about it carefully, and I knew I had to involve my children at just the right time. I wanted to avoid a search party showing up at Nicky's house. As I spoke, Ben nodded and gave me a few of his own suggestions. We talked openly and honestly through our dinner and when we were done, we gave ourselves a high five. Ben ordered a shot of Anisette for me as a congratulatory measure before we left. A man after my own heart!

Twelve

Connie pulled her silver Lexus into an empty parking spot at Peaceful Havens. She wasn't surprised that there were lots of empty parking spots; she knew most of the residents did not drive, and there were not a lot of visitors on a Monday afternoon. It did make her sad and a little guilty to think that Angie probably didn't have a lot of visitors either. Ever since Connie had found out that Angie was at Peaceful Havens last spring, she had only visited her once. It was right after Gina called her to tell her that her mother was placed there after her car accident. Connie stepped out of the Lexus and locked it as she looked up at the front door of Peaceful Havens. She gulped. She remembered the condition Angie was in last spring and what happened when she had visited.

Angie was Connie's next-door neighbor for years when Connie was raising her family. At the time, Angie was probably in her forties. Despite their age difference, they became friends quickly. Angie was a godsend just when Connie needed one. At the time, Connie was working as a school principal and had very little time to bake. In fact, she had very little time to do anything but run off to work every day and try to put out all the fires that erupted in Barrington Middle School—and there were lots of fires, usually requiring Connie to work after hours and even on weekends. Connie's three kids, all under the age of twelve, certainly suffered from Connie's demanding job. To make matters worse, Connie's husband Joe was never home either. He managed four car dealerships, and weekends were his frantic time since most auto sales occurred on weekends. So, on the rare weekend that Connie was not working with some family in crisis at her school, she was running around frantically taking care of all the household chores that never got done during the week. Forget about cleaning the house. Connie remembered that time as a blur of trying to juggle twenty things at once and never successfully.

Angie was such a blessing to Connie. She would appear at her door just when things reached the point of being totally unmanageable with a hot dish in her hand, smiling broadly. Connie remembered Angie saving the day so many times as she would hastily push a casserole into Connie's arms, which were usually filled with a small screaming toddler or a bundle of groceries.

"Connie, I just took this out of the oven, and it's much too much food for us, so here, take a little off our hands," Angie would say quickly, backing away before Connie could object.

Her food was to die for. Connie was Italian, but Angie's cooking was the real deal, even better than her Italian grandmother who was born in Sicily. Angie knew how to make stuffed artichokes with no effort at all, and she made raviolis all the time. She usually had frozen ones in the freezer along with homemade pizza she would also make in bulk. As a result, Connie's family was usually treated at least weekly to something hot and delicious from Angie's kitchen. As the kids got older, Connie tried to reciprocate and helped Angie if she needed something fixed. Joe could usually be persuaded to stop in to fix their broken doorbell or to look at their aging boiler when it refused to work. Joe loved Tony, but he knew his talents did not lie in being a handyman around the house.

What Connie remembered most about living next door to Angie was the great friendship they had. As the kids grew, both women were faced with similar situations in their family dynamics. Joe and Tony were getting older, and both wanted to retire, Tony because of the stress of his demanding job as head of personnel in the federal government and Joe because of the physical stress of managing so many dealerships. Connie and Angie spent many hours over coffee and cupcakes commiserating as they worried about the future. They became close confidants and depended on each other for feedback. Connie remembered Angie's quick wit and ability to laugh at daily stresses, which helped her put things in perspective. Sometimes, Connie thought she never would have managed to bring up three kids, keep Joe happy, and keep her sanity without Angie!

Connie not only admired Angie but she also envied her. Angie had so much energy! Even though she didn't hold down a full-time job, she was able to take care of her household with no effort at all while enjoying it. Angie also worked in real estate at the time. Connie was always amazed at how she could pull it all together with a smile on her face. Angie was a happy person and a warm person. She took the time to listen to Connie and only gave advice after careful thought. She didn't forget any of the kind deeds Joe helped her with either. She always told Connie that she was extremely grateful to have them next door because they were cherished as dear friends. Connie remembered Angie as being loved by everyone. She always had company and welcomed anyone who popped in unexpectedly as if she had been expecting them all day. When the doorbell rang at Connie's house, she usually hid upstairs somewhere!

After Joe retired, he convinced Connie that they should move to the ocean. They did have the means to buy a beautiful retirement home on the beach after Joe sold his car dealerships to his brother. Although Connie and Angie kept in contact, their relationship changed after the move. They saw each other a few times during the year, but their close friendship slowly waned. Still, when Connie reached out to Angie, it was like nothing had changed. She was still bubbling and happy. That is, until the day Tony died.

Connie helped Angie during the wake and funeral but was surprised that Angie didn't seem to grieve. Her life continued despite the fact she was alone in her house. Her kids had moved away by that time, but she still filled her days bustling around with her cooking and shopping. Connie knew that she was lonely and felt guilty she didn't visit more.

When Gina told Connie about Angie's accident, Connie went right over to visit Angie at Peaceful Havens. She was shocked at the change in Angie. Angie smiled and seemed happy to see her but repeated things over and over. She seemed unable to grasp the seriousness of her situation and dismissed Connie's words of concern. Angie's expression had changed to a faraway look of confusion. That was the reason Connie dreaded the visit. It was hard for Connie to see her old friend as a feeble old lady. She didn't want to remember Angie that way.

Connie signed the guest book and continued down the hall to Angie's room. She had left a voice mail that she was going to visit but Angie did not call her back. That also gave Connie a feeling of dread at what she would find.

As Connie rounded the corner to Angie's room, she heard a familiar voice.

"Connie! Is that you?"

Connie turned around and was amazed to see Angie smiling at her, lipstick on, dressed in pink sweater and black Ponte slacks, standing next to the laundry room. Connie brightened up and ran towards Angie, who stepped forward for a hug.

"Wow, Angie, I am so happy to see you! You really look terrific!"

As Connie critically observed Angie from a closer angle, she realized that she really did look terrific. The old Angie was back!

"Bet your feet were dragging as you forced yourself to come and visit, right?" Angie winked and smiled mischievously. "I know that the last time you came, you left here thinking I wasn't long for this world. And I don't blame you. But I am better now, really." Angie's face softened as she gazed at Connie. "I'm so happy you came. How much time do you have for a visit? We can have coffee in the dining room, and I think there are some lemon muffins left over from breakfast."

Relief flooded over Connie as she smiled and nodded. "Sounds good. I have about an hour. Is that okay?" They linked arms and walked towards the dining room. "Wow, Angie, the last time I saw you, you had a walker and kind of shuffled along. No more walker?"

"Well, Connie, that is a recent development. I've been seeing the physical therapist three times a week now. It took a bit of persuading to get Medicare to approve it," Angie chuckled, "but they finally did, and here I am, living proof that therapy does work if you commit yourself to it three times a week. I'll admit it wasn't easy—you know that therapists and doctors were not my favorite people—but I have to say I love Nancy, my therapist. She's gentle and kind but also determined to get me to the place where I don't need that damn walker anymore!"

Connie laughed. "Angie, you always had that stubborn streak! And it ended up working in your favor, right?" Connie sat at an empty chair in the dining room, which was pretty much vacant at the time. "You seem like you are back to being your old self. What plans do you have now? Are you going to move back to your house soon?"

Angie seemed to hesitate a beat too long before she answered.

"No, Gina is selling my house, and she has my permission. I know it's too big for me with all those stairs and bedrooms. We are talking about what the next step is for me, so to speak.... Maybe some kind of independent living situation, but I want to think it through before I do anything in haste. And I do have a lease here until the end of June. So, we will see, but my future will not be moving in with Gina, that I can tell you!" Angie laughed. Connie thought she saw a flash of something deeper in her response, but she couldn't make out what it was.

"Well, Angie, if you need any help while you're making up your mind, let me know. There are some nice places down near the beach not far from us, although I know they're pricey. Still, it would be so great if we could be close to each other again! I'm alone a good deal of the time now because Joe is taking care of his elderly folks in Maine. But my youngest, Sarah, is having a baby in four months and I can't wait!"

Connie smiled broadly as she shared her happy news.

"Oh, that is great, Connie! Your first grandchild! Boy or girl?"

"They will find out soon, but I'm not sure they'll tell us. I hope they don't have one of those dreadful 'reveal' parties!" Connie made a face. "But I don't think so. Sarah is the most private of my kids." Connie reached for one of her pictures of Sarah to show Angie. "Remember how quiet she was as a kid? Well, she still is."

Angie took the picture and gazed at it. "Wow, Connie, it's always incredible to see how the kids you grew up with now are full grown adults with real jobs. She's a psychologist, right?"

Connie was amazed that Angie remembered. "Yes, that's right. And she loves it. Always was focused on helping others. I'm grateful she found an occupation she loves." Connie looked up at Angie again, this time more critically. "You know, Angie, I was really worried about you last time I visited, though I guess you know that. But much to my relief, you look great now. Can I ask you, though, how do you really feel?"

Angie sat back and smiled. "So happy, Connie, *so* happy I made it through that awful time. And I am determined now to make the best of the life I have in front of me!"

Briefly, Connie caught that look on Angie's face once again, but she still could not sort it out. She reached over and held her dear friend's hand tightly. "And no one deserves it more than you!" Connie smiled widely, glad that she had finally made this trip. What a transformation!

Thirteen

Gina finished planting the last of her impatiens in her front yard. She sighed as she surveyed her work with a critical eye. Gina was a weekend gardener who loved seeing rows of flowers planted by her kitchen window—but she was also a lazy gardener and, truth be told, would love for someone else to do the back-breaking work for her.

When Gina first moved into her house with her husband thirty-five years ago, it was fun to do the planting. Her husband planted the red maple on her lawn and the big locust in the backyard. Gina's mission was to plant flowers and vegetables. She carved out a section on the side of the house and made a raised bed for her vegetables long before raised beds became popular. Like her mother, she loved fresh Roma tomatoes for sauce and the small grape tomatoes for snacking. However, after her husband decided to dig up most of their backyard to build a sunroom, space for her flower beds was severely diminished. That was one of the reasons her husband became her ex-husband. Gina expanded her flower beds to the other side of the house under the kitchen window. She also planted a lilac bush, her favorite, under her bedroom window and sunflowers next to the impatiens. The result was a summer riot of colors by late July and August. For now, Gina concentrated on the impatiens and pansies lining the border at the front door.

Gina looked at the remains of the blooms on her dogwood tree above her flower bed. The pink blossoms were stunning but were now beginning to fade. Just as the dogwood began to fade, however, her lilacs bloomed. Gina couldn't help but feel a surge of hope every year when spring brought welcome changes. She needed hope. Her mother's situation cast a daily shadow over her head. It was always there in the back of her mind, reminding her that maybe her decision to move her mother into Peaceful Havens was hasty.

Gina slowly brought herself up from her kneeling place next to the flowers. She wanted to go for her run but felt too tired after all the planting. It wasn't just the planting; it was also hauling the plants out of the back of her car after hauling them in from the nursery. The forty-pound bags of topsoil and mulch were now a problem. She remembered sadly that twenty years ago, these chores did not create any soreness in her back, muscles, and shoulders like they did now. Again, she thought of her mother and how she watched the slow decline in her body as well. Gina was upset about her mother hiding the changes that were happening in her body, but she knew she would have done the same thing. In fact, she was doing it this minute. Planting her spring and summer flowers no longer brought her the joy it once did. Aside from the limitations she felt with her aging issues, Gina had to admit the nagging worry regarding her mother's future was always present and contributed to her general malaise.

Yesterday, Sandy, the realtor handling her mother's house sale, called to tell her they had a full-price offer on the house. Even better, it was a conventional mortgage. The buyers already had sold their own house, but their pockets were deep anyway. The news should have filled her with joy, but Gina's immediate reaction was that of dread. She knew that she could no longer put off the ugly chore of telling her mother her house was about to be sold. What's more, the deed needed to be signed by Angie. Gina had power of attorney, but the house was still in her mother's name, meaning Gina did not have the authority to sign the deed. The closing date of the sales agreement was in three weeks. No longer could Gina afford to procrastinate. Gina knew Sandy assumed Angie had already signed the deed.

As Gina pulled off her garden gloves and stepped into her house, she knew today was the day. As unpleasant as the task might be, putting it off any further would create a tsunami Gina wanted to avoid.

It looks as if running my three miles today will have to wait, she thought ruefully.

Gina pulled her Jeep into an empty spot at Peaceful Havens. Since it was only eleven o'clock, Gina knew her mother was not yet ready for lunch. It was a perfect time to get the task done. She did leave a message on Angie's cell phone that she was going to stop by. She managed to stop at the bakery for a couple of fresh sugar donuts that her mother loved. Gina bought one for herself as well, since she knew her mother would never eat alone. She also snatched a couple of hot coffees to go. Gina was not hopeful that the warm sugar donuts would facilitate a smooth execution of the task before her. As she walked towards the front door, she said a little prayer that all hell would not break loose.

Sharon, the receptionist, seemed distracted as she waved to Gina when she signed in. Sharon was one of the bright spots at Peaceful Havens and was very kind to Angie and also to Gina. She always had time to listen to Gina and seemed to understand the dilemma she was faced with. God knows she must deal with dramas every day, Gina frequently thought. She was so glad she did not have a job like Sharon's where interaction with unpleasant clients and residents filled the better part of the day. Today, though, Sharon was obviously in the throes of a crisis, judging from the look of alarm on her face as she juggled several phone lines at once. Gina briefly wondered what the disaster of the day was, but soon forgot about it as she made her way to her mother's room.

Before she could get to room 323, she saw her mother folding the last of her clean sheets outside the laundry room. Gina instantly felt the usual guilt. She had promised her mother she would wash them for her and forgot. It appeared as if Angie was having no trouble folding them, however, even the pesky bottom sheet. Gina always had a great deal of difficulty with those awful elastic corners.

"Hi, Mom!" Gina proclaimed brightly in a voice that she realized was a little too loud. "It's me, and I brought some of those yummy donuts for us to share!"

Angie looked up, startled. "Well, hi, Gina! You were the last person I expected to see today! To what do I owe this unexpected pleasure?" Angie managed a forced smile as she stacked the sheets into a neat pile.

"I left you a voice mail, Mom. Did you get it?" Gina took the sheets from her mother and pointedly handed her the bag of donuts. She realized, with irritation, that her mother had once again lost her cell phone.

In response, Angie broke into a scornful laugh.

"What is so funny Mom?"

Angie shrugged it all off, as if the cell phone, and even Gina's visit, meant nothing. "Honey, I haven't seen you in days. I'm so glad to see you, but why are you here?

This wasn't going well. Gina smiled at her mother, trying to hide all traces of nervousness. She knew her mother had had no clue she was coming for a visit, but they both knew there was a reason she was here. Gina was smart enough to realize that Angie was probably filled with a sense of foreboding.

"Let's walk over to that family room, okay? I noticed that it was empty and cleaned out. It would be a nice place to have our donuts with the sun shining through the windows. I think these sugar ones are still warm! Remember how they melt in your mouth? You would have been proud of me: I managed to snag the last two. And the coffee is nice and hot, just the way we like it!"

"Okay, I will leave my clean laundry right outside my room. It should be okay until I get back."

Gina agreed, although she wondered what, if anything, her mother was trying to hide from her in her room.

Angie followed her daughter to the room off the dining room known as the family room. It was a large private room they had used for family dinners when Angie was a new resident, but it was also used for family conferences. Gina remembered several such meetings in the past year, especially the one where she had signed Angie's lease, but she tried to put the memory out of her mind. Instead, she plopped the donuts and coffee on the table across from where Angie sat.

To Gina's amazement, Angie did not need any help sitting or navigating the large chairs, and her mother had kept pace with her as she walked down the long corridor. Gina took the opportunity to examine her mother's face. The woman across from her did not resemble the scared and sick woman who Gina had released from the rehab center last year. Angie had the color back in her face. Her hair, with its auburn sheen, was curled and set perfectly. Angie had somehow managed to find her old lipstick, Autumn Rose, which brightened her smile curling at her lips. Her clothes were clean and neat down to the new orthopedic shoes that did not resemble the clumsy ones Gina had hastily bought for her last year. When Angie sat down, Gina could even detect a whiff of Jean Naté, her favorite scent. Gina's jaw dropped open in amazement. When did this remarkable transformation take place?

Angie reached for a warm sugar donut with a smile of satisfaction on her face. "Thank you so much, Gina, this is a wonderful treat! You are the best daughter!" Gina watched her mother bite into the soft pillow of dough then sip her coffee. She was surprised. She seemed so content.

Gina fumbled with her coffee cup, knowing that she could hesitate no more. Now was the time to break the news to her mother. She took a bite and chewed as Angie's eyes locked with hers. She saw curiosity in Angie's bright blue eyes, but Gina was also relieved to notice the look of pure pleasure, and she thought she detected a look of love as well.

"Mom, you look wonderful. I have to say, this is a pleasant surprise to see you so happy! I have some great news for you too. I found out yesterday that your house is going to be sold next month for the asking price! Isn't that great?" Gina tried to keep her voice even because she knew her mother would detect any false gaiety, and being less than honest at this point would frankly make Gina want to upchuck her breakfast.

Angie stared at Gina, chewing slowly. In turn, Gina looked at her mother's face and was surprised at the emotion there. There was compassion and, yes, love. Is it possible her mother understood the conflicts she had because she had them too?

"Wow, Gina, that *is* surprising, and, yes, it is good news. I know you have done so much to make this happen, and I really appreciate your hard work. I didn't have to lift a finger, and I guess I will always regret the fact that this burden fell on your shoulders alone." Angie spoke uncharacteristically slowly, sipping her coffee as she finished her sentence. She put her coffee down and wiped her mouth with the napkin. "Any idea when the closing will be?"

Gina looked at her in astonishment. This was not the reaction she had been expecting, nor was this the mother she had expected to see. What had happened to the disagreeable and unhappy woman that she remembered from last spring? Could it be that the old Angie was back?

Gina found her voice. "Probably in four to five weeks. We're signing the purchase and sales agreement tomorrow. I can let you know exactly when I know, but it looks good—the deal I mean. The buyers are perfect and love the house. The only thing I need today is for you to sign the deed. As you know, I must have this signed because only your name is on it." Gina reached for her purse on the floor.

Angie chuckled ruefully. "Yes Gina, I do remember that from my real estate days."

Gina pulled out the document and placed it in front of her with her pen.

"I recognize that pen! I used it to write out my bills. It's the Coldwell Banker pen I used for years in real estate." She looked up at Gina and smiled.

Gina smiled, too, as she realized where the pen came from. She was amazed again that her mother recognized it too. Angie reached over and signed her name slowly. She left the date blank.

"I know the date will be filled in when the deed is transferred so I will leave that blank."

Angie looked up at Gina and then quickly looked down as she handed over the document to Gina. Gina could not see the expression on her face.

Her mother sighed and stood up. She gave Gina a knowing smile, and Gina responded by impulsively getting up and hugging her mother tightly, a long hard hug. Gina had a feeling that she would not feel this hug again for a long time.

Fourteen

It was a typical Saturday night at Peaceful Havens. The front lobby was being set up for a solo piano player, which was an improvement on the last group of musicians they hired. Last week, a three-piece bluegrass band attempted to play some folk music. There was a power outage earlier in the day so they could not hook up their electric guitars or microphones, resulting in a rather confusing rendition of "Michael, Row the Boat Ashore." I was not deaf yet, but even I had trouble hearing their music. After about a half hour, everyone gave up and went back to their rooms.

There was no power outage tonight, but I was in no mood to listen to chamber music. I made my way to my room after dinner, a meal I was too nervous to eat. Tonight was my escape, and my packed suitcase was already in Ben's car. My train was leaving at eleven o'clock, and Ben was scheduled to pick me up outside the kitchen door at ten thirty. So far, we had tied up all the loose ends we needed to in order to facilitate our departure on time, and I hoped my clever diversion technique would work. I gulped as I unlocked my door for what I hoped was the last time.

I sighed as I looked around the room which had been my home away from home for the past year. It was hard for me to believe it had been that long and even harder to believe that I would finally be leaving. My road ahead was uncertain, and there was a chance my new life would not be what I expected.... What *did* I expect? I had only been to California a few times, and only to visit. I had never lived anywhere but the East Coast. What about earthquakes or those forest fires that popped up every year? As anxious as my thoughts were, however, I did feel a smidge of excited anticipation. The thought of spending the rest of my years at Peaceful Havens in this thankless room was unbearable. Any alternative to staying here had to be a good one. I only hoped my family would somehow, in good time, see that I was right.

The purse I decided to use was small but had enough compartments to carry what I needed for the train. Most of my money was already packed in my suitcase, which was going to be always with me in the train. I felt good about the fact I would have a deluxe super sleeper for much of my journey. Ben had explained it all thoroughly. It was private and had enough room for my suitcase and toiletries. However, these trains did not have elegant washroom facilities. My bathroom was a very tiny room adjacent to my sleeper and only consisted of a toilet and washbasin with a small drain. I had brought my own soap and washcloth, but I would leave everything else up to Amtrak. Altogether, my journey would take about seventy-five hours, not counting any delays along the way. Ben explained that frequently there would be delays, but I was not worried. I was hoping that once I found my plush seat and pulled out of the Providence station, I would not be disturbed.

I looked sadly at all my clothes hanging in the closet. I only packed a few of my favorite outfits for the trip. Most of my clothes were too big for me now anyway. I lost a lot of weight in rehab, and I ate sparingly here. The only time I enjoyed meals now was the rare occasion when I ate out somewhere. As a result, I lost about fifteen pounds, enough to make my old pants and dresses hang on me. They also reminded me of another life. I was glad to say goodbye to that chapter in my life. I was sure I could order whatever I needed from L.L. Bean or Macy's once I got to Nicky's house. I smiled when I remembered how he spoke about his late wife Vivian's obsession with online shopping. I would have to convince him that that would not happen to me!

My good jewelry was coming with me. I didn't have much, but I made sure to put my best gold earrings on today, and I was wearing my Byzantine gold bracelet too. I carefully packed the matching necklace and some of the gold jewelry Tony bought me when we were in Italy. The last thing I packed was my mother's tiny gold Italian earrings that she was wearing when she died. I meant to give them to Gina but never got around to it.

Gina, I thought guiltily.

I fervently hoped my plan was a good one to minimize all the fires that were bound to erupt once I made my escape... but I couldn't worry about that now.

The last thing I packed into my new purse (with my lipstick, of course) was my wallet with all my ID cards, credit cards, and my license. Who knows? Maybe someday in the future I could drive again. That thought gave me new hope.

The streetlights outside my window came on as I finished packing. As I looked around the room critically, my eyes fell on my old cell phone and charger sitting on the bed with my room key.

Ben was nice enough to buy me a new cell phone with a matching charger, the kind I saw advertised in the *Boston Globe* with oversized numbers. It was a flip phone like my old one, but it was easier to press the numbers with my not-so-tiny fingers. The phone number was written on the back on a piece of masking tape in case I forgot it. I was overjoyed when Ben gave it to me as a parting gift. Now I could call Nicky or Ben safely with no possibility of being traced. Eventually, of course, I would share my number with my family, but for now, I needed to remain off the radar. I took my old cell phone and charger and carefully placed it under the mattress. Then I carefully removed the "people locator" from around my neck. This was the device with a big red button we could press if we needed help. Most of the weekend nurses ignored it anyway. They were tired of the residents pressing it when they wanted the blinds opened or the TV station changed. I did not need to hold on to anything that could track me down.

I felt rather naughty as I realized I would basically be a fugitive. I had led such a dull life up until now; this new adventure was giving me a much-needed shot of adrenaline.

It's about time, I thought. *Angie's excellent adventure!*

Fifteen

Sharon sat in her office chair by the window of Peaceful Havens, listening to another disgruntled family member complain about one of the CNAs. From her window on the side of the building, she could see the parking lot, which was usually vacant at this time of the day. From the corner of her eye, Sharon saw Ben slowly walking to his car. If she had not been distracted, it would have dawned on Sharon that Ben usually did not go out driving alone this late in the day.

Sharon loved Ben and his wacky sense of humor. He was the only resident who made her laugh. She was not used to encountering witty remarks working in Peaceful Havens, so meeting Ben was a breath of fresh air. She looked forward to his sharp observations and delighted in his clever banter. Ben always listened to Sharon during their conversations. He remembered that her grandfather arrived from Portugal right around the time Ben's father did and settled in the same town. One day, Sharon brought Ben some homemade Portuguese soup just like his mother used to make. Sharon and Ben were soulmates. Sharon was more than willing to overlook the fact that Ben left the building as it was getting dark. As far as Sharon was concerned, Ben could do whatever he wanted and was certainly entitled to his privacy.

One of the sons of a resident was now loudly complaining on the phone about how his mother was ignored in her room recently when she needed her meals brought to her. His mother had fallen again and couldn't amble down to the dining room as usual. Sharon half-listened to him. As an administrative aide to the director, she had become immune to most of the complaints from the residents, from the staff, and even from the management. She had been working at Peaceful Havens for over twenty years and had seen so many changes of the guard that nothing rattled her. At this point, she reasoned, she could basically run the place single-handedly. There was always going to be the high maintenance director who breezed in with an air of fake authority. Usually, by the time their mistakes became glaring enough to cause a real problem, they were out the door and a new director was coming in as a replacement. This revolving door also applied to many of the staff as well as the nurses. The nurses, who dealt directly with the residents, were frequently burned out and disgruntled. And everyone took their frustrations out on Sharon.

She finally managed to get a few words in edgewise to the latest whiner to calm him down. She promised to have Richard the director call him immediately when he returned. She sighed, knowing that he would sneer at the suggestion that he do his job. That was what Sharon was there for, of course.

Little did Richard know that this whiner was the least of his problems. Now, he was facing a possible nursing strike. Sharon had heard the faint grumblings from the nurses for days. They were not happy with the fact that their medical benefits were going to be cut according to the latest union contract. Some of the seniority rules would also change, making the senior nurses less likely to get the vacations and personal days they were currently entitled to.

In the last day, tensions had escalated. Sharon overheard the union president arguing with several of the senior nurses that morning after breakfast. Although they were whispering, Sharon could make out some of the conversation, and it wasn't good for Peaceful Havens. The nurses were threatening to go on strike tonight at midnight if their demands were not met.

Sharon remembered this happening before, more than once actually. Last time, the strike lasted four days, and it caused bedlam at Peaceful Havens. With limited nurses, the residents suffered and complained loudly. Usually that did not raise any flags, but when they complained to their kids and family, suddenly shit hit the fan and the media was called. In less than twenty-four hours, news cameras had filled the lobby and reporters were standing outside Peaceful Havens with microphones. The mayor called press conferences, and even the governor showed up. A hasty agreement was reached before any resident succumbed as a result of negligence.

Sharon knew this was likely to happen again tonight. She did not relish the thought of coming to work tomorrow and having to push her way through a crowd of cameras and reporters eagerly looking for a story. Not to mention that she would have to look presentable if she was going to be on the evening news. That meant she needed to put on makeup and a nice dress or suit into which she could still fit. Her mood worsened as she realized that, because of the extra fifteen pounds she'd recently gained, most of her nice clothes were out of the question. Sharon had gotten into the habit of wearing jeans and sometimes sweats to work, especially if she knew she would be the only one in the office, which she usually was. Now, things were about to change. Sharon resolved to be strong tomorrow before she faced what was certainly going to be chaos. She would need a good night's sleep and would make sure she had a hearty breakfast to fortify her before she came in.

Of course, she thought ruefully, *food is always foremost in my mind*!

Sixteen

The moon skittered behind wispy clouds and a soft breeze blew through the partially open window next to me. Ben pulled his old Buick into the space reserved for taxis behind the Amtrak station. I felt strangely calm even though I had just managed to pull off the escape I had been fantasizing about for months.

"Whew," I sighed as Ben turned off the ignition. We turned towards each other, and I could see the excitement in his face lit by the streetlight above us. "Can you believe we did it? I almost feel let down because I had anticipated a lot of drama, and in the end, I just walked out of the secret back door and there you were, waiting for me!" I felt a little breathless as I stopped for a minute, my mind swirling with emotions.

"Yes, Angie, you have no idea how happy I was to see you come out that door!" Ben smiled nervously, but I could also see the relief in his eyes. "I guess I kept thinking that this would be the one night that John would have locked the back door..." His voice trailed off in thought.

"Well, Ben, I guess a lot of things could have happened. I can't believe I wasn't detected at all as I walked toward the kitchen. Usually, I see a nurse or someone walking around. It was surreal, like a dream. I really didn't even dare to think that it could work out this easily, but it did!"

"It is strange how Peaceful Havens seemed kind of deserted tonight,"

Ben said slowly. "But I like to think it is divine intervention!" He chuckled. I knew we were still on high alert. "Now, let's get you on the train, so to speak."

Ben opened his car door and came around to my side to open my door. I was relieved I no longer needed a walker or cane. I felt steady and strong if I resisted the impulse to move too quickly. Ben opened the trunk and took out my suitcase. It was the same one Gina had used to bring my clothes to Peaceful Havens a year ago. I had forgotten it was in the back of my closet, and it turned out to be the perfect size. It was a red carry-on and easy to maneuver with wheels that spun around to make it a breeze to pull behind me.

I had packed everything a couple of days ago, making sure my stash of cash was safely hidden in the zippered compartment in the back. All the clothes I wanted to bring managed to fit after I rolled them up lengthwise. I had seen this trick on a QVC television ad for luggage. It was supposed to eliminate wrinkles and provide a lot more space in a packed suitcase. I thought I remembered the saleswoman saying that pilots and stewardesses used that method successfully. In any event, it worked for me, and I found, after some dry runs around my apartment, that it was light enough for me to manage. I knew I would have a few transfers between trains (Ben had carefully reviewed my itinerary several times), but I didn't anticipate any problems if I took my time and walked slowly.

Ben stopped in front of the station and turned towards me. His face became serious as he looked down at me, and then he took both of my hands in his. "Angie, I want to say goodbye before we go to the platform." He looked down, and I could see sadness and loneliness in his eyes. "I have tried to plan every stop along this journey so that you will have total ease in travelling, and hopefully you will be as comfortable as you can possibly be. I managed to get you on Acela trains, which is like first class, whenever possible, and on each leg of your trip, you will have a conductor watching over you, like a guardian angel, so to speak." Ben finished up slowly and took a deep breath, but if he had anything else to say, I didn't give him a chance.

"Ben, *you* have been my guardian angel," I burst out in my typical fashion. "You brought me back to life, and that is not even an exaggeration." I swallowed hard. *How am I going to live without Ben—his smile, his laugh, and his support which was my lifeline?* "I could *never* have done any of this myself.... I know there have been countless hours of planning for you to pull this off. I won't ever forget your kindness, generosity, and friendship...." I began to tear up and had to stop.

Ben wrapped his arms around me, and I could feel his scratchy parka against my chin. It was strangely comforting. I felt his heart beating fast. Mine was too.

"Angie, thank you for your sweet words, but we did this together. I know you must catch this train, but please call me every morning and at night to let me know you're safe, okay? We will be in touch every step of the way. And who knows? Once you are settled in, I can hop a train and visit you!" Ben grinned, and his face lit up at the prospect of a cross-country train ride.

We hugged tightly; I couldn't, wouldn't let him go. I kissed him gently on his cheek. I wiped my eyes, and we both headed to the escalator to track one to New York City. My adventure had begun.

Seventeen

B rian was not used to working the late shift. In the railroads, it was referred to as the "third trick." Amtrak always had staff shortages when it came to conductors (it was not unusual for someone to pull a bender and beg off due to a wicked hangover), and since he had over thirty-five years of experience on the railroad, Brian was used to filling in at the last minute. He liked his job and felt comfortable with the quirky characters he would meet traveling the northeast corridor to New York City and through to Chicago.

Quirky was a kind name for some of these oddballs, he thought.

Last week, he brought a couple of Guinness's to Mayor Giuliani, who was camped out on the club car on the sleeper to DC. What's more, Brian had developed a great camaraderie with the other guys (and gals) on his various shifts. Like pilots and flight attendants on airlines, they spent most of their productive hours together and became a big family. And, like most families, they had their share of dysfunctional eccentrics, most of which were good buddies of Brian's.

Tall and built like a teddy bear, Brian always attracted his fair share of ladies. The admiration was mutual. He still had a full head of dark hair, and his five o'clock shadow imparted a rugged careless attitude that charmed mostly everyone. His handsome face usually sported a lopsided grin, and he was quick to compliment customers even in tense situations. Brian knew his sense of humor was his best asset, but his looks didn't hurt either. Through the years, Brian had had his fair share of lady friends, sometimes overlapping with each other, which was the reason his marriages (two) didn't last very long.

As the ten thirty Acela was boarding track one, Brian looked down at the platform and saw his good friend Ben walking slowly with a spry, redheaded lady next to him. She was wheeling a red overnight bag, and her face was flushed with excitement. Brian stared at her and realized he had met her before but couldn't remember where. Ben had told him that his friend Angie was on a cross-country train trip and would need his assistance on the first leg of her adventure to Chicago. She was already booked in a deluxe sleeper thanks to the insistence of Ben and Brian's ability to finagle reservations. Ben also told Brian that the trip was to be a secret.

Ben and Brian went back a long way, so long in fact that Brian couldn't really remember when he'd met Ben. It seemed to Brian that he'd always known Ben. Ben was a dispatcher when he took Brian under his wing, and they bonded immediately. They shared a crude and wacky sense of humor; both loved the Three Stooges and the Marx Brothers. Through the years, they consoled each other as they navigated the difficulties of their failed love lives, divorces, and alimony problems. It was a deep friendship that managed to continue even after Ben retired. A couple of weeks ago, Ben called Brian to ask for help with Angie's escape plans. Brian was more than happy to step in and keep watch over Angie as a favor to Ben. He loved tasks like this; they always provided a much-needed distraction.

Ben smiled as Brian approached them. "Hi there, Brian. Good to see you!"

Ben reached out to slap Brian on the back of his arm as a sort of man hug. Brian, not to be outdone, took Ben in his arms and gave him a full bear hug, squeezing him extra hard as a sign of his affection.

"Hey, you strong dude, have you been working out?" Brian laughed as he looked into Ben's eyes. "Seems like you've developed some muscle. Is there a lady in your life I don't know about?"

"Yes, here she is!" Ben chuckled as Angie stepped forward with a bemused expression on her face. "Brian, this is Angie."

Angie smiled shyly, then took a closer look at Brian. "Hi, Brian do you remember me?" Angie's smile now turned into a devilish grin.

"Yes, Angie, I do remember you! It wasn't that long ago, right?" Brian quickly tried to recover while his mind spun feverishly, trying to recall where the hell he knew her from; he didn't think he was fooling her.

"Well, Brian, I would say it was quite a long time ago, even though I admit when you get to be my age, time flies." Angie chuckled.

Suddenly Brian's face lit up. "Now I remember, yes! It was at Bill's house when Ben had his seventy-fifth! And I must say, Angie, you look even younger now! Although, I wish I could say the same for Ben." Brian slyly winked at Ben as he took Angie's bag. "Those were really great times, right?" Brian smiled warmly at Angie. "But let's get you to your seat, Angie. We will have plenty of time to reminisce on the way to New York."

Angie turned towards Ben and impulsively hugged him tight.

"Angie, I know you are in good hands, and we will talk soon. Please enjoy this ride, and I will be thinking of you every step of the way—so to speak." Ben released her as he looked into her eyes. "I am so happy for you!"

Angie's eyes filled as she took Ben's hands in hers. "Ben, I love you. Take care. You will hear from me every day, probably more than you want!" She gave him a peck on his cheek and turned to go as Brian hastily led them to the waiting Acela. Ben waved and turned to walk back to the taxi stand where his car was parked.

Angie and Brian chatted happily as they got to the door of the business class car on the Acela. Brian saw Angie turn and look back at Ben walking away. He saw the same look in her face that his five-year-old daughter, Carly, had when he dropped her off at kindergarten for her first day of school.

"Everything okay Angie?" Brian looked at her with alarm as he pushed her suitcase through the door.

Angie took a deep breath and smiled. "Yes, Brian, I'm okay, just a little nervous about this big adventure I'm embarking on. I have to say, I've never done anything like this before, and I'm so appreciative of your help and understanding!" She followed Brian to her sleeper car as the doors of the Acela shut tight.

"Don't worry, Angie. Ben told me, and I will always keep you right under my wing. Think of me as your personal assistant, okay? And as your confidant if you feel a bit overwhelmed about the trip. Let's take it one leg at a time. If I don't tell you later, I think you are an incredibly brave woman to follow your heart this way. Knowing Gina, and I do know Gina, I believe she will feel the same way once she has a chance to process everything. Stay strong!" Brian reached the door of Angie's sleeper car and looked warmly into her eyes. "Remember, I am here for you!" With that, he opened the door. Angie took a step inside her new home for the next few days.

Eighteen

Nicky finished tucking in the sheets of the bed in the spare room. As he topped the bed with a down quilt, he stopped to look out the large bay window adjacent to the queen-size bed. From the spare room, he could see the colors of the mountains shifting as they always did at this time of the day. The palette of blues and grays began to deepen into purple and lavender. At the same time, the cliffs turned bright shades of orange as the sun flaunted its final flash of brilliance before slipping behind the smallest peak. Nicky never tired of watching the sun set over the San Bernardino Mountains. Although he was born on the east coast, steps from Boston's Carson Beach, the sight of those mountains brought a sense of peace no ocean could compete with. Almost every window in his contemporary ranch had a view. Lately, he had taken to daydreaming more often as he looked out over the valley below. He knew that soon he would have a companion to share the views with.

What will that be like? he wondered.

Nicky's independence returned after Vivian died. He certainly had no problem taking care of himself. Despite his arthritic knees, he could still function as he did twenty years ago, albeit at a somewhat slower pace. He was proud of himself. Lately, though, some of his habits had developed into what Nicky realized was scary senior behavior. Nicky admitted to himself that he was troubled by a tendency to be super strict about cleanliness and orderliness, to the point of obsession. He was aware he had a bit of OCD. Nicky was not the type of bachelor who left empty beer cans and pizza boxes lying around the kitchen. Quite the contrary. He became annoyed with himself if he forgot to put the milk away after pouring his morning coffee. His trash cans were emptied daily, usually before they were even half-way filled. After he read his daily newspaper (which he did like clockwork every morning at seven thirty with his coffee), it was immediately discarded in the recycle bin in the garage. Even his refrigerator was spotless. His spices were arranged alphabetically in his pantry, which he cleaned out weekly. Lately, he had even begun to pay his utility bills way ahead of their due date just to get the paperwork off his desk. No one could accuse Nicky of leading the life of a slovenly bachelor.

His traits were partly the reason Nicky felt ambivalent about Angie's upcoming arrival. He knew his life was about to change. Knowing Angie was about to embark on her train journey brought an unwelcome surge of panic. He told himself it was normal to feel that way. However, the twinge of apprehension cast a shadow over the elation he originally felt at the thought of Angie's arrival. Nicky set about examining this recent shift in his mindset. He was determined to explore the reason and find a solution.

For years, the intellectual stimulation he had received from his university life was the fuel he had relied on to give him a sense of purpose. Now that he no longer was working, he missed the camaraderie and conversations. Not that he was a social animal. He disliked the false gaiety of parties among acquaintances with whom he shared no common ground. Small talk bored him, and after a couple of drinks, he became annoyed with all the empty chatter. Nicky disliked wasting time. Instead, his small circle of friends preferred quiet evenings together around a fire, sharing their mutual love of seventeenth century European literature. Such was the stuff that fed Nicky's soul. But Nicky admitted to himself that despite his introverted tendencies, he had become bored with the routine and craved some company, preferably female.

Angie had always made Nicky smile. Her warmth filled up a room as did her ready laugh. She had a quick sense of humor and was not afraid to speak her mind. Back in the days when Tony and Nicky were young men right out of the service, they were not used to meeting women like Angie. Her outspoken and intuitive viewpoints were refreshing. Nicky admitted to himself that he envied Tony when he and Angie became engaged. Ironically, Nicky had introduced them. Nicky would have kept Angie to himself except he was already sort of engaged to his first wife, Carol. Tony had chuckled when he told Nicky that it was hard work to get a ring on Angie's finger. He suspected there were others before him waiting in line. When Tony received a promotion and popped the question, Angie finally said yes. Tony had breathed a sigh of relief. So did Nicky, though secretly he felt a touch of regret that he had not kept Angie to himself. Nicky admitted to himself that although the fire may have ebbed over the years, he still carried a torch.

Nicky was realistic enough to recognize that Angie was no longer the young feisty woman he remembered, but he did believe there was still a spark between them. Nicky abruptly stopped himself. He had to remember that Angie was undergoing a dramatic change in her life. The last thing she needed was a romance thrown into the drama. Nicky had to stay focused on the present.

Take one day at a time, he sternly reminded himself.

Who knows? Maybe after a few weeks of living under the same roof, they would get under each other's skin. Nicky hoped not. He was basically an optimist but realized he must keep his expectations low. It was not easy to do....

Nicky glanced at his reflection in the bedroom mirror as he walked by and stopped. He surveyed himself critically and admitted he was pleased at what he saw. His dark hair, which had thinned considerably over the years, still retained its luster with just a touch of gray. Nicky's trim frame gave him the appearance of being taller than he was, although at six feet, he could be quite imposing. He was as much of a stickler about his body as he was with his orderly home. Every day he spent an hour lifting fifteen-pound weights and doing push-ups and some yoga poses he found on one of Vivian's old exercise videos she had bought from QVC. Nicky usually only ate two meals a day, skipping lunch and preferring a leisurely dinner after the sun had set. He was secretly proud that his pants from his working days at the university some twenty years ago still fit.

Nicky surveyed the guest room with a critical eye. Everything was clean and dusted. The room, unlike the living area and kitchen, had a rose-colored wool rug. It had just been shampooed and traces of cleaning fluid still lingered in the air. Nicky had contemplated pulling up the rug and exposing the hardwoods below like he'd done in the rest of the house, but the warm color and soft carpet underfoot always pleased him on a chilly morning. His own bedroom, the master down the hall with a door to a balcony, also had a soft plush carpet. He hoped Angie would agree with him about the carpet. No doubt Angie had her own ideas about how to decorate, but his house was neat and clean and sparsely furnished. He liked it that way. Clutter made him nervous. He shuddered as he remembered the fiasco with Vivian.

I'll have to keep Angie away from computers and Amazon Prime, he thought ruefully.

Angie's bedroom also had its own attached bathroom, and Nicky had changed the shower curtain and rugs to match the rug in the bed-room. The result was a rose-colored bathroom which complemented the Spanish tiles on the floor. Nicky sighed as he gave the room a last once-over. The only addition he made at the last minute was to add a crucifix over the bed.

The cross was a small gold one he had bought years ago at the Vatican. Nicky's strong Catholic faith did not include weekly visits to church, but he remembered that Angie went to Mass every week. Tony told him he did too, at first, but later he opted to stay home and take care of the kids when they were toddlers. At least, that's what he told Angie. The truth was, Tony preferred to sit and read the Sunday papers with his occasional martini. Church was the last thing on his mind on a Sunday morning. Nicky knew Angie was not fooled by Tony's offer to watch the kids, but Angie let it go, as she did a lot of the picky differences that pop up in a marriage. Nicky admired her for knowing she needed to choose her battles to keep the peace. Angie probably preferred going to Mass alone anyway. Who needs to drag a recalcitrant spouse along in the middle of a somber church service?

For the past few weeks, Angie and Nicky had been speaking off and on and making plans for what would happen when Angie's train trip was over. They spoke easily about Angie's plans and the train schedule, but that wasn't all. Through their phone conversations, they also revealed a lot more about themselves. Nicky was impressed to learn how Angie had managed to get her real estate license after her kids were grown and admired her for her success in such a competitive field. Angie learned, much to her surprise, that Nicky's novels were highly acclaimed in the literary world.

Through their recent conversations, Angie made it clear she was grateful for Nicky's heartfelt generosity, but she wasted no time telling Nicky that she had definite ideas regarding the duration of her stay. Nicky was surprised when Angie informed him that her visit would only be a temporary arrangement. During their very first phone conversation, Angie reassured Nicky that she would only stay as long as it took her to figure out where she would eventually land. She told him she was horrified at the thought of imposing on Nicky. Angie never imposed on anyone, even if they wanted her to.

Nicky was caught off guard. He managed to hide his dismay and instead suggested to Angie that they play it by ear. Nicky hated that expression—as a professor of languages, he did not understand how the expression became popular—but he had used it hastily, not wanting to admit that Angie's decision brought with it a small degree of relief. As much as he loved the idea of welcoming her into his house for a visit, he knew it might not be long before they were both secretly wishing the other would disappear. He did not want that to happen. His last mistake with Vivian had been a disaster he did not want to repeat.

Nicky walked back into his kitchen for a cup of coffee. Lately he had been using his Keurig for an extra shot of caffeine in the afternoon. It helped him stay focused in case he decided to write. His creative streak, which needed a boost several months ago, had suddenly surfaced with a vengeance. He happily navigated to his laptop as the sun was setting, coffee in hand. For years, he had used a Royal typewriter but retired it shortly after Vivian died. Although he loved his Royal, he had to admit he could express himself easier using the Word document on his computer. Nicky was delighted about his recent creative streak. He guessed it was probably fueled by the impending change about to occur in his life.

Nicky sighed and gulped down the remains of his coffee. He would later pour himself his nightly cocktail. He realized that his thoughtful reverie had resulted in a resolution of sorts. Despite his conflicted feelings about a future with Angie, the thought of her arrival filled him with a surge of optimism. This surge of optimism, he was surprised to discover, was something he really craved in his life. At the end of the day, Angie was the type of woman who would fit into his life quite easily right now. That thought filled him with hope.

Nineteen

I was floating down the Seine with Tony on a dinner boat after a night of cocktails. He turned towards me, and his blue eyes were smiling as he opened his mouth to speak. That was when I heard the faint notes of "Moon River" in the recesses of my brain. At first, I thought one of the residents at Peaceful Havens was blasting his TV again, but as my eyes opened, I realized I was not in my familiar bed; I was on a train speeding through the countryside.

"Moon River" was Tony's favorite song. When Ben was setting up my cell phone, he asked me to pick a ringtone.

"Not a boring one," he reminded me with a grin.

So, I blurted out, "'Moon River,'" because that song was my favorite too. Now, the song was my wakeup call.

But wait, I remembered with a start, *it also meant my phone was ringing!*

Quickly I reached for my purse on my nightstand and rummaged in the inside pocket. There it was. I nervously flipped up the top to answer it. I remembered Ben telling me that opening it was like picking up the receiver of my house phone.

"Hi, Angie!" I heard Ben's voice loudly in my ear. "Is that you? Are you okay?"

I sat up and surveyed the scene around me, fully awake.

"Hi, Ben, yes, I am here, and I guess I just woke up!"

The window shade next to me was open, and the sun was streaming through. It was hard to recognize any of the scenery since we were moving so fast. I felt the gentle rocking of the train as it navigated around curves. Was I really on a train heading for the mountains of California?

"Wow, I am so happy you answered!" Ben chuckled. "I have been wanting to catch up with you!"

"What time is it?" I looked around for my watch, then remembered I had slipped it into my purse right before I fell asleep to the rhythm of the rails late in the night.

"It's almost noon on Sunday. Do you know where you are?" Ben asked.

His voice was strong, and I almost felt he was right beside me in my reclining bed—or whatever I was sleeping on. I surveyed the scene around me for the first time in full daylight. The cabin that was my sleeper room was cozy but very small. Next to me was a small lamp which had a table attached to it that I used as a nightstand. My water bottle and purse barely fit on the top. I blinked in the sunlight. Outside my window to my left, I could see the landscape rushing by. I glimpsed a flash of blue and knew we were probably over a body of water, but I had no concept of time and remembered nothing after the small nightcap Brian had brought to me after dinner.

"Well, we must be well on our way to Chicago if it is noon. I thought I would hear the train pulling into the station in Manhattan, but I guess I was in dreamland by that time!" I looked around helplessly for a clue to my location. "I have a feeling I was sleeping so soundly that even Brian decided not to disturb me!"

Now that I was awake, I realized my stomach was grumbling and coffee was foremost on my mind, but I needed to talk to Ben. His voice was familiar and reassuring. I knew he could bridge the uncomfortable gap I was feeling between where I had been and where I was now.

"So, Ben, I am fine." I raised my voice and asked, "Maybe I don't really want to know, but tell me what has happened since last night?" My voice ended in a high-pitched squeak.

"Well, Angie," Ben began slowly, "you will be happy to know that your disappearance has not yet been discovered. Apparently, early this morning, the entire nursing staff decided to strike. As a result, all hell has broken loose, so to speak." Ben ended this announcement with a chortle, obviously happy to deliver the news. "There is virtually no nursing staff anywhere, and the directors and powers that be, whoever they are, are scrambling around trying to figure out what to do. In the meantime, I have a feeling the press just got wind of what is going on. In fact, a Channel 12 news truck just pulled up. Right now, some reporter is hooking up a microphone and slicking back his hair for the camera! I'm looking out the lobby window, Angie," he continued in a near-whisper. "There are a few residents milling around, but at least the Bullhorn is nowhere in sight."

I sat up in my chair and pushed it to an upright position. My mind was spinning with Ben's news. I had been bracing myself for a frantic phone call from Gina and dreaded hearing another report from Ben, but this was not at all the phone call I had expected.

Although I knew Gina did not have my new phone number, I knew that she would figure out that Ben was a conspirator in my escape. It would cause Ben to be dragged into a drama he certainly didn't need or deserve. I immediately felt relieved that, so far, I had not been discovered and Ben was off the hook! Who knew how long the strike would last? For now, at least, there was no immediate danger of anyone detecting my vanishing act. The delicious sense of wickedness I had enjoyed all through my escape so far increased tenfold. Deep down, I had felt very guilty for running away. God knows I had never done anything like that before, but here I was. I had done it. And what's more, it felt great. For the first time in my life, I had acted for me without any consideration of how my actions would impact the lives of my loved ones around me, and, boy, did it feel good! Emotions swirled around me as I stared at the landscape rushing by. There was a huge pause on the line, and I realized Ben was waiting for my delayed reaction.

"Oh my!" I managed to say, all the while trying to form my thoughts into a coherent sentence. "You mean that no one has even been in my room?" I pictured my bed, still made, with Gina's note hidden where I hoped she would find it.

"No, Angie, no nurses anywhere and no staff to speak of. The only people I've seen this morning are a couple of management guys who hastily beat it to their offices and now have the doors closed. Even Sharon is nowhere to be found. But I don't blame her for taking off." Ben said solemnly. "It's not her responsibility to handle a union dispute with management. Especially with all the press breathing down her neck!"

"So, Ben, where are you exactly?" I realized that Ben could be putting himself in danger if he was spotted whispering into a cell phone in the middle of this mayhem. "Is anyone within earshot?"

Ben chuckled softly. "No, I'm sitting across from the office watching this fiasco unfold. So far, there are only a handful of residents here. Most of them are probably sleeping or in their rooms with the TV volume turned on, but that should change shortly. Although there is kitchen staff here, I suspect that the wait staff is also shorthanded. I already went across the street to the Creamery this morning for a bagel and coffee, as I suspect the food situation at Peaceful Havens is about to be compromised as well. When this hits the news, then the shit will fly, so to speak!" Ben cleared his throat. "Excuse the expression, Angie," he apologized. "I'm going to make my way back to my room now," Ben continued. "I really don't want to be observed any more than I should. But I wanted to call and make sure you were okay. How do you like train travel so far?"

I laughed. "Well, Ben, I've spent most of it sleeping, but that is about to change. I think I'll find Brian and have some breakfast and find out where we are. I also need to visit the little girl's room and get cleaned up. But so far, the ride has been quiet and comfortable. I can't tell you enough how grateful I am to you for all your help. I am *so* relieved knowing I have a bit of a reprieve until Gina figures out that I'm missing. I'm determined to enjoy every minute of this ride, even after my secret is discovered." I thought quickly. "Is it okay to call you early tonight? By then we should have a better idea of my situation."

"Sure, Angie. Enjoy the ride and remember: This is a special journey you will always remember. I just wish I were there sitting by your side, watching the world go by!"

Twenty

Brian opened the cabin door just as I finished my bacon and eggs. I smiled up at him as I wiped my mouth with an Amtrak napkin, pushing my plate back at the same time. The food wasn't much better than the place I just left. I realized that I must have wolfed it down without even thinking. My mind was a million miles away.

"So, Angie, looks like you really hated your breakfast," Brian joked as he removed the empty dish before me.

"I guess I was starving," I admitted. "Amtrak must have the same chefs as Peaceful Havens," I quipped. I had even drained my glass of orange juice—and it had pulp! Tony used to joke with me because I hated orange juice with pulp and refused to buy it for him. The pulpy pieces always stuck to the glass, and I would have trouble getting the glasses clean. I smiled as I thought of how important that had seemed so long ago.

"More coffee?" Brian looked around my cabin to see if there was anything else he could do for me. I was amazed at his thoughtfulness.

"Of course, Brian. , I say you can never have enough coffee. You are so attentive. You would make someone a great wife," I joked, hoping he wouldn't take my remarks the wrong way.

I didn't have anything to worry about. Brian laughed and shook his head. "Not what my ex-wife would say if you asked her! Come to think of it, both ex-wives would totally disagree with you there." Brian put the empty plates on a cart outside my door and grabbed a carafe of hot coffee from the bottom of it. "But that's a story for another time, huh?" He winked at me as he refilled my cup. The scent of the steaming brew filled me with happiness. I looked up at him and managed to look shocked.

"Well, they must be crazy, and anytime you want to fill me in with details, I'm all ears. I'm not going anywhere, at least for a few days anyway!"

Brian left the carafe on my table, tipped his hat and was off, closing the cabin door behind him. I took another sip of my coffee, sat back in my seat, and watched the scenery unfold. I was still feeling giddy as the reality of my situation began to sink in.

Here I was, speeding away from the home I always had, about to embark on a new life thousands of miles away, and only two people (well, three including Brian) knew I was an escapee. Ben on his end had masterminded the details, and Nicky on his end eagerly awaited my arrival.

Well, maybe *he was awaiting my arrival eagerly,* I thought uneasily. *What if he was having second thoughts about having me stay with him?*

After all, I could be an unwelcome intrusion for him. Here was Nicky, well into his eighties as I was, living the dream by the foothills of the western mountains, when a voice from the past managed to impose on his privacy. Although it was true that I had not detected any bit of hesitation in his voice during our many phone conversations, I couldn't help but feel guilty that my presence was going to interfere in his life and not in a favorable way.

I sighed as my eyes tried to focus on the blur of highway running beside the tracks, but my mind began to wander again. It was too soon to start ruminating about what would happen once Gina and the nurses discovered my disappearance, so I hastily shoved that thought aside.

What would Tony think about all this? I mused.

At the thought of Tony, my mind drifted back to our last day together.

We didn't know it would be our last day when we rose from our bed, me first as usual, to pad downstairs, put the coffee on, and retrieve the newspaper from the front step. After I had coffee made, I showered, changed, and thought about breakfast. Tony came down shortly after I did and was reading the paper as I made poached eggs and toast. Tony was not really allowed to eat bacon or sausages since his heart surgery (and heart attack before that), so it was eggs and toast for the most part. Tony loved my meals and was always so grateful for the fact that he could step into the kitchen, night or day, and it was constantly filled with the loveliest aromas of cooking.

As Tony read the obituaries, he remarked that it was the one-year anniversary of the death of our neighbor Lorraine Vallente. She and her husband, John, were friends we socialized with occasionally. Lorraine had lost her battle with cancer the previous year.

I remembered thinking, *Has it already been a year?*

Then Tony announced he was going to the library because a couple of his books were overdue. Tony was a frequent visitor to the library, often returning home with several books in his arms.

After breakfast, Tony went upstairs to shave and shower. I finished cleaning up and began to think about dinner. This was my life. One meal was barely done, and I was on to the next even though it was hours away. Tony used to joke about how he lived to eat, and I guessed I was the same way, but lately, Tony had been having trouble with eating and enjoying his food the way he used to. We had been through years of heart problems, starting way back with his heart attack at age forty-six.

On that sunny afternoon in August of 1967, Tony had finished his Sunday dinner (meatballs and lasagna, as I recall) and decided to mow the lawn. It was hot, but neither of us cared. We planned to take a dip in the pool in the late afternoon. All our plans came to a screeching halt, however, when Tony fell to the ground halfway through the lawn mowing. I saw him fall and I screamed. My neighbor Connie heard me and called the ambulance. The rest of the day was a blur. Tony made it to the hospital, and I followed Connie and the kids. The doctors all told us Tony was lucky to be alive. After the initial shock, I couldn't allow myself to wallow in self-pity or even think about what had happened. I immediately acted. Suddenly, my meals were egg- and cholesterol-free. I learned to substitute other less appetizing options for the fat and butter we all loved. Tony spent two months convalescing in the upstairs bedroom, and I became his nursemaid. It was a hard and scary time for me, but we never really talked about how it had impacted *my* life. For the first time, I looked back at this time candidly. As the scenery outside my window flew by, I finally admitted to myself that I had been filled with fear and anxiety. I was petrified. Yet I could not let anyone see my emotions. The Angie everyone knew would never lose her self-control.

My father died when I was nine, and I barely remembered him. My mother was the quintessential Italian martyr who donned black from the day he died until the day she died. There was not much laughter in our house after my father was gone. What there was, however, work to do, and as the oldest daughter, I was expected to take charge of not only my cooking and laundry and cleaning but also my younger siblings.

Laundry, I smiled ruefully, remembering that I only owned two blouses and one pair of Sunday shoes, two skirts, and one dress. The dress was a hand-me-down from one of my older cousins. All our clothes were handmade anyway, and I learned to sew in order to survive. My childhood was certainly not carefree, but I didn't allow myself to think about it or compare myself with others. I saw lots of poverty growing up on K Street in South Boston. Reflecting on it, I understood how it was so easy to fall into the role of caregiver. It fit me well into my adulthood, through my marriage and motherhood. How could I have known that there were other options?

When my youngest sister finally married in her forties, I observed her playing the same selfless role with her widower husband and his six children. She went from being a single carefree career woman to a married mom of six young children overnight. I'm sure it was difficult for her, and she might have regretted her decision many times over, but she never talked about it and neither did I. I knew that in her eyes, taking on such a burden later in life despite the hardships was preferable to being called a spinster. We were brought up that way. We were both a product of growing up fatherless and poor in Southie.

When Tony's heart attack blindsided us, the focus was on him, not me. Tony certainly didn't mind being waited on hand and foot. He enjoyed all the attention. I would bring him books from the library, and he had visitors who would climb the stairs to our bedroom to see him perched in the easy chair next to our bed where he spent most of the time. Meals were delivered to him upstairs on a tray because he could not yet venture down the stairs. I ran myself ragged, cleaning the bedroom for visitors and preparing special meals, all the while continuing my daily routine of shopping, cleaning, and taking care of the kids. After about a week of this, the kids went back to their normal routines. No one noticed that my life had turned upside down.

Tony recovered from the heart attack eventually, but his doctor advised him against any stress that could precipitate another one. At that point, it wasn't difficult for Tony to decide to retire. As best as I can recall, he never even asked my opinion. On the day of his final visit to his cardiologist, he quietly announced at dinner that he was submitting his disability application from the federal government.

"It will be easy to get approved," he declared confidently. His doctor had already completed the necessary paperwork.

Tony's news filled me with both relief and dread. *What would our life be like now?* I hid my feelings and nodded numbly. We resumed our supper of turkey burgers. We were no longer allowed to eat red meat.

So, Tony retired and never looked back. For him, life was just beginning. He didn't seem aware that I was not exactly thrilled about the change in my life. How would he know? I could have told him. I could have sat him down and held his hands, looked him in the eyes, and confessed that I was feeling lost, overwhelmed, and afraid. Did I do any of that? Of course, I did not. Not me. I was a married woman with three children and no job. It was 1967. It didn't even occur to me that I had any options. I took what life dealt me and made the best of it. Now I was beginning to recognize the toll it took on me—on us both.

Not that Tony was difficult to have around. He puttered around the basement and put up some knotty pine paneling. He found an old desk somewhere and set up a little studio for his video camera equipment. Since he had the time, Tony used his video camera to film all family events. The sight of him walking around during holidays and birthday parties became a familiar one to everyone who knew him. He discovered that he loved to edit the tapes and add music to them. Tony was not interested in classroom learning. He preferred to read about how to use his camera through magazines and books. Mostly he was self-taught, spending hours in front of his little boxy monitor that we bought on sale at Murrays. Soon, the basement was filled with gadgets of every kind. Tony amassed a large library of music cassettes to use as background on his videos. He managed to contact a local senior paper and volunteered to run a weekly newsletter column on video cameras and editing. His word processor, next to his monitor, hummed all morning as Tony wrote his column and answered questions. He was just beginning to learn email and became an expert on that subject as well. In addition to all those activities, Tony began writing his memoir. It was something he had talked about for years. I recalled that he began writing it shortly after we married. In those days, he scribbled his thoughts longhand on large yellow pads of paper. Once he retired, he had the time to spend hours writing about his past as he pounded out chapters every day on the word processor. I remembered Tony asking me frequently to read over his writing, but, as I lamented sadly, I never had the time.

As scenes of Ohio farmland whipped by my window, my mind wandered to places it hadn't been in years. I reflected on the changes in our marriage that resulted from Tony's retirement. Up until now, I had avoided any such thoughts. Instantly, I was flooded with intense feelings of sadness and regret, mostly for time wasted. Tony and I could have shared our feelings about the changes we were going through. Tony, unlike me, would talk about his feelings if he was prompted, especially over a martini. This milestone in our marriage should have been a shared experience. Tony's retirement could have been a learning experience, one where we could explore, honestly, my fears and emotions that his sudden change had brought. Instead, I shoved my thoughts under the rug and bravely continued playing the role of dutiful housewife. If Tony were beside me, he would probably be shocked to learn the true nature of my feelings back then.

I had not been brave at all. Up until then, I had been proud of the strength I'd shown in the face of hardship. I realized sadly that I had lacked courage to face my dilemma head-on like I should have. I failed the real test of my strength when it was needed the most.

Woulda, shoulda, coulda, I thought sheepishly as I settled back into the velvet cushion of my cabin seat.

Keeping the peace was more important back then. I remembered an expression Tony used frequently was "Don't rock the boat." We were alike in that way. Neither of us felt comfortable changing anything. Tony liked his role as breadwinner and king of the household. He excelled at making a good living. I fit easily into my role as caregiver and housewife in our early days. I had control over the day-to-day activities of the household, and I managed our three small children. It was rewarding for me to see them leave the house every day in the clothes I had sewn for them, clutching their lunch bags with homemade sandwiches and cookies. The house ran like a well-oiled machine. Dinners, breakfasts, and lunches were all on time. The house was spick-and-span when neighbors or relatives stopped in for a bite. There was the aroma of freshly baked goodies all the time. The refrigerator was stocked with healthy food and plenty of leftovers. I prided myself on having crisp clean curtains hanging over windows that glistened in the sunlight. To the extreme annoyance of my family, the rugs were vacuumed daily, and the kitchen and bathroom floors were mopped as well. I remembered my friends commenting on how people could eat off my floors. I responded to positive reinforcement and loved the home sweet home backdrop of my life. I loved it all—that is, until the kids were not home anymore.

As the nest emptied, all that was left was Tony and me. I realized as time went on that all the chores I loved had become drudgery. What changed in me? I no longer felt needed. Looking back, there were many times I felt as if no one would have cared if I was there or not. I had served my purpose.

I shifted uncomfortably in my seat as I remembered that time. Mario finally bought his own house and moved out, Stacy got an apartment in Boston after graduating, and Gina was already married, being the first to move out at the age of twenty-one. Tony and I were alone. We began to eat out more and travel a bit. Suddenly, the big Sunday dinners were not a weekly thing anymore. Mario came home on Sundays so I could do his laundry. Gina would come on Sundays, too, most of the time, but Stacy was absent except for holidays. I began to get restless and decided to take courses to get my real estate license. I pictured myself driving clients around in our Plymouth Fury (Tony bought it without my knowing. It lacked air conditioning.). My new career decision did not sit well with my family however. All the kids balked at the thought of having to pitch in more during holiday dinners and family birthday parties. Tony was okay with it until he realized that there were no more homemade goodies for his nightly snacks. Surprisingly, it was a good decision for me despite the opposition of my family. I loved being a salesperson. Finding properties for people, negotiating contracts, and managing the financial side of everything felt comfortable to me. I was used to running the show, so running a new show quickly restored the self-confidence that had faded as I became an empty nester. I remembered happily thanking God at church on Sundays that he had allowed me to find my groove at last.

Memories of that time seeped slowly into my consciousness. Tony was left alone a lot more. I didn't take much notice of his activities. Tony could be very self-sufficient if there was food in the fridge. He happily spent his time at the library writing his video column and experimenting with his video camera. He had fun sending and receiving emails when he could get online through our AOL connection. When I was out of the house and not tying up the phone line, it was easy for him to connect to the World Wide Web. So, I wasn't really concerned that he would miss me. As it turned out, that was the last thing I had to worry about.

It was about that time that Tony finished his memoir. He was proud that it was finally completed to his satisfaction. I remembered he did spend a few weeks editing it, but when that was done, he managed to print the whole thing out by taking it to the copy store. I had just gotten home from a real estate seminar one afternoon when he proudly walked in the door with a large bundle under his arm.

"Here it is," he announced with a flourish as he plopped the manuscript on the kitchen table. "Read it and weep!" He grinned at me like a little kid.

I admit I was not really paying much attention. It was close to dinnertime. I still had on my work clothes and needed to change before I figured out what to cook for supper. I was distracted by my textbook and barely looked up.

Why wasn't I more supportive? I could have given him the slightest sign that I was even paying attention, but I didn't. He stood silently for a few minutes watching me, then took off his jacket and hung it in the closet. After another sidelong look back at me, he quietly picked up his book and retreated to the basement.

Tony needed uninterrupted time with his thoughts to form ideas. Too much chatter and noise around him did not give him the opportunity to speak quickly. For that reason, he usually sat back and observed. That was why he was so comfortable playing the role of a videographer. He didn't have to speak. He just walked around and let everyone else do the talking.

Tony was never the kind of guy to call attention to himself. Unlike me, he loved quiet times and solitude. His voice was low, his conversation was subdued. He managed to get his point across with very few words, but his words were thoughtful and full of meaning. I recall the many birthday and anniversary cards he gave me. They never had lots of flowery verses or meaningless monologues. One line would usually suffice, but the sentiment was more powerful than any fancy card embellished with hearts and flowers. He did not express his thoughts easily. I knew he was uncomfortable when I blurted out whatever was on my mind. That was not his style.

There were only two times when Tony became talkative: when he had a martini in his hand or through his writing. Sometimes both activities came at the same time. Alcohol loosened him, resulting in a very chatty Tony. His writing revealed a guy who was quite entertaining and witty. When I finally read Tony's writing, I was amazed.

Was this the same guy I was married to?

Tony on paper was almost an extrovert. His clever observations of the people around him were frank and right on the mark. Sometimes they even bordered on offensive. Tony's style was ingenious. His sharp humor softened anything that could be perceived as a character assault. Tony's writing was delightful, full of humorous anecdotes and interesting observations.

One day after Tony had been gone for about a year, I was cleaning out some of the books and videos in the basement. I put them carefully in boxes, where they still were today. Gina had them in storage somewhere, I realized guiltily. I didn't know where they were even though I remembered she had told me. At the time, I didn't care. Truthfully, I didn't let myself even think about all the memorabilia in front of me. It hurt too much to pick up photos of us together, our trips and smiling faces from a time when everything was carefree, times when I didn't have to think too much. I was on automatic pilot, as I was for most of my life.

What a boring wife I must have been.

Maybe that was why Tony had secret thoughts that he harbored through most of our marriage.

That day, I picked up Tony's memoir. I leafed through the early parts of his life. I was intrigued at his descriptions of lusty feelings during puberty. I eagerly read through his first few chapters. As I continued through his teens into early army days, I was stunned by his confessions.

It was as if I was observing a car accident about to happen in front of me. I could not take my eyes off the pages.

Dazed and shaken, I pulled up a chair to finally read his memoir. Slowly, I became reacquainted with the man who I had married.

Twenty-One

Tony hung up the phone in his office and slumped back in his chair. For the third time that week, someone called him for a favor. It was always the same: a friend of a friend (of a friend) knew he oversaw personnel for the government and needed his help. Could he possibly help a cousin, daughter, or nephew who needed a job? The person was always down on his luck (why was it always "he"?) but promised he would work *very* hard to prove himself to be the best candidate for the position. Such a position always required a high score on a civil service exam, but this "friend" wanted him to bypass this step. Why not? Weren't friends supposed to help each other? He knew a guy. It never changed. Tony could predict the sob story; he had heard them all. And it was only Tuesday.

Tony sighed and gazed out the large window in his office that overlooked the state house. The dome was resplendent in the afternoon light. Usually, the sight of the city spread before him raised his spirits, but his mood had sunk to an all-time low.

For a guy who got off the boat at age two and couldn't speak a word of English, he was proud of how far he had come. No one in his office knew he was a first-generation Italian raised in the hood of Southie. People would never suspect he used to pay a nickel every Saturday night to use the bathhouse down by Carson's Beach for a weekly bath crammed in with dozens of other guys. And, he realized guiltily, no one suspected he had not gone to college. Not even for a day.

After his discharge from the army, Tony heard there were hiring opportunities at the federal government. He was able to score high points on the civil service exam because he had learned shorthand and typing in the army. It was rare for a guy to have those talents, so he was quickly hired as an entry-level clerk stenographer. Tony loved sitting at a keyboard, even if it meant typing out boring letters and repetitious memos. Once he grew familiar with office work, he had no trouble moving up the ladder. Despite his somewhat auspicious start, Tony never took his fortunes for granted. He was grateful that he had climbed the corporate ladder so quickly. From the very beginning of his career, his good looks, shy smile, and quick mind brought him instant popularity. His calm demeanor and command of the English language allowed him to talk himself in and out of almost any situation.

At first, Tony was flattered and amazed at the same time. Growing up in a third-floor, cold water flat with two parents who only spoke fractured English, he was not used to flattery. He was used to being ignored. He had easily excelled at schoolwork and graduated with honors in high school, but he knew there was no money in his family for college. So, when he began to earn serious money, his parents were thrilled. It pleased him to please them, and he happily turned over half his paycheck to them for household expenses. With the remainder of his salary, he opened a bank account. Every week, he was delighted to hand over his passbook to the teller at Industrial National Bank. He watched his balance grow to a staggering sum. As his salary increased, so did his responsibilities. Tony enjoyed a few years of euphoria at the beginning of his career, but the honeymoon dissipated after his third or fourth promotion.

He had gotten to secretly hate his job. No longer could he spend his time typing while his mind wandered across town to the beach. His day was spent mostly putting out fires and negotiating with disgruntled unions who resented upper management. He realized with a guilty start that he *was* upper management. Almost overnight, he had turned into a faceless bureaucrat in a three-piece suit.

Tony's dream was always to paint, draw, or write. On a whim, he bought some art supplies, and in his spare time, he began to sketch ocean scenes down at Carson's Beach. He was aware that artists lived a rather bohemian existence. If his parents even knew what his real ambition was, they would have frowned upon it. Or maybe they would have just laughed. No one would have taken him seriously.

No one except for the women on the beach that is....

He discovered quickly that a young attractive guy with dark curly hair and dimples when he smiled became a babe magnet sitting on the beach in swim trunks with an artist's easel. He didn't even have to make clever conversation because he could pretend to be engrossed in his artwork, which was considered a serious endeavor. It also helped that his paintings and drawings were very good—a bonus. Soon, curvy blondes and brunettes in skimpy bikinis frequented his blanket more and more often.

Tony was delighted that one of his loves led to another. Being soft-spoken and timid suddenly proved to be an advantage. Women apparently liked the silent type—especially the kind of women who were brazen enough to be comfortable approaching a strange man on the beach while wearing a swimsuit that revealed more than anything Tony had even seen while flipping through the "Foundation Garments" section in the Sears catalog. Besides the pinup posters hung in the barracks in his army days, Tony had little expertise on what a naked woman looked like. The sight of curvy, bouncing flesh was almost too good to be true. He managed to sneak extra peeks while pretending to search for a clean brush or different watercolor for whatever landscape he was working on. Most of his completed paintings looked similar, varied only by an occasional beach umbrella or seagull placed into the scene on a whim, but none of the babes on the beach were really focused on his artwork. They made no pretense: Their primary interest was Tony.

At first, Tony worried about his lack of expertise in the dating department, but it soon became obvious that inexperience was not a problem. He quickly learned that the women clamoring for his affection did not demand more than a few words of flattery and some hugging as the relationship progressed. They were not ladies who expected to be wined and dined at a fancy restaurant. Instead, all that was required of Tony was a physical demonstration of his feelings, and he was all too happy to oblige. It wasn't long before Tony had the names and phone numbers of several of the more willing women in his little black book. He had bought a used Ford with some of his savings, another big plus in his favor. Soon, he found himself spending more and more time by the beach on weekend nights without his easel. Instead, he was usually accompanied by any one of the friendly beach ladies who admired his lean and tanned torso, among other things.

It didn't take long for Tony to lose any inhibitions he might have had. His 1937 Ford Coupe was suddenly transformed into a very different kind of vehicle, mostly providing erotic pleasures that until then Tony had only dreamed about. He became familiar with lovers' lanes that had been beyond the scope of his imagination even a few weeks prior. After a few awkward moments in the front seat of his car mostly involving the gear shift, he and his companion opted to use the back seat, which proved to be most comfortable. It was springtime, and the nights were filled with an earthy fragrance that set the mood for romance. As the weather warmed, it helped to keep the windows opened. Driving home afterwards was a little challenging since he had to keep stopping to wipe down the windows that had fogged up considerably.

Tony was careful to wear protection and look out for cops, two potential complications that could put an end to his favorite pastime. From talking to other guys down at the bathhouse, he learned which places to avoid because of heavy police patrols. Guys talk, and Tony had a way of eliciting information without divulging much. He could be friendly and amusing but at the same time, he wasn't a braggart. Tony always chose his words carefully. His talents in that regard helped him secure important information regarding police presence. More importantly, Tony found out about Trojans.

Condoms, as Tony soon discovered, came in many varieties of colors and materials. The first time he shuffled into a drugstore to buy a package, he simply pointed to the box behind the counter. He was new to it. He also knew that his inexperience in that department would not be looked upon favorably by the druggist or anyone else shopping in the store, especially a woman. But he was lucky. On his first visit he managed to find a younger guy behind the counter who took Tony under his wing. After Tony pointed to the box of condoms, the guy waiting on him, whose name was Mike according to the tag on his blue shirt, gave him a quick rundown on what kinds to buy.

"You don't want the cheap rubber ones. They break, especially if you're kinda large." Mike glanced at Tony slyly. "You know what I'm getting at, right?"

Tony laughed. He was grateful for the knowledge, especially when Mike recommended the ribbed red ones because "the ladies love them." Of course, they were a little pricier.

But who cares? thought Tony.

The last thing he needed was to use a rubber that was cheap. He shuddered to think of the consequences of a broken one after a steamy night in his back seat. He eventually found a brand he liked, and it quickly became his favorite. Now all he had to do was swagger into the drugstore and knowingly point to the red condoms that came packaged in a discreet brown box.

He was relieved to solve that problem. His amorous nights continued, mostly during the weekends. Tony found it too difficult to extract himself from his bedsheets early enough for work after a weeknight of contortions in his back seat, as satisfactory as they proved to be. Sometimes the ladies put up a little fuss since it appeared most of them did not hold down regular jobs. Tony was not too familiar with the personal lives of the women. He suspected they mostly were waitresses or lived at home with their parents, perhaps pursuing some kind of degree to fill the time. After a while, his trysts had narrowed down to three women: Sally, Paula, and Donna.

Sally was his favorite. Happy and bouncy in both the figurative and literal sense, she was totally at ease with her body. Apparently, she was at ease with Tony's as well. Tony learned moves he knew could be very useful to him in the future. Paula was a demure brunette with a throaty voice and a laugh that turned him on. Her body was leaner than the others, but she was athletic, a fact that brought new variations to his back seat encounters. Donna was blonde and willowy with a sharp sense of humor and wit. Tony could relate easier to Donna intellectually but preferred the company of Sally. When it came to encounters of the libido, he realized he wanted little intellectual stimulation. The physical part was all he could handle.

Tony discovered a new-found freedom and sense of accomplishment as a result of his new relationships. He developed self-confidence, which up until then had eluded him. Despite his high-paying job, he frequently felt inferior, as if he had somehow cheated his way to the top. Most likely his feelings of inferiority stemmed from his poor upbringing and lack of social skills. His parents could not be expected to help in that department. They both were immigrants and were satisfied with their lives. Like many of the families surrounding them in their third floor flat, his parents' aspirations consisted mostly of having enough food on the table and a solid roof over their heads. Heat in the winter was a bonus; their flat had no central heating. The gas-on-gas stove in the middle of the linoleum floor in the living room was where they all huddled on winter nights. Up until he began his career, Tony gave all of it little thought. His world had consisted of kids like himself without any aspirations or motivation. It was generally expected that after high school you would find a job, usually one involving menial labor. Never did he remember his mother working. It was a full-time job cooking, cleaning, and keeping Tony, his father, and his sister in clean clothes. The truth was Tony's mother didn't even like cooking, accounting for the slim waistlines of everyone in his family. Often, supper was sandwiches or fried eggs and peppers. Tony secretly longed for his home to be full of tomato sauce and garlic with meatballs frying in the pan in the kitchen. Nevertheless, this was Tony's world growing up, and until recently, it had seemed it would be his lot in life. He hoped, however, that now, things were looking up and all kinds of new possibilities awaited him.

Then one day, Tony saw Angie walking down the street as he met his friend Nicky on the corner. Nicky and he were close friends, having met in the army. Somehow Nicky knew Angie. Tony didn't remember how or where they had met, but he got the impression they had never dated. Nicky was dating a blonde named Marjorie at the time. Tony remembered Angie was wearing a short red dress and a wide-brimmed white hat that day. She was dressed for work and had just left her job for the day. As she scurried down the street towards them, Tony was smitten by her smile and good looks. A broad white belt accentuated her curvy figure and tiny waist.

Nicky made introductions and that was that. Up until then, Tony had not seriously dated. He was still in the throes of his juggling act between Sally and Donna, who had recently been joined by Lori. He wasn't quite sure what had happened to Paula, but she had dropped out of sight. Lori was a sultry redhead with large breasts. She could be moody but was not averse to a quick booty call, which Tony appreciated. Tony had been playing musical chairs with these women for quite a while. It was a boost to his libido which had been sagging and badly in need of a lift up until then. He felt that all his women had played a huge role in his sexual awakening. He would always be grateful for the opportunity that somehow had landed in his lap, literally, while painting on the beach. Someday, he knew he would use that chapter in his memoir.

Quite frankly, though, Tony was getting tired of the games he had to play. Frequently, he found he was mixing the women up and had, several times, almost blurted out the wrong name in the heat of passion. The initial excitement of having a bevy of women had faded. Lately, living a triple life had become too much work. The minuses began to outnumber the pluses. Tony always kept a mental list in his head: one column with the cons of a situation and one column with the pros. His list proved to be a guideline for many decisions he made in his life. At this moment, the cons column for multi-dating had grown larger than the pros column.

That was one reason Tony was so attracted to Angie. She was easy to be with. She was not an easy woman to pin down however. At first, they only met for coffee or a walk down by the Charles River. Angie worked in the garment district as a secretary to one of the owners. Tony was impressed by her ambition, and Angie was impressed with Tony's high position in the government as well. He took it slowly with Angie because he knew she wanted it that way, and he discovered he did too. It was proving to be difficult to extract himself from the clutches of the women who had been taking up all his spare time.

Soon they were dating. At least Tony called it dating. They saw each other at least once a week for the obligatory Saturday night date. Tony picked Angie up at her home and chatted with her mother, who instantly loved him. Tony could remember some of the Italian dialect he grew up with, and it proved helpful. Angie's mother, Carmela, spoke only limited English, although she could understand more. Every night, she listened to the news on her tiny radio. Tony's parents, on the other hand, had no idea what was going on in their country or the world. Sometimes, they would receive an air mail letter from a cousin in Italy, and Tony had to respond while his mother told him what to write. Tony had not brought Angie over to meet his family. He was ashamed to admit he was embarrassed by their ignorance. Every day, he stepped out of their world to his working world, where sophistication and intelligence replaced illiteracy.

Tony would never admit his feelings to anyone, especially Angie. He would have moved out of their flat months ago, but he knew how hurt they would be. Angie, on the other hand, seemed unaware of her own mother's limitations. She joked with her brother and two sisters about Carmela's imperfect English. They all gently teased one another but in a friendly way. Tony could tell they had a close bond with each other stemming from a genuine respect. He was envious of Angie's relationship with her family since he knew he neither appreciated nor admired his parents' values and never would. He felt he could introduce her to his parents without judgement. Angie was easygoing and possessed a remarkable ability to find the good in everyone, even Tony.

Whenever Tony had allowed himself (admittedly not often) to picture his ideal wife, Angie came close. In fact, she was nearly perfect. Smart, sexy, and witty—and she could handle her siblings and all the responsibility at home while working full time. She was able to take everything in stride and maintained a cheerful attitude despite her meager upbringing. She never displayed any of the moodiness of his own mother, who was prone to days of silent brooding. Her depth of knowledge and intelligence surprised him. They were evenly matched. And Angie was gorgeous. What else could a guy like him want in a wife?

However, Angie was frequently unavailable on other nights besides Saturday. A few times, Tony asked to pick her up from work and take her for a walk or out to Castle Island for a hotdog and beer. His overtures were rejected with vague excuses. He was puzzled by it, mostly because he was used to women falling all over him. Angie often mentioned her boss, Frankie. Tony had never met Frankie, but Angie seemed to have a great deal of respect for him. They also had lunch occasionally, and Angie told Tony that Frankie had once walked her home, which was at least a two-mile walk. Tony brooded about it for a while. He was not sure why her boss would walk four miles out of his way with his secretary. He suspected there was another reason that Frankie walked her home, but he also knew the last thing that would bring him closer to Angie was to display a jealous streak. Instead, he played it cool and decided to prove to Angie that he was the real deal.

One Saturday night, Tony was lucky enough to find himself with Angie in his Coupe driving back from a picnic on Castle Island. It was getting dark enough for his headlights, and Angie was happily sitting next to him, her hand lightly resting on his knee. On a whim, Tony decided to take Angie to one of his old haunts down by the beach.

He nervously glanced at her and asked casually, "Feel like going for a ride?"

Angie looked surprised but nodded anyway. Tony felt strange bringing his Ford and Angie to the place occupied by the ghosts of the four women from his past. He guiltily worried that somehow one of them would be there to divulge his lascivious secrets.

He turned his car into the lane leading to the beach, not daring to look at Angie's face. He found a spot that used to be one of his favorites with a view of the water but not close to the other cars. He knew that cops did not frequent this spot—at least he hoped not. He turned off the ignition, and there was an intense silence in the car. No one said anything for a moment. Then Tony turned to Angie, who looked at him with an air of bewilderment.

"Seems like you're familiar with this place," she said softly.

Tony thought quickly. "I've come here a few times to paint during the day. The views are nice." He finished lamely.

Angie kept her hand on Tony's knee, and Tony held it firmly. He looked into her eyes and winked. Angie squeezed Tony's hand in response, and Tony knew as she smiled up at him that he had made the right choice.

Twenty-Two

I woke with a start, feeling my head beginning to slump below my head cushion. My mind was full of a dream that skittered away as I pulled myself to an upright position.

I have been dreaming a lot, I thought suddenly.

I was never a dreamer. During our marriage, it was Tony who awoke full of dreams. He delighted in giving me a full update in detail, usually while I was scrambling around the kitchen to make breakfast. I admit I was usually too distracted to pay attention to his ramblings, but secretly I wished I had dreams. Usually, Tony's dreams involved some kind of erotic escapade from his past. I would tease him about how he was attempting to reclaim his lost youth. Quite frankly, I had thought Tony's harem of willing women existed mostly in his imagination.

Was I fooling myself all along? Or did I choose to ignore the obvious truth about my husband?

My dreams now were full of characters from my past as well. My latest dream involved my old boss, Frank, or Frankie as I used to call him. In my dream, Frankie looked just as he always did when we were together: dressed in a three-piece Italian suit (usually designer) and close-shaved, smelling wonderful. Frankie towered over me as he walked me home after work. In my dream, we were holding hands as we approached my shabby third-floor flat. My brother Giuseppe (we called him Joey) was playing ball outside in the street with his pal Rico, their sweaty faces red under their baseball caps, dodging the occasional car that dared to interrupt their game. Suddenly, however, Frankie and I were transported in a dreamlike way to Frankie's house instead.

I had only been to Frankie's house once. It was no secret that Frankie was well-heeled. His parents were immigrants from Ireland but managed to land a job immediately after they arrived in the United States by joining their cousins in their small construction business, which quickly grew with the hard work they contributed. His whole family were skilled carpenters from the old country. His mother was not above getting her hands dirty as a house cleaner, washwoman, or whatever else put food on the table. Frankie told me how he grew up in a large tenement house filled with family members who saved every penny by eating potato soup and bread for every meal. Soon, his father began buying houses, and fixing them up. It was an American dream come to life. Frankie was able to go to college, and his father helped him buy the textile factory where we both worked. Although Frankie spoke about his past, he never bragged. The first and only time I visited his house, I tried not to look as impressed as I was.

It was a grand Italianate brownstone on Beacon Hill in Boston. At the time, I had never heard of Beacon Hill, and I doubted any of my friends had either. It was a far cry from Southie, I realized, as Frankie unlocked the double mahogany doors to the entrance. Even the stairway was impressive, with shiny iron railings adorning the stone and brick front stoop. Inside, the crystal chandelier was lit as if it was already dusk. He gave me the grand tour that left me speechless. I did remember carved cornices, gold painted ceilings, and wide pine floors, but my mouth dropped open when I saw the furnishings. Up until then, I had never even dreamed people lived like that. As Frankie led me into the last bedroom (there were four or maybe there were five), he pulled me towards him. My heart quickened as I felt his lips meet mine....

In the dream I had two days ago, we were walking on Carson's Beach, hand in hand. It was after work, and we were alone. The sun had begun to set, and the soft air was fragrant with beach roses. I thought it was early fall, which was our favorite time to walk the beach. Frankie had just bent down to pick up a seashell. I looked out into the distance to Castle Island and felt a surge of happiness. When I turned to Frankie, instead of a seashell in his hand, he held a large diamond ring. His face was full of anticipation and happiness. That was when I woke up.

All sorts of emotions were swirling inside of me. I hadn't thought of that moment in years. It belonged to the part of me that I kept hidden. I was beginning to realize there was a huge vault inside of me where stuff was hidden. As painful as it was to pull out the memories and emotions and examine them, I realized it was time. Taking the memories one at a time and caressing them, stroking them, feeling them once again was what I really needed. I felt alive for the first time in years.

Why and how could I have denied such delicious memories?

My reverie was interrupted by the click of the door handle of my sleeper quarters.

Brian popped his head in, tipped his hat, and grinned. "Well, sleepy-head, how are you? I didn't want to disturb you, but thought you might be getting hungry?"

I sat up straight and realized I needed a lipstick refresh. "Oops, sorry, Brian. Yeah, I guess I dozed off.... For how long?"

I just realized that we might be approaching Chicago already.

Chicago! How exciting, I thought childishly. I realized I had never even set foot in Chicago in my whole life.

"Good catch, Angie. We should be pulling in around four-fifty or five this afternoon." He glanced at his watch. "It's around two right now. How about lunch? I'll bring you a menu, okay?" He winked and was gone.

I took a deep breath, trying to process everything. In a way, I almost felt like I was still deep into the dream of a few minutes ago. I almost had to pinch myself to realize I really was on a train speeding into a mid-western state to a destination across the country. Up until the present,

I had led such a banal existence with the four walls of Peaceful Haven as my only backdrop. I craved the kind of adventure I was immersed in, but I never imagined it would happen. The old Angie was frightened and apprehensive. I pulled my rosary beads out of the worn bag next to me and began to silently pray. As it usually happened, I felt a peaceful calmness overtake me as my Hail Mary prayer formed a silent chant in my mind.

I wasn't preachy about my faith, but it had never failed me. I began to envision a new and improved Angie, the lady I had always wanted to be. She was taking shape before my eyes.

She does need a pep talk now and then, I admitted to myself. *I guess I am a real work in progress, as Tony used to say about his abilities to use his computer.* I suddenly felt a strong need to talk to him.

Tony had his faults, but one of his greatest assets was the way he showered praise on me—not that I needed it very often. Most of the tasks I took on around the house were of the domestic variety, and I certainly knew how to cook and clean, but when I began my real estate venture, he was more than complimentary about my ability to adjust to such a stressful occupation.

"Angie," he used to say with pride, "you could sell ice cubes to an Eskimo!"

I felt a warm glow of appreciation when he told me that I excelled at something, even if it was my homemade coffee cake or apple pie. I shifted in my seat with a pang of guilt, as I recalled that I rarely told him how happy he made me. Even when he left for work each morning, sometimes looking as if he were going to the gas chamber, I failed to smile and tell him he looked handsome in his pressed olive-green suit and yellow tie. He smelled great, too, but I couldn't even remember giving him a hug goodbye most mornings as I scurried around the house with the carpet sweeper. It was so important for me to comb the rugs because I disliked the look of footprints.

Could I have been that shallow?

I gulped as another memory popped into my mind. Tony had just come home on a Friday night. I usually picked him up from the train station, but that night I was busy, so he took the bus. What was I busy doing? The girls from the neighborhood (consisting of my three friends, Connie, Millie, and Lois) and I had spent a good part of the afternoon sitting at my kitchen table chitchatting while we shared coffee and a lemon meringue pie. They left around four thirty (no one wanted to be late when her husband arrived home for dinner), and I needed to clean up the kitchen. I vividly remembered I was washing the floor when Tony trudged through the back door, looking sad and disheveled. On my hands and knees, I looked up and ignored the disturbing expression on his face. I knew he was tired, and his day was probably filled with frustrating meetings and upsetting confrontations. From his appearance, it seemed as if that Friday was a particularly distressing one. Of course, he could have used a supportive spouse in the situation, one who could sit down with him, pour him a drink, and let him vent, but I was not that spouse. I realized with a guilty start that I had never been.

That Friday, I ignored Tony and concentrated instead on washing the floor until it shined. I even waxed it and told Tony in no uncertain terms was he to walk on the floor until I told him it was dry. Tony did not say a word. He stared at me for a minute, took in the whole situation, and left me to change his clothes in the bedroom. I remembered him shutting the bedroom door with a little more force than usual.

That night in the bedroom, Tony reached for me after he turned out the light. He smelled good, and his embrace was warm and comforting. I hugged him lightly but then I pushed him away. That morning, I had had my hair done, and I didn't want it to get messed up with any kind of amorous thrashing around—although, to be perfectly honest, I seemed to recall that we rarely thrashed at all. Our sexual dalliances, if you could call them that, consisted mostly of a quiet and reserved twenty minutes in the missionary position. I rarely moved from my spot on my back. You could say I was less than a willing participant in our monthly sexual liaisons and usually grudgingly acquiesced only after Tony plied me with a couple of glasses of rosé wine. There wasn't much kissing going on and even less passion. Looking back, I can't imagine that our sex life could have been anything Tony looked forward to. In fact, he must have felt insulted because I regularly dismissed his advances. His manhood was regularly stomped on because I thwarted any romantic attempts he made to get me into bed.

For my birthday and Christmas, Tony would buy me sexy lingerie and Chanel No. 5. The lingerie remained in my drawer with the tags on it, and that was where Gina found it after Tony died. Gina stared at it in disbelief, but I thought she was even more surprised at my lack of emotion, discovering, not for the first time, a startling but revealing piece of evidence about her parents' lack of intimacy. What other clues did Gina have that her parents had grown apart? Thinking back, I cringed at the fact that there were many. I was cringing because, in my selfishness, I had become blind to the fact that I was responsible for the lack of intimacy in our marriage.

Tony had his first heart attack two weeks after that Friday night when I rebuffed his advances for about the hundredth time, but nothing changed. I even used his weak heart as an excuse for abstaining from sex even more than before. After a while, Tony stopped reaching for me. He didn't hold my hand anymore when we walked into a store or restaurant. Even his compliments dwindled down to nothing. He stopped buying me sexy things, and instead his gifts consisted of gloves, handbags, and an occasional vacuum cleaner.

I tried to think back to the woman I was then. Even though I felt Tony slowly moving away from me, I was too absorbed in my house-wifely mode to care. My life revolved around fulfilling the role of the matriarch of the house. The truth was that my horny days mostly ended after I'd given birth to Mario. My total focus after the kids were born shifted from wife to mother. The repercussions of my actions, or lack thereof, never dawned on me. Tony, in his quiet thoughtful way, never once acted like it was my "wifely duty" to accommodate his needs.

Good thing, because I would have put him in his place, I thought wryly.

Tony didn't think of conjugal relations as a duty. His sex drive was never lacking, and he flirted shamelessly with attractive women we knew or met. The gleam in his eye and his witty subtle playfulness turned a lot of women's heads. I could see they envied me because Tony was a catch. What a fool I was!

I suddenly remembered chatting with Connie next door one morning. She casually mentioned that she slept late that morning because of date night the night before. She winked and blushed and I laughed. Then she asked me how many times we had a date night, giggling as she crossed her legs and threw her head back. Her large diamond ring shone as she pulled her hair up in a mock ponytail, waiting for my answer. At the time, I felt a little flustered, and not really knowing how to be coy, I told her it had been a while. She stared at me, waiting for more information. There was silence as I tried to figure out what to say, but I didn't have to think long. I figured every woman was like I was, making jokes about having a headache at bedtime. In fact, "Not tonight honey" could have been my mantra; it was certainly a familiar refrain in our bedroom. I crisply informed Connie that neither Tony nor I had much use anymore for messy sex and preferred to just cuddle. Of course, this was stretching the truth because cuddling, like sex, had become nonexistent in our house as well. Connie looked down and changed the subject. I could tell my response made her uncomfortable. There was even a bit of pity in her eyes. My reaction was to make a hasty retreat, telling her I had a pie in the oven.

I used to enjoy sex. Just admitting that to myself caused my heart to pound a little harder. Those early days with Frankie were luscious. The feeling of him holding me, looking into my eyes while his arms tightened around me could make me tremble. Deep kisses that traveled way, way down, almost bringing me to my knees. Wanting more and more... and giving more and more. Later, I had nights like that with Tony. We would park at Carson's Beach and watch the lights across the shore as Boston came to life. Our passion also came to life when Tony pulled me into the back seat of his old Ford. I thought if I inhaled Old Spice right then, I would be transported back to those days when Tony's dizzying kisses could spin me into a tizzy. Every night, the windows were fogged up as Tony lit a cigarette for us to share. We sat naked under his wool army blanket feeling wicked. We laughed about possibly getting caught *in flagrante*. We murmured sexy promises to each other, and usually that resulted in igniting our steamy passion, leading to another round. Tony would joke about how I wore him out, but I never did. I couldn't get enough, and I let him know it. What I would do right now to be transported back to a time like that when I felt so loved and so loving. It was beautiful.

Suddenly the door opened, and Brian appeared with a menu. He looked harried but smiled as he tipped his hat again. "Angie, here is the menu. It's getting busy, but I will be back to take your order, okay?"

I knew what I wanted, my usual diner lunch. "No fuss, Brian. I will have a BLT on toasted wheat, light on mayo, and coffee, light cream." It occurred to me that I should change my usual and think outside the box, but part of my brain was still with Tony in the back seat of his car....

"Sure, Angie, be back soon." Brian shut the door behind him.

I could hear other passengers chatting and the clink of utensils on plates. I settled back in my seat again, took a deep breath, and got a whiff of coffee. I felt strangely lethargic.

Up until that point, I hadn't allowed myself to think about the fact that I had begun to have sexual dreams for the past couple of months. They started after I talked to Nicky. Our conversations since that first one was not flirty. Well, maybe they were a little. The difference was that now I *wanted* to flirt and was hoping he would initiate it. The feeling was strange and unsettling to me. I had become so practiced at pulling back at the first signs of any intimacy that I wasn't even aware I didn't want to do that anymore. My dreams centered mostly on amorous embraces that left me breathless. My suitors in the dreams were sometimes faceless, but I could feel the delicious warmth of their bodies and even inhaled a hint of aftershave. Whose aftershave I didn't know, but I didn't care. A scratchy beard and strong arms to hold me were what I remembered from the first dream. There was giggling in the second dream and hesitant exploring on both sides. I was wearing a rose-colored mohair sweater, a sweater I had a long time ago (before Tony?), that was pulled up gently as I could feel a hand reaching to unhook my bra...

Wow, where was that coming from?

I squirmed in my seat, which had become warm from the heat pulsating inside me. I didn't remember feeling so frisky since menopause, which was now a distant memory.

What is happening with my hormones? I wondered.

Back when I first experienced the signs of menopause, I felt a huge relief. My periods were always ghastly, with cramping and heavy bleeding. I refused to wear tampons. They were not the old-fashioned pads I had grown up with. My time of the month meant I had to trudge down to the Rexall pharmacy and discreetly purchase a huge box of super Kotex. They were fashioned with a flimsy belt that had hooks on the end to hold the strips from the end of the pad. It was archaic beyond belief. Years later the pads developed a sticky underside to fasten to underwear with wings to protect panties. None of it worked for me because blood poured out of me. I felt weak and became anemic a few times, which was the reason I loved being pregnant. No periods for nine months! So, when the change began and my periods became sporadic, I was ecstatic. I could even wear white skirts during my time of the month!

I didn't tell Tony I was going through the change. One of the reasons I gave Tony for abstaining from sex was my period. Tony was guileless and did not pay much attention to my monthly cycle, thank God, so my go-to excuse to keep him away from me was that it was my time of the month. Like most men, Tony was uncomfortable with the mystery of women's monthly cycles. All I had to do was mention that Flo was in town (yes, I really used that expression) and Tony pulled away quickly. He also assumed I was off-limits for at least a week because that was how long I told him it lasted. Sometimes I stretched it out to ten days or even two weeks.

Poor Tony, I thought guiltily. He had no idea what a devious woman he'd married. *Or did he?*

Unlike many women I knew, menopause was an easy transition for me. There were no hot flashes to speak of, so there was no visible evidence of the change that was beginning in my body. I was happy that I didn't have to buy super Kotex any longer, but I kept that a secret as well. I continued to use my periods as an excuse to abstain from sex. Looking back, I realized how sneaky I had become. A feeling of deep sadness engulfed me as I realized I cheated both of us out of some of the best moments of our marriage. Then I discovered I was not the only one keeping secrets.

I envied the Connies of the world who seduced their husbands with sexy negligees and used sex toys I saw advertised on the back pages of magazines. Those magazines were the *Playboys* that I discovered one day cleaning out the bedroom. I was shocked at first to find one hidden under Tony's side of the mattress. It looked well-worn as I thumbed through it in disbelief. I don't know what shocked me more: the women posing completely in the nude (lacking pubic hair that, from the looks of it, had been previously shaved) or that Tony had savored each page. I picked through the pages carefully, not wanting to leave any evidence that I had intruded into Tony's stash of porn. I need not have worried about being discovered; the pages were so worn and creased that I began to fantasize about Tony and the magazine. The more I gently thumbed through the pages, I more fascinated I became with the images. I also was aware of a depression settling over me. My husband had turned to porn! And why? Because his wife, who he had once thought to be very sexy, no longer was the object of his affection. The issue of *Playboy* was not a new one. I had no idea how long Tony had been using adult magazines to satisfy his sexual urges. I knew Tony's urges were strong, strong enough that glossy pictures in a magazine were not going to be enough to satisfy him in the long run.

That day I put the *Playboy* back hastily when the doorbell rang. Later, I finished making the bed and did not allow myself to think of our lack of sex again. I stopped having to make excuses because Tony rarely initiated any kind of intimacy with me anymore. Instead of feeling sad,

I was relieved I no longer had to think of a reason why I didn't want to have sex. Now I realized how selfish and stupid I had been. Tony got the message, but he wasn't going to beg me for sex anymore. Why should he? I knew now he discovered he was still an attractive sexy guy and if I didn't want him, there were other cute women who would be more than willing to jump into bed with him. I wouldn't have been surprised if I forced him into the arms of another woman. I wished I could talk to him, but it was too late. Tony died thinking I no longer wanted him or loved him.

I didn't want to think about sex and the lack thereof, but now I couldn't stop.

What was lacking in our marriage was me.

Spurning Tony's advances for years had consequences. I had evolved into the stereotype of the matronly wife who traded sexy nightgowns for flannel pajamas once the babies came along. I remembered in the early days, before the kids, Tony and I would sleep in the nude. We didn't have air conditioning but even in the winter, it was fun to cuddle under layers of covers giggling as my feet curled around Tony's thighs, eventually making their way higher and higher. I used to enjoy the look on his face when eventually I reached those secret erogenous zones. I certainly didn't call it that. I learned all by myself the power I could wield when I cupped him in both hands. It was fun to experiment when I was young and hot. Well, maybe I wasn't that hot, but Tony sure made me feel like I was desirable. It didn't take him long to finish, a fact we used to joke about. He blamed me and jokingly complained that he couldn't wait for me in the heat of his own passion. I never really admitted to Tony that I wasn't satisfied most of the time, and I never quite figured out how to tell him how to help. I couldn't really talk about any of it. Good girls did not talk about orgasms or how to become aroused.

I had my first orgasm accidentally. Frankie, who was a man before his time now that I thought about it, was determined to make me happy in bed. Being a submissive sex partner, one night I was all set to make him happy in bed—and I did—but unlike most men, Frankie wasn't finished afterwards. He began to manipulate me gently, all the while cupping and sucking my breasts. He did it slowly, and soon I felt a swirling, unfamiliar rush of passion burst between my legs. As I cried out, Frankie increased his thrusting inside with two fingers, and I finished in a soggy heap of happiness. Frankie was very pleased with himself.

After that time, our sex life improved immensely. I had never understood there was an actual reason women enjoyed sex, and once I realized it, I was in heaven. Most days, I walked around in a daze, feeling as if I would burst from the giant secret I held inside. It was not just the powerful feeling of intimacy Frankie and I shared, although that was certainly unlike anything I had ever experienced, but it was also the strange, sweet, and secret knowledge that I had discovered that part of myself, the place in a woman's body that was sacred and sexy and oh so delicious. I felt like I had discovered the secret to life. Tony and I also had quite a sex life in our early years, but quite frankly, I never again felt the way I did with Frankie after that one night.

The door opened, and Brian appeared with my BLT and coffee. I straightened up quickly, hoping he didn't realize my face was flushed. I glanced at his face and was relieved to see he was distracted enough not to notice. He smiled quickly, tipped his hat again and was off, the door closing behind him.

Twenty-Three

Ben woke from his nap and noticed the quiet right away. Normally he would hear bustling noises from the hallway and would be interrupted at least once by a nurse barging into his room to help him with his medications. If he knew he was going down for a nap (he still used that expression as if he were a two-year-old at naptime), he would take out his hearing aids in order not to be disturbed. He didn't expect to sleep but dozed off as he listened to the Red Sox play their first spring training game in Fort Myers, Florida. He never missed the first game, especially since he knew his sister Theresa was there with her husband, Alan. Theresa and Alan had a small mobile home in a park with other seniors, which was very close to Jet Blue Park where the Red Sox played.

He slowly sat up and put on his shoes. He hadn't been asleep for long; the game was still scoreless. He realized that the lack of noise in the corridors and the absence of a nursing presence meant that the strike had not yet been resolved. He smiled to himself, thinking that it couldn't have come at a better time.

It is fate, he thought, *that Angie would choose to leave when the culmination of a nursing strike meant there would be no one to notice that she had vanished.*

Ben felt a twinge of sadness. He realized he could no longer visit

Angie. More than ever before, he felt alone. He was all by himself with his thoughts and just about everything else. Ben had become accustomed to ambling down the hall to room 323 to speak to Angie in hushed tones. Her planned escape had been an exciting diversion for him, allowing him to forget his health problems for a while. Now the reality of his situation was beginning to sink in.

His bedside phone suddenly played the *Titanic* theme song. The tune was Ben's ringtone, chosen because of his devotion to ocean liners and all things nautical. Ben changed his ringtone every month. Last month, it was the theme song to *The Three Stooges*, another one of Ben's favorites. The *Titanic* ringtone was specific to Angie. Ben knew how to set the ringtone for different callers, and since he had bought Angie her deluxe cell phone with the large numbers for her journey, he also chose the *Titanic* theme song as her ringtone. It didn't really matter since Ben's phone seldom rang anyway except for phone calls about his upcoming doctor visits.

Ben flipped the phone open. "Hi, Angie!" His voice squeaked a bit as he tried to project his voice as high as he could. Despite having had a cell phone for years, Ben still thought that he had to practically scream into it to be heard.

"Hi Ben, it's Angie! Am I calling at a bad time?" Angie's voice came in sweet and strong, just as she was.

"No, not at all, Angie. I was just thinking about you. How is everything going, so to speak?"

"It's been great, Ben. I just finished a late lunch. Brian is wonderful. I admit I have been dozing and daydreaming a lot and just realized I have sort of lost track of time! That was why I was calling, to check in to see how everything was." Angie sounded a little breathless, but excited too.

"I'm glad you did. Everything here appears to be the same. I am in my room now, but the nurses are nowhere to be seen. I haven't been outside, but I was going to check to see if the news cameras are still stationed there. I would guess that right now the strike has not been resolved, and that, of course, means your absence has still gone undetected." Ben lowered his voice considerably as he finished the last sentence even though he was pretty sure there was no one within earshot. He shuffled over to his door and cracked it open. He saw no activity whatsoever, not even a resident hobbling by.

"Wow, Ben, it's almost as if this was meant to be." Ben thought Angie sounded relieved and even relaxed. "Of course, I know the strike will not last forever, and I guess I am just delaying the inevitable, but I will take whatever reprieve I get for now!" Angie lowered her voice also. "I hope you are okay. Are you feeling all right? I miss you!"

"Sure, Angie, I am thinking about you a lot too. I sure miss being with you, but the important thing is that you are safe and in good hands, which you are. Do you know your destination right now?" Ben ambled back to his bed and plopped down on it as he tried to remember the timetable for the Acela Cardinal routes.

"I'm not exactly sure, but Brian is still here. I think he is supposed to switch off outside of Chicago. I will ask him as soon as he returns; he seemed very busy when he dropped my lunch off a while ago. I can't tell you how nice he has been and how protected I feel right now with all you good fellas watching out for me!" Angie chuckled. "I can't help but think, 'If Tony could only see me now!'"

Ben laughed. "I know. He would be proud of you, I'm sure. No way would he have wanted you to stay here. I can tell you that even though I never met him. He is surely watching over you, so to speak." Ben glanced at the Thomas the Train clock next to his bed and realized he was overdue for lunch. "Tell you what, Angie, why don't I check out the situation here by going outside and seeing what the scuttlebutt is. I will call you back later, maybe early evening?"

"Sure, Ben. In the meantime, I'll try to find out where we are and what our next stop is. It is so good to hear your voice."

"Me, too," Ben said, his throat catching. "Glad you are a-okay." Ben tried to sound upbeat, but hearing Angie's voice made him realize how much he missed her. His existence suddenly felt meaningless, but the last thing he wanted to do was let Angie know, even in the tone of his voice, how he felt. It was not about him.

Realizing that he still had a lot of work to do, he was suddenly filled with purpose. He got off his bed and flung open the drawers to his desk. He had to make sure he had the timelines correct. Even though he knew he could probably check the schedule online, Ben was old-school. He had just about every timetable for every train in the country, and even some of the Canadian ones. Chuckling to himself, he remembered he even had some of the Italian trains' schedules from long ago, but they were, of course, in Italian. He shook his head as he realized he should toss those in the trash—if he ever found them. After rifling through some Amazon bills, he found the stack of timetables in his bottom drawer. He grabbed the one for the Southwest Chief, pulled up his suspenders, and decided to go over the schedule while he savored a coffee milkshake from the Creamery across the street. On the way out, he could check out the progress of the nursing strike, he decided, killing two birds with one stone....

After grabbing his car keys, Ben left his room and headed to the lobby. Although his mind was on what to order with his milkshake, he understood the corridors were silent. As he passed Angie's closed door, he noticed no sign that anyone had even been around the nursing station next door or even the laundry across the hall. He headed to the elevator, hoping his luck would hold out, and he would not encounter the Bullhorn.

So far, so good, he thought as he entered the lobby. He could see the Channel 12 news camera off to the side of the parking lot and several reporters milling around, but Sharon's seat at the reception area was vacant and the office doors of the director and staff were firmly shut. Peaceful Havens was eerily quiet, a blessing now for Angie and Ben, but still, it was strangely unsettling. Ben quietly slipped out the side door near the hair salon past the library. The last thing he needed was to be harassed by someone from the media. Besides, he had fish and chips on his mind.

Twenty-Four

The coffee was hot and the BLT was toasty and warm, just as I like it. I might've I broken a new record by finishing the whole sandwich in five bites. Usually, it took me forever to finish my meal, a fact that annoyed Gina. I was not always like that. Before Peaceful Havens, I did everything fast, too fast, but I always thought of myself as extremely efficient. I knew it really annoyed Tony when I began clearing the dishes when he was only halfway through his meal. Typical of Tony, he liked to savor his food with his nightly martini. Also typical of him, he never mentioned his irritation, but I could tell from the terse look on his face that he wished I would sit down and relax until he was finished. After I was placed in Peaceful Havens, however, I began to mimic, unconsciously, the habits of the other residents. They moved at a snail's pace, not just at the dinner table, but everywhere else as well. I knew there was not much incentive to gobble down the garbage disguised as dinner, but I knew their tediously slow movements were the reason they were there in the first place. I cringed as I finished off my sandwich, thinking of what it would be like to be back in my dingy apartment. With no kitchen staff, the food there would be even more dreadful than it was before.

Even harder to believe, I thought as I munched on my Lay's chips, *is*

*the fact that I escaped and pulled off a stunt I never had dreamed possible
a few months ago.*

My thoughts began to drift back to the delicious memories of Frankie
that still lingered in my mind. It had been years since I had thought of
him. Remembering how his body felt was like a delightful daydream I
wanted to savor over and over. More powerful than those sensations,
however, was the transformation in me for which Frankie was responsible. Up until I met Frankie, I had little confidence in where my life
was going and lacked any ambition to figure out where that would be. It
never occurred to me that I was pretty or, as Frankie said, a knockout. I
always thought knockouts had to look like Marilyn Monroe, who posed
in provocative poses. Then I would see the look in Frankie's eyes when
I walked through the door. That was all I needed to make me feel like a
real woman. As I looked back, our days and nights together formed the
basis of my own mental image of myself. I developed a whole bunch of
self-confidence just stepping into Frankie's arms every night.

We dated for about a year. Then I met Tony. At first, I gave Tony the
brush-off because Frankie and I were in love. Well, I had convinced myself
I loved him, and he did tell me (usually in the throes of passion) that he
loved me too. It was true that my heart did skip a beat when I saw him,
and didn't all the songs say that was how you knew you were in love? I
finally told my mother we were going steady after she became suspicious
of my absences late at night. I tried to keep Frankie a secret at first, but my
activities were closely monitored by my mother. She knew I was usually
home from work at five thirty, which was how long it would take me by
trolley. So, one day I told her I was interested in my boss and he was going
to take me out to dinner after work. I didn't, of course, reveal the fact that
he had lured me to his Back Bay mansion, but I did tell her he had money.
That fact alone was enough to please Mom. Forget school or work. My
mother only wanted me to find a rich husband, settle down, and have
babies. I sighed. No wonder domesticity was in my genes!

Frankie and I didn't become intimate right away. I resisted at first
because I didn't want to appear to be "easy."

"Why buy the cow when the milk is free?" my mother always smugly declared.

Frankie was smooth and unassuming. If it seemed like I wasn't going to succumb to his charms, he didn't make a big deal out of it. I was sure he knew it was just a matter of time, and as he said later, "Good things come to those who wait." I appreciated his patience and willingness to let me call the shots. I felt respected as a woman. He didn't immediately give up on me as other guys did when I didn't put out. No, Frankie was a different kind of guy. Looking back at the situation, I realized he probably was used to getting what he wanted—and what he wanted was me.

I had stars in my eyes during the whole time I was with Frankie. I never dreamed that a poor little Italian girl, living in a third-floor, cold water flat with a widowed mother and three other siblings would not only attract a guy like Frankie but would keep him interested in her.

What in the world did he see in me? I wondered at first.

As time went on and I became more self-confident (Frankie gave me that), I stopped thinking of myself in such an unflattering light. Sometimes I felt like I deserved him, but other times, and there were many other times, I not only failed to see what he saw in me, I was convinced that a prettier, more sophisticated woman would snatch him out from under me at any moment. Those feelings of inadequacy, I realized, mostly stemmed from my background. Frankie had not yet met my mother or seen where I lived. I knew it was only a matter of time before he became aware that I was the poor Italian girl from the other side of the tracks.

Frankie's background was the opposite from mine. He was a wealthy Irish guy who had money, good looks, and an enviable job in his own business. The fact that he was Irish and I was Italian shouldn't have mattered to me but it did. It seemed to make no difference to Frankie because he never mentioned it. He wore his wealth and good fortune the same way he wore his Italian suits, with casual indifference. His unassuming unpretentiousness made him, in my eyes, even more desirable.

I had never met anyone like Frankie. Frankie, despite his many riches, was loved by everyone he met.

The appearance of Tony in my life, however, put a dent in the Frankie-Angie story. At first, I gave Tony vague excuses about long hours at work to thwart him. I did mention Frankie was my boss but revealed nothing more. Tony, however, was persistent in his attempts to win me over. He accomplished this by being sweet, thoughtful, and very available, characteristics that at first annoyed me but then disarmed me. He would show up at my house with roses (my favorite) and take me for long rides to Nantasket Beach. Tony didn't wear designer suits, but he was intelligent, kind, and *very* cute. More importantly, he possessed the one attribute Frankie did not: He was Italian.

During Tony's visits to my house, he would speak Italian to my mother as they sat together at our little metal table in the kitchen. My mother happily poured him coffee and brought out her pizzelles to snack on along with some pizza she had made that day. During their visit, my brother Giuseppe and sister Felicia would also come by to show Tony the homework they had just finished. Tony, who loved schoolwork, patiently corrected their math and science questions and even taught them a few phrases in Italian. Tony would also listen to them as they reported their adventures in school that day. Their schoolwork improved, and I noticed they smiled more. My family fell in love with Tony long before I ever did.

As Tony became more of a fixture in my family, his family did too. Tony's mother Elvira met my mother and, soon, was also a frequent visitor in our kitchen. It turned out that Elvira and Gus, Tony's father, lived two streets down from us. Gus's job as a chef meant our icebox was stocked with beef and pork, items which had been virtually nonexistent up until then. Tony's flat was almost identical to ours, a fact that endeared me to him. What's more, his sister Albina and I hit it off immediately, sharing cigarettes, martinis, and secrets together in her tiny bedroom adjacent to the kitchen in Tony's flat. Albina had just discovered she was pregnant, a fact she divulged to me as she puffed away on a Pall Mall. She confessed that she now had to marry her boyfriend, Mike Testa, and scrunched up her face as she revealed this information. Mike was not a favorite in the eyes of her parents since he was an unemployed busboy, but he was the father of the baby Albina could feel kicking her under her red, oversized dress that doubled as a beach cover-up. I felt very privileged to learn of the impending birth and soon-to-be wedding before anyone else did. As she shared her feelings about suddenly looking at motherhood, I listened attentively, all the while trying to hide the look of alarm obviously written all over my face. My close friendship with Albina made me happy, more so because I really didn't have any girlfriends to share stuff with.

Albina was funny, open, and encouraged salty dialogue. We practiced some vulgar language together as we giggled conspiratorially. Albina was two years older than me. Besides being a good example of why birth control was necessary, I learned some valuable lessons from hanging out with Albina, and I began to confide in her as well.

Coincidentally, my relationship with Tony deepened as my friendship with Albina grew. It was also a relief to have my mother finally develop a relationship with someone other than the guy at the butcher shop. She loved Elvira and was happy when Gus quietly took care of some of the manly chores that had piled up around the flat. That, and the fact Gus's occupation substantially broadened our range of mealtime options, sealed the deal. In my mother's eyes, Tony was the one, and she made it very clear that Frankie, who she knew about all along, had to go.

The only problem was that Frankie was still in my life and certainly in my heart. I felt myself drifting away from him slowly, but having had little experience in ways to end relationships, I had no idea what to do. I knew things would end badly if I didn't cut the cord with Frankie before either one discovered that the other existed. Life suddenly became very complicated, and in my attempt to figure out what to do, I solved the problem by doing nothing.

One afternoon, Frankie appeared as I was packing up to leave for the day. I had just put the cover on my Olivetti typewriter when I heard his voice behind me.

"Hey, Ang, how about a quick bite at O'Sullivan's?"

O'Sullivan's was the take-out joint at Castle Island where we loved to go and watch the planes land at Logan Airport. It was also a great place to sip beers, munch on foot-long hotdogs, and walk on the beach. O'Sullivan's had become "our place."

I quickly agreed, and we headed out to Frankie's car. I loved riding next to Frankie in his new Chrysler with leather seats. Inside, the world belonged to just us. Frankie smiled as he opened the door and I happily settled into the lavish seats, feeling like a princess. As nagging thoughts of Tony popped into the back of my mind, I quickly dismissed them.

I need a break from my good girl behavior, I thought. *Time for me.*

The sun had already begun to set as we arrived at Castle Island. I loved looking over the expanse of Boston Harbor down to Carson Beach. Sometimes I pretended I was on a tropical island, maybe in the South Seas, far away from my little world on K Street. Frankie let the car idle as he ran into O'Sullivan's to pick up some hot dogs and beer for us. I remembered as he shut the door behind him that I had a few chocolate chip cookies left over from lunch.

Those would be good for dessert, I mused.

Food was never far from my mind. I guiltily remembered that Tony loved my chocolate chip cookies.

Stop it, I told myself sternly. *This is no time to think of Tony.*

I thrust all thoughts of cookies and Tony to the back of my mind as Frankie returned to the car. Delicious aromas of hot dogs, which we called wieners, drifted from the greasy bag Frankie brought in, along with French fries and a couple of beers.

I smiled at Frankie, and we took off to the end of the island, which afforded us views of airplanes and boats. It was a private strip of land we had found behind the fort, which took up most of the island on the west side. It was great for sunsets too. Almost on cue, the sun began to dip behind the backdrop of East Boston on the other side of Boston Harbor. It was a gorgeous night with a soft breeze, but my arms were still warm from the day. Frankie opened my door for me, and we headed to our spot near the fort. Even though it was a lovely night, there was an empty bench waiting for us.

"We are in luck, Ang." Frankie grinned. "Looks like we beat everyone to the best seat in town."

I looked up at him and my heart lurched. He towered over me, handsome as ever, with the sun as his backdrop. There were moments in my life, I realized suddenly, that would stay with me forever, and that was one of them.

We devoured our dogs, beer, and fries with gusto. I had skipped lunch and I knew Frankie had too.

"I don't think any meal, even one at Anthony's Pier 4, could compare with this," I said, my mouth full of the last of my fries.

Frankie wiped his mouth on the last napkin and nodded in agreement. "I always say, it's the best things in life that are free." Frankie suddenly looked serious.

I thought that remark, coming from a guy as well-heeled as Frankie, was peculiar. *Welcome to my world*, I thought, knowing cheap eats had always been a necessity in my family. The fact Frankie couldn't relate to that part of me managed to distance us. Frankie might be referring to his parents' humble roots, but he had no idea what it was like to count every single penny that came into the household.

These thoughts were in and out of my mind as I watched the sun set while jets flew over our heads. I sat back and closed my eyes, feeling the last of the sun on my face. It was Friday. Frankie's hand closed over mine and suddenly I could feel myself drifting off, the sights and the sounds of Boston Harbor fading into the distance. How long I sat there I don't know, but I woke with a start as I felt Frankie take both of my hands and hold them tightly. That was when I knew he had something on his mind.

"Ang, this night is perfect, you are perfect, and right now, my world is perfect." Frankie's voice was low and intense. My relaxing evening with Frankie was now turning into something ominous. I sat up straight; my first instinct was to bolt off the bench, into the car, and back home, but

I didn't have time. "You know I love you, or at least, I hope you know that. I can't remember being with a woman like you before, Angie. It's more than just thinking about you all the time; lately my thoughts have been turning towards the future. After all, I am not getting any younger. I've sowed all my wild oats, excuse that expression," Frankie smiled sheepishly, "and I guess what I am trying to say, Ang, is, you are the one." Frankie stopped and gazed into my eyes. I could not remember ever seeing him so serious. "I hope I am the one for you, too, because I want you to be my wife, Angie, and hell, I am asking you to marry me!" Frankie fumbled in the pocket of his designer slacks and pulled out a small jewelry box. It was turquoise, and it was from Tiffany.

It was a good thing that Frankie had released my hands because they had grown clammy. They began to tremble along with my knees. *Marriage? To Frankie? Where were my instincts?* I had not seen this coming in a million years.

I watched with horror as Frankie opened the little box. There before me, a large, round, perfect diamond winked temptingly in the waning sunlight. I stared at it, a symbol of love, perfect love, the love that Frankie thought we had—and the love that I knew, with my heart sinking into the sand, that I did not have for Frankie.

I felt wretched and scared, and all the time my mind was racing. I couldn't imagine what was showing on my face, but I wished with all my heart that I could put the night into reverse and go back to work—or better yet, go back to the morning where I had the opportunity to call in sick and avoid such a disaster—but here I was.

What do I do now? I thought desperately.

My first instinct was to somehow mitigate the damage, kick the can down the road, without hurting Frankie, but I realized that I could not avoid the truth, and any further attempt to lie my way out of the situation would result in even more of a disaster than the one I was facing.

I looked up at Frankie and met his eyes. I smiled weakly but Frankie's expression, at first questioning, began to change. As the knowledge that I was not jumping up and down with delight began to sink in, he grew quiet. My heart sank as I tried to find the words to let him down and somehow salvage our relationship. I knew it was impossible, but I took a deep breath anyway.

"Frankie, I do love you. I think you know that. I am so flattered that you want me to be your wife. I really, really mean that. I had never dreamed that you were at the stage in your life where marriage was a possibility because I have to honestly admit I am not. There are many reasons that I have to say no, but my feelings for you are not among them...." I tried to slow down, and not stammer. "You have never met my mother or my family, but if you did, you would understand that our backgrounds couldn't be more opposite. I am the poor Italian girl supporting my widowed mother and young siblings, living from paycheck to paycheck, in a tiny third-floor flat. Your family, your peers, expect more of a future wife from you than someone with my lack of social skills and upbringing. Honestly, Frankie, I have nothing to offer you. I would be an embarrassment to you. It would, in time, create a divide that would only widen as we tried to begin a life together." Frankie looked troubled so I stopped. "Can you understand where I am coming from?"

I grabbed his hand, which was still clutching the ring box. The box was still open, but in the darkness, the ring was no longer visible. There was a huge silence. I felt like I was going to throw up. I waited for Frankie to say something, anything. Inside my head I was screaming, *Is this really happening?*

Finally, Frankie wordlessly closed the box, grabbed all the greasy bags, and walked back to the car. I had no choice but to follow him. After he silently dropped me off, we never really spoke again.

—

Brian opened my roomette door, and I was transported back to my life as a fugitive. "Hey, Angie, sorry I was so busy, but now things have calmed down a bit. How was lunch?"

I composed myself and sat up. "Best lunch I have had in, like, forever. Thanks, Brian. You have been so attentive; I really appreciate it. You know, I could really get used to this royal treatment." I passed him my empty dishes. "As you can tell, I really disliked the food."

Brian chuckled and rested for a minute against the door. "Angie, you are a model traveler, the kind I wished I had more of. It's always the regular coach travelers, who I see all the time, who are the most maintenance. But I am used to it, and it's kind of fun to navigate through a busy day. Never a dull moment, that's for sure. Tomorrow morning we reach Chicago, and we have a shift change. It's fun to see new faces, and I am happy to tell you that my replacement is a guy you know. Remember Bill Bates? Well, of course you do; you remembered that you met me at the party he threw for Ben. He dated Gina, right? So, you two are old pals! He was in Chicago, so he volunteered to be on the next shift with you after Ben filled him in about your situation." Brian looked really pleased with that last remark.

I loved Bill. He and Gina parted as friends a year or two ago (wasn't it right after my accident?), but Bill always helped me out after Tony died. For some reason, he enjoyed hearing about growing up in Southie and took an interest in poring over old family albums. He had an almost photographic memory and remembered all our old relatives, even some I had forgotten. Once, I had my cousins from Australia visiting, and he talked to them for hours, never tiring of listening to their history.

"I can't think of a person I would rather have accompany me on the last leg of this trip, Brian, other than you, of course." Dredging up all my old memories, ones I really wanted to forget, had put me into a funk. Hearing about Bill, though, perked me up. I smiled nervously as Brian nodded.

"I know this is probably hard for you, Angie. All this upheaval would do anyone in, especially in light of your, er, situation...." Brian looked at me with concern. "I want to make this as enjoyable for you as possible. After all, I know you will remember this journey forever, for many reasons. Now, just settle down and enjoy the rest of the day. I'll let you know when dinner is served. More coffee?"

I laughed out loud. "Sure, Brian, when you get a chance. You are a real sweetheart. Ben was right."

Brian laughed too. "I'm not sure that sweetheart would be the word Ben would use to describe me, but thanks." He tipped his hat and left my cabin with a flourish.

Whew, I thought. This trip so far has been an emotional ride. I knew there was going to be way more drama as soon as Gina and the rest of the crew in Providence found out I had escaped. I got up slowly and decided it was time to make myself more presentable. I headed to the toilet, all the while still thinking of what was to come.

Twenty-Five

Gina hung up the phone with a sigh. She stared at it, trying to process the news she had just received. The call was from Nancy, her realtor. In a breathless flurry of excitement, Nancy told her the closing of Mom's house was all set for next week, all the while congratulating herself on how she had singlehandedly negotiated the deal. Although Gina had been hoping for that outcome, now that it had happened, she felt deflated and confused. She had always mixed feelings about selling her childhood home, and those conflicting emotions now swirled around her head.

She never really wanted to sell it. It was forced upon her because her mother ended up in that awful place. All through the cleaning, sorting, packing, and getting the house ready for sale, she had never let her real emotions take over, but they did now. Tears filled her eyes. She couldn't believe the house would no longer belong to her family. Even though the house was part of the very fabric that defined her childhood, someone else would soon be living in it. Someone else's footsteps would soon dominate the stairs leading to the little porch to the garden backyard. Children would wake in her bedroom and look out below to the street as she had for many years. The house would have new scents belonging to a new family, which would transform her house, her family's house, into a place that was unfamiliar and strange.

Gina also felt resentful that she was alone with her sentiments. Her brother and sister obviously did not share any of her concerns. They were so far removed from the whole saga with their mother that to them, the event was no more than a house sale. The same way the yard sale, dubbed an "estate sale" to attract wealthy buyers, was just a way to dispose of a lot of the dishes and household items for which they had little attachment. But Gina did. Half of the stuff laid out on the table for the sale ended up back in the trunk of Gina's car. How could she possibly part with her mother's Corning Ware pie dishes? Or her Lenox candy bowls that always held chocolate eggs at Easter and red and green M&Ms at Christmastime? Gina was horrified when Maria had stacked the sale table with her mother's old pizzelle maker and rolling pin. Those also ended up in her trunk, where most of the items remained.

Gina didn't dare reveal even a trace of her sadness to anyone. For one thing, she would have little sympathy. Maria briskly counted the money after the estate sale, smiling about their success. Mario hastily retreated once the last customer walked to his car, mumbling something about having to run to the store before dinner. Gina was left with the house just as she was left with her conflicting emotions.

She knew she should not feel so angry and hurt. Other people, she knew, had to sell their childhood homes, oftentimes without a quick sale like hers. She tried to tell herself that her resentment was unfair; after all, the house had to be sold to pay for Peaceful Havens. Even her mother agreed that she didn't want to live there anymore. Still, Gina couldn't shake her deepening depression. It seemed so unfair that the only one who seemed bothered by any of this was her. She knew her siblings would be genuinely thrilled when she told them about the full price offer.

Gina walked over to the large picture window overlooking the street. Dusk had started to settle, and the pink dogwood blossoms that had bloomed last week were beginning to fade and fall onto their lawn. The late-blooming tulips were already spent, and their stems had flattened into the ground around the lilac bushes.

I won't ever watch the lilacs burst open here anymore, she thought.

Gina remembered her father planting the little bush when they had just moved in because lilacs were her favorite flowers, not roses, her mother's favorite. They had several rose bushes in the back for her. Even though the roses were usually eaten by Japanese beetles by August, Gina would miss those as well. She knew that the new owners would probably not want the maple tree, the one her father had planted in the backyard, because the leaves made a mess in the driveway in the autumn. All the azalea bushes along the side of the house would probably face a similar fate and be uprooted and tossed in the junk heap. After the closing, Gina would have to rely on her memories when she wanted to revisit that slice of her childhood.

The house was already bare, but some furniture remained. The upstairs bedroom set was claimed by the Carnevales, mostly because Gina offered it to them for free.

At least I know it will go to a good home, Gina thought wryly.

One of the remaining spinsters, Grace, decided to claim Gina's mother's sewing machine that sat covered in the basement. Everything else was pretty much picked over except for the TV set, which was an ancient console that sat kitty corner in the living room for as long as Gina could remember.

There wasn't much of a demand for a heavy furniture piece like this one, Gina thought as she walked over to it. This might be the only thing she would have to leave on the sidewalk with a *Free* sign on it hoping some junk collector would take it away.

Feeling a wave of nostalgia, Gina picked up the remote and flicked on the TV. It took a few seconds to warm up, as it usually did, then flickered to life. Gina realized the TV had not been played since the day her mother had left the house before her accident. The channel was still on a local TV station for the news, her mother's favorite—and what appeared on the screen, big as life, was Peaceful Havens, the top story of the day. Gina's eyes widened as she stared at the reporter standing outside the main building, a light wind blowing her lacquered curls despite the hood over her head. The twenty-something beauty queen reporter was excitedly pointing to the main building, where disgruntled-looking women in nurse's scrubs were walking around with signs while reporters and important-looking men in suits scurried back and forth nervously. She caught a glimpse of her mother's most recent CNA, Cheryl, marching outside along with the rest of the staff, looking as if she would rather be anywhere else than in the hastily formed picket line.

What the hell? Gina thought with growing alarm. So Peaceful Havens was having a nurse's strike, and this was the first time she'd learned of it in how many days? No one bothered to clue Gina in on any important information, least of all her mother, who must be holed up in her room like all the rest of the residents. After her first flash of anger and confusion, guilt flooded through her. What in the world has her mother been eating if the kitchen staff were also on strike? Of course, Gina's mind, like her mother's, jumped immediately to food.

Gina didn't stop to hear any of the details that the reporter was eager to tell. She grabbed her cell phone, pulled up her mother's smiling face, and hit Call. Gina's heart was racing now. She rehearsed the frustrating rant she would launch into as soon as her mother picked up, but no one picked up. The phone rang and rang and finally went to voice mail, which was a recording of Gina's voice in a calmer frame of mind asking herself to please leave a message and someone would get right back to them. Gina did not bother leaving a message since her mother, as far as she knew, had no idea how to retrieve any of her messages—or at least she pretended she didn't. Gina suspected all along that her mother, being cagey and not quite as helpless as she pretended, just didn't feel like listening to her messages, especially if she knew they were from Gina.

Gina scrolled down to find Peaceful Haven's main phone number, all along knowing that, too, would probably be a futile effort. Obviously, no one was working, and even if management *was* in the office, they would be insane to pick up their phones. Gina could just imagine that the phone lines had been ringing off the hook for days. As she had suspected, after pressing one for the director, she reached the voicemail, politely asking her to leave a message. She didn't bother pressing all the rest of the numbered options, certain they would all yield similar results. In fact, she was informed at the end of the message that the voicemail box was full.

Gina stuffed her phone back into her purse and grabbed her keys.

Looks like the only solution to this latest fiasco, she thought, *is to head over to Peaceful Havens myself.* She clicked the Off button on the TV remote, and the image diminished and vanished. *I wish this problem could vanish as easily*, Gina thought grimly.

Twenty-Six

Bill unwrapped his Italian sandwich, careful to remove the oily wax paper that dripped on his lunch box. The sandwich was sausage and peppers, his favorite, and he had made it the night before. As he bit into the spicy sausage laced with his marinara sauce, it reminded him of the mouthwatering meals Gina's mother, Angie, used to prepare. The sausage and peppers sandwich was one of Angie's favorites and became Bill's after his first bite.

When they were dating, he and Gina would be invited to Angie's house at least once a week, a fact which delighted him, and Gina too, although Gina pretended she was annoyed at how Angie doted on Bill. Angie doted on everyone who came into her kitchen. She had the uncanny ability to remember what meals everyone liked and what they didn't like. She knew, for example, that Bill hated tomatoes, so she always prepared a special salad for Bill with no tomatoes, which of course irked Gina even more.

Gina and Bill traveled together often, and usually their trips had to include a stop at Disneyland, Bill's favorite place in the whole world. On the eve of their many trips together, Angie would always prepare a going-away dinner for them. Those were the absolute best of times. Bill also fondly remembered some great conversations with Tony while they nursed their martinis before dinner. Bill didn't have a great relationship with his own father, and Tony, through the years, stepped into that role easily. When Tony died, a bit of Bill did too. Gina and Bill remained good friends, but their relationship fell apart after Angie became a widow.

Bill was looking forward to seeing Angie. When Ben asked him to switch his schedule to take over Brian's slot on the Acela, he jumped at the chance. He was thrilled to not only see her again but to be part of her great escape. Ben and Brian filled him in on what was going on, being careful to warn him of complete secrecy. *No problem*, Bill thought. He was always great at keeping secrets. The whole adventure made him feel like a wicked coconspirator, and he was happy to fulfill that role.

Bill did feel conflicted about keeping the secret from Gina however. He still cared for her, more than he would admit even to himself. No one since Gina had even come close to filling her shoes. He suspected she felt the same way, although she was always careful not to show that side of herself. Ever since Angie had ended up in Peaceful Havens, Gina had more on her plate than she could handle. Sometimes, in frustration, she shared her feelings with Bill. Their late-night phone calls, although infrequent, gave Bill false hope that they could somehow pick up where they left off. During one particularly emotional conversation in which Bill suspected Gina had indulged in a few cocktails, Gina confided that she felt guilty depositing Angie on the doorstep of Peaceful Havens. She hinted that Angie, recovered from her accident, no longer belonged in a place meant for the old and feeble. Gina had to deal with the scornful wrath of her aunts, who insinuated in no uncertain terms that Angie was imprisoned in a nursing facility against her will. Several of the neighbors, especially the nosy ones across the street, were also happy to put a huge guilt trip on Gina. Bill knew that Gina tried to remain stoic, but the stress of the situation showed on her face and in her demeanor. She appeared tired and jokingly remarked to Bill that she had lost weight, a silver lining to the dark cloud constantly looming over her.

Bill realized that when Tony died, their relationship did too. It was such a time of intense sorrow that neither one seemed to know or care what to do about it. Bill only remembered the fog of grief that lasted for months. After it cleared, a different Gina emerged. She became sullen and showed little patience toward Angie and everyone in general. The change was subtle but hard to ignore. Bill had changed too. He no longer cared about anything and began to make reckless choices. Bill still felt intense guilt about stepping out on Gina one night, which was the end of them.

Bill hastily finished his sandwich, wiped his mouth, and stood up. Lunch was over. It was time to see for himself if, indeed, the old Angie had returned.

Twenty-Seven

Gina flew up the driveway to Peaceful Havens in record time. Her heart was pounding, and her face was flushed with anger. Taking a few tips from her yoga teacher, she tried deep breathing to calm down, but it only resulted in her hyperventilating even more. It didn't help to see the parking lot filled with news cameras surrounding the handful of nurses who were still picketing the building, looking more bored than determined. It took Gina several turns around the parking lot to find an empty spot, and she finally settled in the last spot way over in the end, mostly reserved for food delivery trucks, which obviously hadn't appeared for days.

She grabbed her Yeti filled with iced coffee, realizing that the caffeine was not helping her to maintain any sense of composure she needed right now. To add insult to injury, she realized that she hadn't eaten since the previous night. Dinner was a hastily prepared baked pasta, heated up in the microwave. It was accompanied by her nightly chardonnay while she enjoyed a rerun of *Sex and the City*. Her stomach rumbled as she headed for the entrance, and she prepared herself for the onslaught of reporters looking to pounce. She felt like a lamb heading for slaughter.

The first reporter to accost her was, of course, the one Gina saw on TV. Her hair had wilted since Gina saw her on TV, but her makeup was still intact. Her high heels clicking purposefully on the cement, she strode up to Gina with a smile plastered on her face and microphone in hand. Gina wondered what shade of lipstick she was wearing; it looked purple and was not at all flattering with her skin color, which was most likely altered, not in a favorable way, by frequent visits to the local tanning salon. She put these negative thoughts to the back of her mind, reminding herself that her priority was her mother, who was somewhere behind the walls of the ghastly building.

"Let me introduce myself," the reporter began happily. "My name is Jessica Lopes, and I am here with Channel 12 news to cover the very unfortunate strike we have here at Peaceful Havens. May I ask your name and what your business is here this afternoon?"

Gina knew she had to maintain her composure and silently gritted her teeth. She managed to look Jessica in the eye (heavily covered with Maybelline mascara, she suspected) and attempted a shy smile. "Sorry, I would love to talk, but I am rather in a hurry right now. I'm sure you can understand." Gina spoke quickly and stepped up her pace to almost a power walk, being careful not to jostle any equipment or step on any of the various wires snaking through the doors and even an open window. She managed to slither successfully between two cameramen who were focused on the picket lines and were fortunately unaware that she was being pressed by Jessica to speak into the microphone. Relieved that she managed to evade the clutches of their key reporter, Gina practically ran into the front door while Jessica, obviously annoyed at her cameramen's inability to capture a key moment with a disgruntled family member, whipped around to find someone to help her. Gina took advantage of the reporter's turnabout and scurried into the building, shutting the door behind her with a bang.

Whew, she thought, *that was close.*

After all that drama, however, the inside lobby, usually bustling with activity, was silent. It was an eerie silence, and Gina's apprehension increased with every step she took towards the elevator. Where was everyone? Did she somehow manage to miss the fact that all the residents were removed by their family members immediately after the strike began? This possibility only provoked Gina's rage. The old guilt reared its ugly head as she suspected, once again, that she was the last one to know that Peaceful Havens was no longer peaceful, or a haven.

Gina's shoes, an old pair of Doc Martens she had hastily slipped on before leaving her mother's house, echoed in the empty hallways as Gina emerged from the elevator and strode towards her mother's room. The corridors were eerily silent, as if she were part of a giant apocalypse, like in a dream. Gina had had many dreams like this, and the endings were never happy. She knew the dreams were manifested in her fear that she would find her mother comatose, mostly as a result of Gina's own negligence.

Gina frequently had flashbacks of the day she found her mother lying on the kitchen floor. That time, Gina saved her mother's life, but she was forever haunted by the ghastly scene, which she relived over and over in her mind. That trauma, which troubled Gina more frequently than she wanted it to, was the reason Angie ended up in Peaceful Havens. Gina was petrified that the next time would be the last and did not want to be in that position ever again.

And here she was, at the door of Angie's room, once again facing the possibility that her worst fears would be realized when she opened the door. Gina's plan to keep Angie safe in this godforsaken place had backfired. Despite Gina's best intentions, Angie was not cared for here; she was not loved here. The nursing system had broken down. In the end, her mother was an unwilling victim of power and money and greed. Gina unlocked the door, closed her eyes, said a silent prayer, and entered Angie's room.

—

Gina opened her eyes. Angie's room was neat and orderly and smelled like Jean Naté. The bed was made in the perfect way her mother liked it with the corners neatly tucked in and the comforter folded at the foot of the bed. The window blinds were partly open, letting in the afternoon light, and a quick look in the bathroom did not reveal anything amiss. But Angie was gone.

Gina walked around the room slowly, trying to figure out where her mother was. Her mind was racing, yet she felt a deep relief that she had not encountered the scene she was most dreading. Okay, so her mother appeared to be safe, but where had she gone?

Gina went into the bathroom and noticed her toothbrush and toothpaste were gone. She pulled back the shower curtain and saw the shower was dry; obviously no one had used it in at least a couple of days. Her towels, hung neatly on the racks, were also dry. Absent also from the bathroom was Angie's brush and comb set.

One of Angie's most cherished Christmas gifts from Tony was a mother-of-pearl brush and comb set that fit into a lovely satin box. Gina always remembered the brush and comb sitting on her mother's bureau. She eyed it enviously as a little girl. Many times, when her mother was not around, Gina would play with it like she did sometimes with her mother's lipstick and nail polish. Gina packed it along with her mother's treasured clothes when she moved her to Peaceful Havens. Angie still used it every day. Gina looked in a few drawers in her mother's bureau and in her bathroom closet, but the mother-of-pearl brush and comb were gone, along with Angie.

The relief that Gina initially felt was gradually replaced with a growing pit of fear in her stomach. Her mind raced as she tried to put the pieces of this puzzle together. Trying not to panic, she told herself that there had to be a simple explanation. Angie couldn't just disappear. And she wouldn't go anywhere of course, without telling Gina. *Would she?*

Gina tried to think back to Angie's behavior in the past couple of weeks and could not recall anything that could remotely be considered a red flag. Trying as hard as she could, she honestly could not remember the last conversation they'd had. Maybe it was a week ago? Gina grew increasingly alarmed. Of course, her emotions were fueled, as they always were, by guilt.

Suddenly Gina noticed a faint beep coming from somewhere in the room. At first, she thought she only imagined it and waited silently. Then a few moments later, she heard it again. Puzzled, she moved towards the sound, which seemed to be coming from the bed. She paused and stopped right over the bed—and there! The sound was coming from the bed covers, or maybe under the pillows? Gina tore the sheets back from the bed, but there was nothing there. The beep came again, a little louder, seemingly from under the sheets. In desperation, Gina flung over the mattress, and there, lying between the box spring and the mattress, was Angie's cell phone plugged into its charger with the power cord extending under the covers to the outlet behind her bed.

Gina's eyes widened in disbelief. What was her mother's cell phone doing under her mattress for God's sake? Did she put it there herself, and, more importantly, why? Gina grabbed it and flipped up the phone. There were all of Gina's recent calls, all, of course, unanswered and unread.

So, that was the reason she hadn't answered her calls, Gina mused. *Wherever it was that Angie had gotten off to, she had decided not to take her cell phone with her.*

Gina narrowed her eyes and thought carefully. The discovery of the cell phone changed everything. No longer did Gina feel as fearful as she did foolish. Angie obviously planned to leave Peaceful Havens and did not want to be disturbed. She had escaped silently without taking her phone.

Despite her growing sense of frustration, Gina felt a sudden rush of love and empathy towards her mother. The old Angie was back. She did not want to be found right now. By anyone, including Gina.

Gina shook her head in utter amazement as she had frequently done over the years with her headstrong mother. Angie always wore the pants in the house and ruled the roost her own way. Now Gina had to find her, and it was not going to be easy. There were no staff or management to be found at Peaceful Havens, that she knew.

First things first, she thought as she reached for her own cell phone.

She scrolled down her mother's phone first to find Ben's phone number.

Ben might know where she was; it was certainly worth a shot. Plan B was to visit Ben down the hall if he didn't answer his phone, which was a good possibility. Gina knew Ben's hearing problems and the fact that like most of the residents, his cell phone was usually either uncharged or lying at the bottom of an unused bureau drawer.

Gina carefully punched in Ben's phone number and waited. It rang several times, and then stopped. It did not go to voicemail, which puzzled Gina. It was as if Ben had declined the call. Gina tried again and got the same result. Putting her phone back in her pocket, she decided to go find him. After all, he had to be somewhere around the facility since his family, who basically ignored him, was obviously not interested in rescuing him from the fiasco at Peaceful Havens. Or did they? Could he be gone as well? Strange days, indeed! Gina rushed out the door and down the corridor.

Twenty-Eight

Ben reached for his wallet as the waitress cleared the dishes from his table. The fish and chips were just what the doctor ordered. He had asked for extra ketchup for the fries (usually he kept extra packets in his car) and some vinegar. He planned to take the leftovers back with him for his dinner, but he couldn't help himself. The large portion was gone before he knew it. He was ravenous, and since the kitchen at Peaceful Havens was virtually empty, he had been relying on leftovers and sandwiches in his room. He always had some bread lying around, and his Amazon Prime account kept him supplied with a steady stream of peanut butter, honey, jam, and even marshmallow fluff. Ben's culinary palate stretched from gourmet cuisine to that of a nine-year-old.

Marsha was his waitress, and she grinned at Ben as she picked up his bill and credit card. "No ice cream today, Uncle Ben?"

Most of the waitresses, along with the staff at Peaceful Havens, called him Uncle Ben because he asked them to. He liked having a nickname that gave him a special significance. Everyone on the railroad had always called him Uncle Ben, and they still did.

Ben was thinking of ice cream, mainly a banana split, but decided to save that for dinner. "Thanks, Marsha, but I don't think I have any room left in the caboose, so to speak!" Ben patted his stomach and smiled. "Maybe later, though!"

"Okay, sweetie, see you later!" Marsha twirled away and was gone. At that moment, Ben's cell phone played the theme song to *Titanic*, startling him as he was putting his wallet back into his jacket pocket. He reached for it quickly to see if he recognized the number before he flipped it open and was taken aback to see that it was Gina calling. Normally, he would be delighted to hear from her and would answer eagerly, usually with a witty comment, but this time Ben froze at the sight of Gina's number on his phone.

He could guess why she was calling him. Gina had finally discovered her mother was missing and was probably in a panic. Ben's face grew long. He pressed the decline button on his phone until he could figure out what to do. Letting the call go to voicemail would only make things worse, he figured, since Gina would leave a frantic message. Of course, Ben had the option of not listening to Gina's message, but he knew he would, just as he knew that he knew he would be filled with remorse and regret if he did not help Gina find Angie. Both Angie and Ben had discussed at length how to approach Gina when she discovered her mother was missing.

Lots of compassion and tact would be necessary, Ben thought woefully.

Ben gulped and walked slowly back to his car. As he did, his phone rang again. He didn't need to look at it to know it was Gina again, but he did anyway. Again, he pressed the button to decline her call. Ben knew that it was critical that he made the right decision now. He couldn't kick the can for very long, Gina being the can—or was Angie the can? He knew one thing for certain: If he didn't respond soon, it would be his can getting kicked down the road. Of course, he would have to talk to Gina, but first, he needed to talk to Angie and let her know the jig was up.

Twenty-Nine

The door to my cabin opened slowly, and I smiled in delight as Bill entered my little room. I was glad I had just finished refreshing my face with a little lipstick and rouge and felt so happy to see him. He obviously was thrilled as well because we both came together in a giant bear hug. I could feel his tight embrace, and the familiar aftershave he wore brought me back to happier times in my old kitchen. I knew that Bill felt that connection. He wouldn't let me go, and I felt tears coming. When we finally parted, his eyes were also wet, and we were both smiling.

"Wow, Angie, long time." Bill gulped as he tried to regain his composure and grinned sheepishly. "I can't remember a more wonderful reunion or one I've looked forward to more either. And I have to say, you look wonderful." Bill stopped and stared at me in astonishment. I knew from the look on his face that he meant every word.

"Thank you, Bill. You know how much you have always meant to me and still do. I feel like you being here is almost prophetic, like a perfect place for us both to be right at this time. You know what I am going through right now," I paused to wipe my eyes, "and what I am facing might be difficult in the next couple of days. But for the first time, I feel strong because I have good friends who are right by my side, you included. Brian was great, and, of course, Ben has been an angel. I couldn't have asked for better accomplices to assist me in my secret escape, so to speak."

Bill chuckled and wiped his eyes with the back of his hand. "Yeah, Angie, I hear Ben in your words. After hanging out with Ben for a while, we inevitably start talking like him. Good old Uncle Ben. I know he has been a huge help, but you know, Angie, you have done so much for him too. Right now, Ben is facing some tough health problems, and being with you was what he needed to take the focus off himself. You really have given him a new spark in his life. I'm not too sure if you realize that." Bill's eyes grew dark and serious.

"I noticed he has more energy and is happier, yes. I didn't really think it was because of me though." I looked out the window, deep in thought. "I was worried at first that I was causing him too much stress, which of course he doesn't need after being through so much before he got to Peaceful Havens. Are his health problems related to his vision? I remember he mentioned he was going to his eye doctor last week." I guiltily realized I had forgotten to ask him what happened at the doctors. Ben's offhand way of dealing with questions about his health had had the effect he wanted on me, because I had dropped any more conversations about it. Now I realized I should have pressed him further.

"Well, Russell, his nephew, told me he is going blind. Ben, of course, refuses to believe this, and until he cannot pass his driver's test, he is never going to give up his car keys. You know Ben. But soon there will come a time when he must." Bill looked down sadly. "My own mother is going through that right now too. It's like we've reversed our roles, now I am her guardian telling her what to do, and she is acting like a spoiled teenager." Bill managed to smile but looked sad.

"Of course, Bill. You're preaching to the choir, you know. I don't have to tell you what went on between me and Gina and the battles we had and are still having. Not to mention the battle we will have when she finds out I am missing, which I suspect will be sooner rather than later." I managed to laugh, but it was hollow, lacking conviction. I looked up at Bill who was nodding in agreement. It was so good to talk about all of it. Worry still filled my head as I thought about what was to come.

Bill sat down next to me and balanced on the arm of the chair. In typical Bill fashion, he took both my hands and looked at me. "Angie, I know you are worried. When I found out what you were going through and what your plans were, I knew I had to keep quiet, and not telling Gina has been difficult, I must admit. But I have thought about this a lot, and what I feel now, especially after seeing you and talking to you is, you will be okay. Gina will be upset and will probably react the way you expect her to at first. But here you are, living your life, deciding to be safe and happy in a place where you need to be surrounded by love. I must tell you something." Bill cleared his throat and lowered his voice. "I think Gina realizes she made a mistake putting you in assisted living. She hinted to me a few times that she acted hastily because she was afraid for your safety. We even talked about how difficult it would be to undo that decision, especially since your house will be sold soon. I know you won't tell her this, but I'm telling you because it's something you need to know. Gina might not be as unhappy about what you are doing as you think."

I stared at Bill in amazement. His words rang true in a lot of ways, especially considering my recent interactions with Gina. We had settled into a polite way of talking without dealing with any of the hard stuff.

"Do you think that she really thought she had made a mistake? Why didn't she just tell me, so we could clear the air and maybe find a solution?"

Bill sighed. "I don't think she thought there *was* a solution. It would mean admitting to everyone, including your relatives, that she had acted hastily and perhaps selfishly. Think about what Maria and Mario would say. They were all sold on the solutions offered by the so-called health care professionals. Not to mention the battle she would have with the nursing staff at Peaceful Havens. Talk about World War Three." Bill shook his head in disgust. "I know I probably shouldn't say any of this stuff, but Angie, I am so glad you escaped from that place."

Relief flooded through me, and I laughed nervously as I squeezed his hands. "Bill, you don't know how much I needed to hear this. What a relief to think about the fact that maybe, just maybe, our relationship can survive all of this. Because, you know, that's my main worry. I'm not saying that I'm not worried about what Peaceful Havens will do, or what my other relatives will say, or even what will happen to me now. My number one worry has been what this will do to the relationship I have with my oldest and most faithful daughter. I really don't want to be one of those old ladies whose kids refuse to ever talk to her again." I felt myself choking up, so I stopped.

"No way, Angie. Don't forget, Gina loves you very much. I know you might not think it was love that put you here, but put yourself in Gina's place. She was under a great deal of pressure to make the decision she made, even if she realized too late that there were better options. Love is also the reason that now she will accept that she really wants more for you, because you deserve it. We all know you have been an amazing mother who should be happy, especially after all you have been through. I think if you can remember the love, above all, you and Gina can get through this and come out the other end stronger, wiser, and happier. I really do."

Just at that moment, my phone went off. We both sat up to the sounds of "Moon River." I looked at my phone in dismay. "It's Ben. He isn't supposed to call 'til later." Bill and I shared looks of alarm. "I think I've been found out, my friend," I said. I reached for my phone and verified it was Ben. "Hi, Ben, what's up?"

I knew right away that it wasn't good news. Usually, Ben had a chipper retort when I first saw him or called him on the phone. This time, there was silence and then I heard Ben clear his throat.

"Hi, Angie, how are you? Got a minute?" I looked at Bill, and he rolled his eyes. He didn't have any trouble hearing Ben even though he wasn't on a speaker phone. Ben's voice could probably be heard in the next car down from me.

"Sure, Ben, I am okay. Actually, Bill is here with me." I hesitated for a minute. "He is giving me moral support, which I assume I might need by the end of this phone call. Am I right?" I tried to sound lighthearted, but my heart was pounding a mile a minute.

"Yeah, Angie, I'm afraid I am calling to tell you that I am pretty sure Gina knows you left, and she is frantically looking for you. She called me twice, but I did not pick up. I need to know how to proceed at this point, but I think we need to take the bull by the horns, so to speak." Ben stopped and waited. "That is, if you agree."

Bill was watching me, and when I looked up at him, he had a concerned look on his face. Then he nodded.

"Ben, I understand. I am so sorry to put you in the middle of this situation. It's my drama to deal with, and deal with it I will. I am going to call Gina when we hang up and tell her everything. All I can say is I hope she doesn't fly off the deep end, but I want her to hear about all this from me before she does something rash, like maybe call the police." I gulped and closed my eyes. I was picturing a very disturbing scenario that could be playing out, maybe this very minute.

"Okay, Angie. I am not at Peaceful Havens right now, but if it helps, I can meet her after you two hash it out. I can kind of maybe calm her down and tell her that you are certainly safe and happy. Is that something you would like me to do?" Ben lowered his voice and seemed calmer. "I'm across the street at Smith Hill Creamery. After you talk to her, ask her to meet me here. No sense me going back to my room since I would probably have to beat down a whole bunch of nosy reporters at the front door."

"That's a good idea, Ben. Okay, let me call her now. This conversation might take a while though...." I let my voice trail off as Bill squeezed my hand in support. "I don't want to keep you hanging, but it could be a long one. Are you sitting in your car?"

"Yes, Angie. Don't worry. It's a nice day, I'm in the parking lot, and I have nothing else to do. Take your time. I will say a prayer that your conversation will go well. Things *will* be okay, Angie. How are you feeling right now?" Ben had returned to his booming voice as I heard loud motorcycles in the background. We waited a second until they passed, all the time I needed. This was the moment I had dreaded, but there was no escaping the fact that D-day had finally arrived.

"I'm nervous, but strangely relieved if that makes any sense. Ben, don't worry, and please, I am sorry you are in the middle.... You know I appreciate you being there for me. I'll talk later, if that's good for you?"

"Okay, Angie, over and out." With that, Ben hung up.

I felt shaky but didn't want Bill to be worried. Nonetheless, he looked at me with concern, and said, "Angie, do you want me to stay here with you? Just for support. Gina shouldn't know I'm here. I can stay in the background, mute my phone, and make sure you are not disturbed...." Bill looked nervous. All the excitement had brought high color to his cheekbones, and despite my dilemma, I had to admit he looked very attractive. I had always felt he was just right for my daughter.

"As long as I am not taking you away from your duties, Bill, that's great. It really helps to have support. I must admit I am nervous, but I have been practicing what I would say to Gina, and now is the time before she does anything foolish. So, here goes...."

Thirty

Gina strode purposefully down the corridor after closing her mother's door firmly behind her. She didn't bother locking it. Her mind was racing wildly. Maybe, she thought, her mother had decided to hole up with Ben for the duration of the strike. That could explain Ben's refusal to take her call. At this point, she had no other option than to see if Ben was in his room. She pictured herself opening Ben's door to find them in some kind of compromising position on his bed.

Stop it!, she told herself.

Gina knew the idea was wildly irrational, but at least it would provide a reasonable explanation for her mother's absence. Deep down, however, she knew if that was the case, her mother would never bring her toothpaste and toothbrush to Ben's. Come to think of it, her mother would never entertain the thought of becoming romantically involved with anyone, especially Ben. *Next thing you know*, Gina thought to herself, *I'll start to suspect they both ran off together*. Gina knew that idea was just as ludicrous, especially if they used Ben's old Buick, which had about 250,000 miles on it.

Ben's door, number 342, loomed before her. Gina knocked loudly. The corridor was silent as if everyone had somehow disappeared. Gina felt as if she were in some kind of dream and knocked again. She knew there was no one in the room but still hoped that maybe Ben was asleep or forgot to put his hearing aids in, which had happened before. His door was always unlocked, so Gina timidly turned the knob and called out his name. There was still no sound, so she entered the room. Nervously, she glanced over to the bathroom, remembering that Ben liked to sit on the john reading his train magazines. Ben had a morning routine he called SSS (shit, shower, and shave) that lasted until about nine o'clock. He shared this information with just about anyone he knew, grinning widely. Gina walked around the room, still calling out Ben's name. She felt like an intruder once she realized Ben was not there, but she didn't want to leave. She could smell his Old Spice aftershave, and his presence was strangely comforting. His bed was made, and there was a sloppy pile of train timetables on his nightstand. His drawer was open as if someone had been rifling through the contents. On his desk, he had scribbled some notes. Gina peered at them closely.

What does it mean, she thought to herself, *that Ben has written down different times and destinations for the Southwest Chief?*

Gina remembered that she and Bill had taken that train on a cross-country trip once to Las Vegas. The train went all the way to California. Her mind whirled in ten thousand different directions at once. Gina sat on the edge of Ben's bed.

Focus, she instructed herself. If Angie was headed west, she certainly had a destination in mind. *Where? And who,* Gina wondered, *was she going to see?* Gina tried to think like her mother did and was still as she racked her brain for answers. Then the realization began to dawn....

She was so startled she jumped as her phone vibrated to life. Gina dug in her pocket and pulled it out, staring at the unfamiliar number. It was a Rhode Island area code but not anyone in her contacts. Usually that meant a spam call. Gina hesitated to answer but quickly realized that it could have something to do with her mother being missing, so she hit accept.

"Hello, Gina here," she croaked into her phone, her mouth dry with fear.

"Hi, Gina, dear, it's Mom."

At the sound of her mother's voice, Gina was flooded with emotion. First, she felt relief (her mother sounded unusually strong and even happy), but that emotion was quickly overshadowed by anger (*how could she do this to me?*) and hurt (*didn't I deserve to be in on her secret?*) along with the usual intense feeling of frustration that she was placed in the situation in the first place. She pictured her brother and sister blithely unaware of this catastrophe, going about their lives with not a care in the world.

"Mom!" Gina sputtered and then couldn't help herself. "Where the hell are you?" She normally didn't use any expletives around her mother, saving her salty language for her friends. Gina knew her mother hated swearing. Even during times of huge anxiety, her mother would spell out swear words instead of saying them, a fact that annoyed Gina immensely.

Angie didn't speak right away. Gina could hear her clear her throat and her voice was a little shaky. She started slowly. Then her voice became stronger. It was full of love.

"Gina, please don't be angry with me. I am so sorry I've worried you. I've been worried sick too. I hated having to hide everything from you.... I have been planning this for months actually.... You know I love you.... I know you had the best intentions when you brought me to Peaceful Havens. It may have been the best place for me at first, we both know that." Angie hesitated, then continued. "Now it isn't. I know, we should have talked about this, but it was hard. You haven't been super-approachable, and I can imagine I haven't been either. But please, if you love me, listen to me. I don't want to go back. Sell the house. I'll never forget everything you have done for me, you know." Angie took a breath. "I am going to start a new chapter in my life now. I am happy, with friends, and on my way to somewhere safe. I know one thing: I am never returning to Peaceful Havens." Angie's voice was full of emotion. "I hated my life there. It is where everyone goes to die, and quite frankly I am not there yet. Not even close. I want you to trust me." Angie stopped, paused, and then finished her speech. "This is a conversation I have had in my head for a long time. I'm sorry it took me so long to get these words out."

Gina paced around Ben's room as her mother spoke. She listened, shocked at what she was hearing. She stared out the window, seeing a few reporters walking around the back of the building. She wanted to yell, to scream, to rant, but at the sound of her mother's tearful voice, she stopped. She suddenly felt drained, and somehow quietly relieved, as if she had been waiting for those words for months. The fact her mother was voicing the very emotions that Gina had felt lately but hadn't allowed herself to say softened her resolve to resist. Her mother had it right, she had everything right, but still, how dare she just get up and leave?

"Mom, it's okay, don't cry. I'm crying too." Gina felt her tears coming and looked around Ben's room unsuccessfully for a Kleenex. "I wish we had talked; in fact, I wish you were here right now so we could look at each other and have this conversation in person, which brings me to my first question: *Where are you?*" Gina tried to keep the emotion out of her voice but wasn't very successful, and her last words came out as a squeak.

Angie was silent.

Gina waited, and then asked timidly, "Mom, are you on a train?" Gina heard what she thought was her mother dabbing her eyes with a Kleenex.

"Yes," she replied softly.

Thirty-One

Ben had been sitting in his car for over an hour consumed with thoughts of doom. Many times, he thought about taking off. But where? As the clock on his dashboard ticked away, he grew more and more alarmed. Worst of all, there was nothing he could do. He had to sit there stewing in his own juices. His last conversation with Angie was all he had to go on, and she asked him to wait for Gina. Ben was afraid Gina would be so upset that meeting Ben would be the last thing she'd want to do. Why would she, after discovering Ben had been a willing accomplice in the escape plan? Was he in big trouble? Was his deep friendship with Gina at risk? Worst of all, was he going to go to jail for obstructing justice and harboring a fugitive? He knew he was exaggerating the last part, but who knew what the authorities would do with the information that Ben had helped a resident escape? *Was that a crime,* he wondered. He was just an old guy, going blind, and they most likely could throw the book at him and no one would really care.

Ben wasn't really worried about himself, but he loved Gina and Angie, and their happiness was uppermost in his mind. He was afraid he had sabotaged both relationships, the worst-case outcome. As he pondered the gloomy state of his life, he looked up to see Gina's Jeep pull into the parking lot of the Smith Hill Creamery. Silently, he murmured a prayer of thanks and fingered the rosary beads he kept hanging from his rearview mirror. He watched her park her Jeep and, miraculously, rush over to his car with a smile on her face. There were no words for the relief he felt. All his fears had been unfounded, and in a moment of joy, he opened his car door and walked towards her with open arms. The next thing he knew, they were in a giant embrace.

"Oh Ben, I was so wrong.... I'm so happy you are here with me." Gina buried her head in his shoulder, and he could feel her body relax against his. His hearing aids squealed as they always did when she spoke too close to him, and they both laughed at that. Ben wouldn't let her go. For several minutes he just stood there, basking in the moment. Then he looked down at her face. She had been crying but now looked happy. She looked relieved.

"Come on, Gina, let's sit."

The picnic bench out front where kids usually ate their ice cream was empty in the middle of the day. They plopped down, and Gina collapsed in a tiring heap.

"Ben, I guess you know that now I know where my mother is?" Gina began with a question and then continued when she saw the look of confusion on Ben's face. "I went into Mom's room because I found out about the strike—saw it on TV on the midday news—and rushed over here. When I couldn't find her, I called you and ended up in your room. Hope you don't mind." Gina looked at Ben sheepishly. "While I was there, I saw the Acela timetables, and I put two and two together. Then Mom called me just as I had figured everything out. Things got emotional, but now I know." Gina began to cry again. "You know, I can't believe I am saying this, but I am so relieved."

Ben felt the beginnings of tears in his eyes, too, but tried to blink them away. Hearing the joy in Gina's voice made him so happy he felt like a new man. Silently, he said a small prayer of thanks. He wasn't going to be arrested after all.

"Gina, we are probably both feeling equal amounts of relief. You have no idea how it felt to keep all this from you. It was painful, I can tell you that. I have been waking in a panic, feeling awful about the pain I knew you would feel, but also knowing I might be putting Angie at risk. Although, in all honesty, I felt like Angie was making the right choice. She carefully considered her options, we talked about it, and she made sure there would be no surprises on the other end, so to speak." Ben looked at Gina hopefully, still not sure how much she knew about Angie's plans.

"It's okay, Ben. I'm sure you would understand that initially, when I called you, I was pretty upset, to say the least, mostly due to fear, because I realized when I found my mother's cell phone under her mattress that she did not want to be found. After all I have done so far to keep her safe, I felt like a complete failure; she slipped through my fingers and escaped anyway. But you know, that's my mother. Headstrong to the end. And you know what?" Gina stopped to wipe a tear that had escaped down her cheek. "I probably would have done the same damn thing."

Ben smiled in relief. He looked at Gina, filled with love and admiration for her. When he'd met her years ago, he secretly had wished he was fifteen years younger, and Bill was out of the picture. The truth was, she always reminded him of his dead wife Sue, and he would carry a torch for her forever.

"It took a lot of planning. We had to be very cautious, but the strike was not planned. We were kind of lucky it just happened that way, and it bought us some time. You know how she feels about that place, and frankly, I feel the same way, but I am grateful I could help her find happiness and even more grateful that you are in my life.... I admit I was terrified you would never speak to me when you found out I was part of this secret mission, so to speak." Ben shook his head and managed to smile.

Gina touched Ben's arm with affection. "At first, I was, but then all of this happened so fast. And when I just talked to Mom, it turns out Bill was sitting next to her the whole time. That, too, made me feel very emotional, and you know, some of the emotions I felt talking to Bill just a few minutes ago were jealousy. Jealous that I couldn't be there holding

Mom's hand and giving her the support she needed. Bill and I talked a while, and I think we will be talking again real soon." Gina looked at Ben slyly and smiled.

"I hope you do. I think you know how much Bill thinks of you. But I guess I will let him tell you that." Ben looked at Gina carefully. "By the way, should I ask the question that has been in the back of my mind? Or is it none of my business?"

Gina looked thoughtfully at Ben. "I guess you mean, what the hell am I going to do about Peaceful Havens, right? Well, Ben, let's talk that one over. I would like your advice. While we ponder that question, how about if I treat you to the ice cream you passed up for dessert?"

Thirty-Two

I felt the train slow to a crawl as we pulled into the station at San Bernardino. Looking out the dust-streaked windows, I saw miles of desert hills, the landscape that would now be the backdrop of my new life. Although I was dying to finally get off the train, I felt a little sad. The train had become the link from my old life to this new one. From my little cabin, I had experienced a spiritual journey of my own. While the train wove its way through the Midwest, I was finally able to reflect on events of my past, events I managed to bury for years. Issues that had haunted me were finally laid to rest, or at least resolved somewhat, in my mind. Throughout it all, I felt like Tony was by my side, listening to my confessions and coming to terms with some of his own demons from his own past. I recognized an unfamiliar emotion: peace. I welcomed it with a renewed sense of hope.

Five days ago, the doors to the train had closed behind me on the East Coast. Now, the doors were about to open on the opposite coast to new beginnings. I gulped. I wasn't afraid, but my emotions were swirling all around me as I gathered my purse and my overnight bag.

Randy, who was the last conductor to help me through my journey, opened the door and smiled at me. "Angie, you are all ready, willing, and able, right? Here we are, and away you go! I wish you so much luck, sweetie!"

Randy had a rather corny way of communicating, but I was used to it. Ben and Brian also talked that way, which I called "Three Stooges Talk." It was endearing, much like Randy himself. He was short, wiry, and had his hair shorn in a crew cut. On his left ear a large diamond winked wickedly. He dressed like a dapper young gentleman; the only hint of his masculinity was the tattoo that was partially visible under the starched white cuff of his shirt sleeve. It snaked up to his arm. Last night, I had the courage to ask him about it, and he pulled up his sleeve to reveal a long vine of tiny pink roses with the name Sandy etched in the middle. He told me Sandy was his German shepherd, who saved his life about three years ago in a house fire. Randy and his husband, Glen, narrowly escaped from their burning house, but Sandy didn't make it.

I would miss Randy, just as I missed Brian. I didn't have to miss Bill though. He continued to ride with me after Gina and I had our giant showdown as I called it. It did take several additional emotional conversations with Gina, some early-morning and late-night discussions, to finally resolve most of our issues. Bill ended up flying back home right outside of Flagstaff after he helped referee the discussions Gina and I waded through to come to the place where we were now. During that time, Bill and I also had many heartfelt talks, many about the past. Bill confessed to me that he and Gina were almost at the point where they both wanted to start over. Bill always lacked a filter, blurting out secrets, but that news made me happy. Gina didn't reveal that to me yet, probably because we were too busy hashing out old grievances. After several tearful conversations on Facetime, I felt closer to Gina than I had in years. I told her how I was indebted to her. I admitted to her that she had once again saved my life. She confessed that she was consumed with guilt, knowing I was stuck (she thought forever) in Peaceful Havens and she had been the one to make that happen. I suspected that Gina emerged from our talks happier than I have seen her in a long time. Probably the biggest relief for me on my journey was the knowledge that I didn't have to return to that dreadful place. I still had some dreams of being trapped there, but I hoped these would fade away in time.

I told Gina to do whatever she could to terminate my lease. "Throw some money at the problem," I said. "Seems like money always talks."

It worked. After a few meetings with Gina's friend Nancy, who was a no-nonsense attorney, Peaceful Havens let me go. It did help that they had a waiting list (imagine people were standing, or rather sitting in line waiting to get into that dump), so it was not a problem for the director there to agree to let my room go to a higher bidder. I also told Gina that once the house was sold, the three kids could divide up the money. I did confess that I had a secret stash of my own money that I had squirreled away for years. It seemed she was so relieved about Peaceful Havens that she didn't even ask how much money I had.

I let Gina figure out how to deal with the relatives and neighbors. Maria and Mario were told a watered-down version of the aftermath of the whole affair, but I haven't talked to them yet. Apparently, they would be fine if I was fine. Frankly, if Gina hadn't found out I vanished, they wouldn't have even noticed.

My focus now was Nicky. Nicky, who I had been talking to daily, was happily waiting right outside the train, on the platform of the station in San Bernardino. Or at least I hope it was happily....

Thirty-Three

The sun was bright, and it was quite warm as I found my way to the open door at the front of my train car. To my surprise, a few of the conductors had gotten wind of my crazy adventure, and they were all gathered at the door to help me off. I hugged each one, including Randy, who gave me a red rose and a kiss on the cheek. I felt like a rock star but knew I had to exit quickly or the train would depart. I could feel tears begin, so I turned and stepped onto the platform and into the sunshine.

The first thing I noticed was the dryness. The air was not like New England; there was a different smell, dusty and unfamiliar. There was no humidity which surprised me. The air was clear and very refreshing. I stood still on the platform to take in the scenery. There were more people than I had expected, and I watched passengers rushing to get on the train and some last-minute travelers hastily getting off. Already the train was beginning to leave the station. I watched it slowly curl around the corner, out of sight.

I turned to focus on the people hurrying around me, anxious now, hoping Nicky was somewhere in the crowd. Suddenly I spotted a tall lanky figure walking towards me, his face looking long-ago familiar. He still had a good amount of dark hair, combed straight back, and he appeared quite tanned. He was dressed in a yellow striped polo shirt, pressed crisply on the sleeves, and a pair of olive-green chinos. As he approached me, he grinned and waved. I knew it was Nicky and dropped my bags to greet him. The next thing I knew, we were hugging tightly. I felt his strong arms around me and smelled his musky aftershave, with hints of lavender and eucalyptus.

I heard his throaty whisper in my ear. "Ang, you haven't changed a bit!" I relaxed into his embrace.

Here, I suddenly realized, was where I belonged.

Thirty-Four

Nicky sat on his balcony watching the sun set, his nightly cocktail in his hand. The day was warm but now the cool Santa Ana breezes chilled the air enough for a sweater. It was almost time for dinner, a typical Friday afternoon at five o'clock. Nicky looked across at Angie, the reason his world had been transformed in the last few months. Angie was sitting next to him, holding her glass of Kendall Jackson chardonnay. She looked happy and smiled as the sun cast its last glow of the day on her face. The deep lines of worry and doubt she had brought with her from the east had virtually disappeared.

Angie's appearance caused other delightful changes in Nicky's world, including the tempting aroma of Angie's marinara sauce which she was serving with homemade pasta for dinner. In addition, a caprese salad waited for them in the refrigerator along with a lemon meringue pie. Nicky was amazed at the way Angie produced such wonderful food out of thin air with hardly any effort at all. She was the happiest when she was cooking, usually to the sounds of Pavarotti or Frank Sinatra, crooning out her favorite songs. What a difference from Nicky's existence in the last few years when takeout or frozen Stouffer's were his usual choices for dinner.

Nicky discovered that beneath Angie's practical demeanor, she was a romantic at heart. She adored the roses Nicky brought her (several times a week) and loved having coffee brought to her in the quiet, early morning. When she first moved in, she quickly gravitated to her usual role of domestic partner, but Nicky put a stop to that. He insisted that he play the role of doting partner as well, which took some getting used to. At first, Angie balked at the thought of Nicky shopping for their food. Although she hadn't been inside a supermarket for a couple of years, Angie couldn't fathom the idea that any man could successfully accomplish the task of grocery shopping. It turned out Nicky could. Of course, Angie insisted on giving him a list, complete with comical pictures, to ensure there were no errors. It was a work in progress. Angie didn't like to admit it, but Nicky could tell that she was happy that she could concentrate on just cooking, her real love, and leave the tedious work of shopping to someone more suited to it.

There were other compromises as well, some not so easily negotiated. When Angie first met Juanita, Nicky's cleaning woman (Angie refused to call her a maid), she was horrified at the thought that another woman would be the one responsible to sweep, vacuum, and even change her sheets. To Angie's amazement, Juanita completed the laundry in record time. Angie had not recovered from her unpleasant memories of the washer and dryer at Peaceful Havens. It took a while for her to accept the idea of domestic help, but when her clothes arrived smelling sweet and freshly folded, she was a happy convert. Unlike Tony, Nicky was almost fanatically organized and clean. His bed was made within five minutes of arising, much to Angie's wonder. Soon her earlier resolutions of staying at Nicky's for just a couple of weeks were a distant memory to them both. They both quickly became accustomed to their new life, loving every minute.

Nicky would admit to himself that he couldn't have imagined such domestic bliss existed, especially at this stage in his life. Every day, he anxiously expected the other shoe to drop, but it never did. Angie was a dream companion. As the days passed, they shared stories and secrets of their past. It was easy to confide in Angie; she was a great listener.

Nicky began to feel a closeness to Angie that really surprised him. It didn't take long for them to realize that their deep and comfortable connection was as close to any intimate relationship as they could ever have imagined. But they weren't there yet....

Nicky's master suite with a balcony and Angie's cozy rose-colored bedroom down the hall still served them well. Nicky was very careful not to intrude on Angie's private abode, fearing he would scare her off, but Angie seemed less and less afraid of any intrusion as the days passed into weeks and into months. Their familiarity became comfortable enough that Angie began to creep into Nicky's bedroom late at night or in the wee hours of the morning. Nicky was delighted to wake up and find Angie sleeping next to him, an occasion that became more commonplace as time went on. Still, Nicky was very cautious. He remembered his old cat Rufus, who would have no problem coming to cuddle up to Nicky on his terms but would skitter away if Nicky made the first move. Nicky suspected Angie was like Rufus, and he worried about how a false move would scare her away for good.

Deepening shadows surrendered the sun as the sky turned golden. Angie loved twilight time, when the day was done, and they could enjoy the sun setting before them. After years of living on the mountainside, Nicky was used to the changing scenery before him, so he was enchanted by Angie's obvious delight. She was used to oceans, not mountains. It had been many years since she savored an evening sunset, she'd told him, referring back to nights at Carson Beach long ago. Now, her twilight time was the best time of the day. *Their* twilight time, she corrected herself.

"You know I feel like I died and went to heaven," Angie said slowly after a sip of chardonnay. "Literally," she added.

Her face took on a wistful look as she glanced up at Nicky. Nicky took her hand in response and squeezed it gently. He loved holding her hands, which still seemed so youthful, her nails long and tapered even without any polish. He fingered the gold band still on her left hand. Nicky never mentioned the gold band. He admitted to himself that he had mixed emotions. On the one hand, he secretly admired Angie's devotion to Tony and her desire to keep that devotion alive. On the other hand, Nicky felt a certain amount of jealousy that it wasn't Nicky's ring that graced Angie's left hand. Of course, he realized he was being foolish. Nicky had not proposed to Angie yet, although the thought was beginning to appeal to him more and more. Nicky knew better than to bring it up to Angie, however, and kept his thoughts to himself.

"You know, I almost feel as if you have been with me, here, on my balcony, and in my life, forever," Nicky blurted out. He glanced quickly at Angie, afraid of what his confession might elicit.

But Angie looked calmly out at the mountain vista and nodded. "I know, isn't it strange?" Angie seemed to have no trouble finding her words. "I have to admit, Nicky, that I didn't expect any of this, you know."

They both looked at each other and smiled.

Nicky squeezed her hand again. "What didn't you expect, Ang?" he asked quietly, waiting for her answer.

Angie was silent for several minutes more. The golden streaks of the last of the sun deepened to red, then purple. Soon it would be dark, and they would head inside for dinner.

"I didn't expect to fall in love with you." Angie looked at Nicky with such tenderness that Nicky knew the moment was one he would remember forever. Together they put their drinks down and fell into a delicious embrace.

Epilogue

Gina hurried across the street at the sound of the church bells, resounding in the sweet autumn breeze. Our Lady of the Rosary Church stood tall and imposing in the sunlight, overlooking the river on one side and the narrow streets of three-deckers on the other. This was Ben's church; she had come here once before for his sister's funeral many years ago. Now, it was Ben whose life would be celebrated today. Gina felt a deep sadness at the recent loss. Since Angie had moved to California, Ben and Gina had grown close. It didn't take long for Ben's eyesight to fail to the point where he could no longer drive. Gina quickly stepped into the role of caregiver for him, but this time she had help. Bill was by her side, unwavering in his devotion to both.

Ben was the catalyst that brought about all the recent changes in Gina's life. She made sure he knew how indebted she was to him, but he just smiled and shrugged. He often spoke of how Angie had brought joy and life to him when he really needed it. In a way, Ben felt he had accomplished his great mission in life, his last hurrah, as he put it. He planned everything for her and was unwavering in his determination to get everything right. And he did, right down to each station stop along the way. It was the perfect coup, he said, so to speak.

As sad as Gina was about Ben, she could take solace knowing that his last months were happy. Bill and Gina made dinner for him every week and took him to all his favorite places. They were their favorite places too. Bill took him for rides exploring old rail beds; sometimes Gina joined them. Gina wouldn't admit that she never tired of hearing Ben pontificate about all the things that delighted him, which invariably included trains, boats, and, of course, food. Gina felt tears begin as she realized how much she would miss his love, which had sustained her throughout the whole Angie adventure.

Gina thought back to last year when Angie left. Everything seemed to happen at once. Selling the house, moving the rest of Angie's stuff to her new house in California (Gina still couldn't believe she lived there), and managing the disbursement of Angie's assets was like a blur. Throughout it all, Ben was there. It seemed like a miracle to Gina that everything seemed to fit into place so seamlessly. For the longest time, the whole situation with Angie had looked so bleak that she never thought there was a way out. Most of the time, Gina had wandered around in quiet desperation, hoping a solution would appear. The overwhelming feelings of guilt were something she didn't share with anyone, although Bill said later, he knew from her face how conflicted she was.

Gina made the sign of the cross and slipped into the first row of pews. She pulled Angie's old rosary beads from her handbag and fingered them thoughtfully. She felt blessed, thinking of all the friends she had who had helped her navigate this voyage. But the best gift of all was Nicky.

Since Angie moved, Gina spent hours on the phone talking to Nicky (Thank God there were no long-distance charges anymore). Right away, Gina was captivated by his gentle nature and quiet manner. He was so easy to talk to that Gina found herself confiding in him before very long. Gina loved the fact that he had an imperfect history and some baggage, which he shared unabashedly. Pretty soon they called or texted each other regularly (Angie was still not proficient at texting, but Nicky was trying his best to convert her). Nicky's calm voice comforted Gina, as if he were in the next room instead of two thousand miles away. *How could it be*, she wondered, *that she had never met her godfather, this wonderful man, up until now?* Gina knew his appearance in her life was no coincidence. He has become a second father to her.

Angie and Nicky. It still seemed unbelievable. At first, Gina was skeptical that Nicky and California could be the solution she had prayed for. Gina admitted to Ben and Bill that it all seemed too perfect, so there had to be a flaw in the whole plan. How could it be that two people on opposite coasts, forged only by a connection that was fifty-five years in the past, could come together so effortlessly? The aunts couldn't believe any of it. Friends and neighbors, doubtful about something that sounded too perfect to be true, badgered Gina with endless questions. Finally, she stopped even trying to explain it, and let Angie and Nicky take over. Gina learned to let go. As Ben would say, "The Lord will provide, so to speak...."

The inside of the church was cool, and the smell of incense calmed her. Ben's sister had asked Gina to sit in front with them; her husband and Bill were pallbearers along with Ben's nephew, Russ. Gina suspected that most of the guests would be old railroad workers from Ben's past, mostly guys she had never met. She imagined the luncheon afterwards, held at Luigi's, full of old railroad stories and lots of laughter. Ben would have loved it—especially the dessert, which was his favorite: tiramisu.

Lost in thought, Gina heard the big church doors open. Throughout Angie's disappearance and Ben's illness, Gina and Bill rehashed the demons of their own past. Gina hadn't realized how much Tony's death had impacted Bill. She discovered he was still grieving as much as she was. Tony's sudden death would always be a nightmare. Gina came to realize she reacted badly, assuming the role of caregiver to Angie in order to gain some control of her life. Her actions helped no one. Her health and personal life suffered greatly as a result. So did Angie's, until she devised her own escape plan. Gina shuddered to think that Angie could still be stuck in Peaceful Havens if she hadn't taken the bull by the horns. Gina smiled ruefully. In the end, Angie knew what she needed, and thank God she had the will to do it.

Gina heard the footsteps ringing down the church aisle, and they stopped at her pew. As she dropped her rosary beads, she stood up and looked, expecting to greet Ben's family. Instead, Angie and Nicky stood there before her holding hands and grinning mischievously.

Gina stood there dumbfounded. Then they all fell into an embrace, Angie's familiar scent engulfing her once again. Gina could have hugged her forever.

"What... Okay, why didn't you tell me you would be here?"

Gina finally pulled away and looked closely at Angie. She was shocked at the change in her. Gone were the deep furrows and lines around her eyes and mouth. They were replaced by a face softened by happiness and love. Gina glanced at Nicky, who smiled sheepishly.

"Don't blame me, I had nothing to do with it. I wanted to call you and give you a heads up, but Angie wanted it to be a surprise."

"Well, surprise is a huge understatement! I am *so* glad to see you. Do you have any idea how much I've missed you?"

Gina's voice started to squeak before she remembered she was in church. Many questions remained unanswered, but they could wait. Gina looked down and saw they were holding hands tightly. Mom's gold wedding ring was replaced with a silver band studded with small diamonds. Gina gasped and grabbed her hand to look at it closely. Mom didn't pull away; she looked at Nicky shyly and smiled.

"I missed you so much, and what better time to come back to honor Ben?" Nicky squeezed her hand. He looked at ease, gazing at the sun streaming through the stained-glass windows. They both appeared none the worse from spending the last eight hours on a plane.

Gina sighed and signaled them both to sit beside her. "I agree, we all have a lot of catching up to do."

About the Author

Born in South Boston, Joanne Perella grew up in Providence Rhode Island in a closeknit Italian family.

After retiring from over forty years of government work, she has been an antique fanatic and appraiser for twenty years. Joanne began writing as far back as she can remember and was reading novels by the first grade. She has been published in several anthologies. Her work has also been featured on NPR.

Her passions include photography, travel, antiques, biking, hiking and of course writing. She now lives on Bullocks Cove in Riverside Rhode Island.

Made in United States
North Haven, CT
02 January 2025

63884081R00124